THE WRITING ON THE WALL AND OTHER STORIES

THE WRITING ON THE WALL AND OTHER STORIES

PENNY EDWARDS

Matador
9 Priory Business Park,
Wistow Road, Kibworth Beauchamp,
Leicestershire. LE8 0RX
Tel: 0116 279 2299
Email: books@troubador.co.uk
Web: www.troubador.co.uk/matador
Twitter: @matadorbooks

ISBN 978 1785891 397

British Library Cataloguing in Publication Data.
A catalogue record for this book is available from the British Library.

Printed and bound by CPI Group (UK) Ltd, Croydon, CR0 4YY
Typeset in 11pt Aldine401 BT by Troubador Publishing Ltd, Leicester, UK

Matador is an imprint of Troubador Publishing Ltd

To my husband and daughter

CONTENTS

THE WRITING ON THE WALL

1

BERLIN 2006

Peter Bayer was seventy-three. He'd taught at the school just up the road for most of his life and, when the wall came down, saw no reason to move. Nobody could say life had been easy and when it was built, he'd lost contact with many friends, but he'd learnt to enjoy life as best he could and had had the good fortune of a happy marriage to Elsa.

This evening they'd had a good meal of beef stew and boiled potatoes, the sauce slightly salty, perhaps, but the consistency good and the meat tender. He wiped the tablecloth several times. A few drops of dry sauce on Elsa's side were persistent and difficult to ease off. He got the spray from underneath the sink and put a liberal amount on the plastic cloth. It successfully removed the stain and he placed the vase of flowers back in the middle. He yawned. He couldn't help himself, but once he'd started he couldn't stop and by the time his mouth opened for the fifth or sixth inhalation, a tear began to trickle down his face with the sheer effort of it all. It had been a long day. But there was nothing unusual in that. In fact, these days it was difficult for him to distinguish day from night and he guessed the only real clues were turning on the lights and pulling the curtains. For instance, at three this morning Elsa was tugging the jacket of his pyjamas and he'd woken to discover they were both lying in her urine. He'd probably nodded off in a cat-nap kind of way sometime between four and six, after he'd sorted out all three of them – Elsa, Peter and the poor old bed – but three was when it all really began.

A few years ago, a time that now seemed untouchable, they'd wake at about half-seven or eight, or maybe a bit later if they were particularly tired, smile and look a little perplexed as dreams merged with reality. He'd offer to make them both a cup of coffee, and bring the drinks to bed where they'd quench their thirst and plan their day. He liked the fact that they were always good at listening to one another, taking it in turns to give in a little bit and do what the other wanted and enjoying it anyway because they could see the pleasure on the other's face.

This morning, at six-thirty, he'd brought Elsa a cup of coffee, but she'd taken a sip, decided she didn't like it and chucked it across the room. His own coffee was cold by the time he'd cleaned the floor as much as he could. It was beginning to rebel, fed up with being washed and scrubbed and no longer prepared to play ball by allowing the offending liquid to completely disappear. When he managed to get round to gulping down his own, it was a disappointing experience, offering nothing of the gently sipped and quietly thought-over one that had helped him make those plans with Elsa.

She lifted herself from her pillow, scrambled her legs away from the duvet, and then swung them round to reach the floor. He told her to wait as she began to lift herself from the bed, but he knew there was no certainty that she would.

He went to the bathroom to prepare a bowl of warm water to bring to her, but as he'd come to expect, he could see her worried face behind him in the mirror. It was his shadow and it barely left him. So instead, he just filled the sink. Like milk from a baby's bottle, he tested the temperature on his own skin first so it wouldn't distress her, then soaked a flannel, squeezed it and washed his wife's face. She smiled up at him.

"That's good, Daddy," she said. "Please wash my face again."

He stroked her cheeks with the flannel. "Close your eyes," he whispered and he gently wiped across first her left eye, then her right.

They went back into the bedroom, Elsa holding his hand for guidance, and he sat her on the bed. He went to her chest of drawers and pulled out a white bra, but she said she wanted the pink one. He put this on the bed, then looked for some pants and a petticoat. She showed no objections to the ones he chose. It was hot and he thought she wouldn't need anything on her legs, but she demanded thick tights, so a pair was taken out and placed by the other things. He opened the wardrobe door, picked out a cool, cotton dress, the pink and blue floral one she wore that evening in Freiburg. Elsa grinned.

"Freiburg," she giggled. She wanted a cardigan, the orange one; she would be so hot, he thought, but didn't argue and so, like the dress, the cardigan left the wardrobe as well.

Slowly, he helped her take off her nightclothes and, when she was naked, she started to put on her dress.

"No, my darling," he said quietly. "You put these on first," and he held up the bra, pants and petticoat. He held her in his arms and kissed her forehead. "Otherwise, you'll have to wear your underwear on top of your dress. You'll look like a pop star."

She laughed. She was rather taken with this man's idea that she might look like a pop star and danced a little jig, still wrapped in his arms.

He remembered them dancing; in the early years it was part of who they were. Elsa was always one of the first up at the local dances, taking his hand and pulling him towards her with such an enthusiasm it left him quite breathless and unsure that he could ever live up to her expectations. All he could see was the other blokes eyeing her up and it was a long time before he could allow himself to believe she seemed to be keen on him. They laughed a lot because the rock 'n' roll was

3

fast and full of an energy that came easily to Elsa but not quite so much to him, so he was constantly a second or two behind. He loved her laugh: it never ridiculed, only instilled a level of confidence in him that he hadn't experienced before, so he enjoyed his inability to catch up as much as she did. There was a lightness to their life that seemed to either not recognise any worries or treat them with an air of indifference if they were spotted.

When they'd eaten some porridge, he half a bowlful, she a few spoonfuls less, he told Elsa they needed to go to the flat. The English woman was due this evening and he needed to make sure the flat was ready. Alke, he was sure, had done her usual excellent job of cleaning it, but he always liked to just look around and put the final touches to it before any holidaymaker came.

He started to put her coat on for her, but, and this was quite normal, she resisted ferociously, with flaying arms and angry words, every utterance causing a twitch or a tightening in his body.

"It's a lovely day, the air will do you good," he tried to cajole her, while thinking – and this was selfish, he knew it was selfish – the air would do him good. But he was unlucky.

"No, no, I don't know who you are. Mummy tells me not to go anywhere with strangers."

The house, the house, it was always the house. But he knew somehow that today she wasn't going to move.

Her face always looked at his with such an urgency and an unbearable earnestness that, despite his frustration, it was sometimes very difficult not to just pick her up and say, "I know, sweetheart, you're absolutely right, it's true," for it held such a heavy weight, mouth quivering, eyes wide and full of tears, he could almost feel a disaster of unthinkable magnitude would be the inevitable outcome if he didn't agree with her and act upon what she said. So maybe some terrible outrage might occur if he didn't say to the stranger in the supermarket, a young man probably in his thirties who had just brushed past them to reach for a few mushrooms, that Elsa was very angry at the way he'd been so outrageously flirting with her and didn't he realise that this was her father? Or that the woman in the blue coat by the bread was one of her dearest school friends. But the problem was this could be true. They were about the same age and Elsa's recollections of decades he had trouble conjuring up could contain the odd enviable accuracy.

Such was the confused life they now inhabited that he often questioned his own sanity, a doubt that crawled upwards inside him like poisoned ivy because he didn't spend enough hours in the company of the sane, who would hopefully reassure him that his fears were nonsense. They understood every word he said, as did he them.

And so he gave up. It was the seventh time he'd relented in as many days. He took her to her favourite armchair where he sat her down and from where she stared at him for some time afterwards.

After her last bite of bread at lunchtime, Elsa had asked him what the time was, an innocuous question in itself and a perfectly reasonable one. She'd never been one for watches and so, over the years, it had become a question he was accustomed to. He told her it was five past one. At six minutes past, the question came again. And at seven minutes past he had the same enquiry. He was sitting opposite her, on what they'd both come to know as his armchair. He had a pen in his hand – it was as if years of marking school books from this very chair had never really left him – and a notepad on the little table next to the chair. He was always making notes, something that caught his eye on the telly, a thought he had, something he had to remember, et cetera, et cetera, but this time, he drew a matchstick each time Elsa asked him the time and after six, he scrawled a diagonal line across them, like a prisoner calculating their release date by counting off time already served. When there was finally a silence and it was no longer of any interest to Elsa what time of day it was, he calculated that he'd served seven weeks and three days. And it was only just two o'clock.

He rang Alke. He was so sorry to bother her, but could she possibly come and sit with Elsa a bit later on? Mrs Thompson, the English woman, would be getting to the flat about six. Would it be possible for her to come round about five-thirty? It's just that Elsa wouldn't go out. Alke said that would be fine, happy to help. He put the phone down and smiled at his good fortune in knowing Alke. Where the hell would he be without her? And Elsa, thank whoever it was he thanked, was OK with her.

When he got to the flat, it was, of course, beautiful. Alke had scrubbed it to within an inch of its life and it looked wonderful. Poor thing, he'd given her a particularly busy summer, what with the World Cup and Karl getting him properly set up on the internet. He smiled and drank in the memory of going to a World Cup Match, only three months ago, but it felt as if it had happened more like years previously, when Karl had taken him to see Germany against Ecuador, something he once never thought imaginable in his lifetime. Oh, the sheer joy of seeing one's own country. Marvellous. And Karl's wife, Ingrid, had looked after Elsa. She wasn't as bad then.

He glanced round again. The flat was fine. All he needed to do was wait. At ten past six there was a knock on the door.

2

However universal the world had become, Helen had never got used to drinking from a mug at home, then picking up an almost identical one thousands of miles away. It seemed unfair, somehow, to travel such a distance, listen to music you didn't like in taxis that were late, face hundreds of people you wouldn't see again and play waiting games at airports, only to find yourself sipping from the self-same vessel. Surely this effort deserved the reward of something significantly different.

She found herself, therefore, looking at the photo of the single lavender, slightly out of focus, with a little disappointment. It was the same single lavender that hung opposite her bed at home, the one she saw last thing at night after she'd sprinkled a few lavender drops on her pillow and the first thing she saw every morning before she stopped her alarm.

Herr Bayer coughed politely.

"It's a beautiful flat," she enthused quickly coming out of her musings, "and on such a lovely street."

"Thank you," he replied. "We like it and it's quiet here most of the time. But you have to be very careful of the dog mess on the street."

She was grateful he spoke such fluent English. Apart from a little French and an even smaller amount of Latin, the latter having equipped her to occasionally understand the medical name of an illness and to read tombstones, she was unable to communicate with nearly all non-English-speaking peoples. Her universality was pretty limited.

She scrambled for the agreed cash that would secure a three-week stay. Herr Bayer took it from her and walked towards the kitchen table where he quietly counted the money. He took what seemed like a small notepad from the left pocket of his cardigan and then a biro from his right. Without saying a word he wrote out a receipt for her, then carefully tore it out of the book.

"Thank you, Mrs Thompson." He smiled and handed her the flimsy piece of paper. "There are books and maps on the table by the sofa and the rubbish goes into the courtyard. Left out of here and left again. It's not very far. If you need to contact me, we're in number seven. Do you think you'll be OK?"

She said she was sure she would.

"Before I go, I'll show you the keys." He picked up two keys, held together by a silver ring, from the table and walked towards the glass front door. "You have to use both keys to lock it," and he demonstrated twice how the door was to be locked and unlocked. He smiled again and then, as if suddenly remembering something, said, "I have to go now." He seemed agitated, tapping his back trouser pockets quite sharply; a panic had, without invitation, woken him from a peaceful interlude. "Please knock on my door if there's anything you need." He looked awkward. "I hope you enjoy your stay."

"Thank you. Thank you very much. It's lovely." She put the keys in a glass fruit bowl on the table. They rattled to the bottom and she realised how still everything had become; a traveller no more, she'd arrived at her destination.

She scanned the room. It was pleasing to the eye. The front of the flat, including the door, was entirely window space, made discreet by fine cream linen curtains that ensured complete privacy. It was a large room, with a bed in one corner facing the street. A duvet cover, full with bright reds, oranges and purples, looking as if a modern art gallery would be proud to call it their own, left her feeling Herr Bayer had had a younger eye to help him furnish. In another corner, near the window, were a sofa, table and TV. A pine and Wedgewood blue kitchen sat at the back and in the final corner was a spacious white wardrobe, which she couldn't bear the thought of filling until the morning. She peeped in at the bathroom, tucked neatly behind the kitchen and it was, as with everything here, beautifully clean. She liked the red towels, which made a welcome change from the usual white or pastel shades offered holidaymakers. The information she'd received from Herr Bayer when she booked was that the flat was a converted shop and as she sat on the bed, listening to people's feet and conversations she couldn't understand, she wondered what sort would have sat on this East Berlin street. She was breathing the air of spy novels and it felt peculiarly exciting to be sitting comfortably in such dangerous territory where suspicion and fear pervaded every corner.

It was seven. She needed to eat. Opposite the flat was what looked like a very fashionable restaurant and hotel, but it suggested a special occasion and her travel weariness dictated that this wasn't it. She plucked the map out of her handbag, opened it and searched for Tieckstrasse. Luckily, she wasn't far from a main street. She picked up the keys, stepped out and double-locked the door, as instructed by Herr Bayer, pushing against it afterwards to be certain no one could enter without breaking in.

She needed only a light jumper and she'd picked out her navy crochet one that she'd almost discarded in the winter sale, then thinking it wouldn't be warm enough but ideal for the weather they'd had recently. It had been a long hot summer, which had drifted into September quite easily. She walked down the street. She hadn't lied to Herr Bayer. It was very attractive, wide with old buildings either side and young trees placed equidistantly on either side. She suddenly felt disorientated, almost not believing she'd walked down her own street only this morning. It was always the first night away that troubled her, filling her with a nostalgia for home comforts and friends. Her cautious excitement was tempered by a feeling of alienation and a peculiar anxiety that normality would never be hers again. Now, she felt it acutely. This was her first holiday on her own, not since her twenties or since the time when she decided she'd had enough of Stephen and the children and took herself off; no, this was her first holiday on her own, ever. She belonged to a generation in which lone female travel wasn't taken for granted and was considered not to be the done thing for it perhaps suggested an aloneness not of one's own making or a separation from some quiet moral code.

She walked through the streets somewhat adrift, bereft of company and familiar language, yet strangely heartened by the fact that no one she passed knew anything about her relatively new status of widow. In that sense, and this did make her smile slightly, it would truly be a break. Normality, after all, could be horribly claustrophobic with its pressure to behave within the perimeters of what's considered acceptable grieving behaviour.

She sat at an outside table of a café that seemed as good as any and ordered a pizza. It had probably been a very hot day because the evening air felt as if it was slightly relieved and was breathing out a sigh of gratitude that the sun was finally waving goodbye. This country, she thought, had a familiarity about it like no other, even though she'd never been here before. It felt as if it was inside her somehow, part of who she was through listening to parents and grandparents and through the experiences, not of those she knew particularly, but of their relatives, people who knew people who knew people. The war, the war before that and a cold war that used to give her mother a shudder whenever the very name Russia was mentioned. She couldn't remember exactly how old she was when she first became aware of what was always referred to as the last war, which, in her young mind, she initially interpreted as the last war that was ever going to happen and if that was the case, she supposed she could see why it was so talked about. But she could, without much effort, conjure up the remembrance services she used to have to attend at primary school. It was always an icy day and there was invariably a slight fog. They would all stand, frozen, around the memorial in the churchyard, their poppies pinned firmly to their coats, and listened to the last post, although they didn't really know it as that then; it was just someone playing an instrument, though it was very sad. They were just a few yards from school, but the warmth of the classroom felt a world away as they remained still, not daring to move. Her mother stood a little behind her. Fay was opposite. Her long plaits, as ever in place, and her German mother, Mrs Harris, was next to Fay, firm and proud, her blonde hair long for mothers then and her bright blue eyes staring into the distance. The ceremony ended and she remembered on this particular day people started talking more quickly, perhaps because they were frozen and thought speech might help, though no one spoke to Mrs Harris. When nearly everyone had gone, Mrs Harris approached her mother.

"We didn't know," she said, but she didn't think her mother, who'd heard this before, ever quite believed Mrs Harris. "Where did they think everyone was going?" she used to say, though it was a few years before Helen registered who the everyone were her mother was talking about. Back then, she probably just picked up that her mother didn't always quite believe what was said to her.

She looked around the café and wondered who the grandparents and great-grandparents were of those sitting around her. What had they done, what had been their responsibilities during the war? She'd heard of others doing something similar when visiting countries that were former adversaries, but she hated herself. It was none of her business and why should people be scarred who weren't alive then? Nevertheless, she couldn't help herself and her mind began transporting their features to another time.

"Could I have the bill, please?" she asked of the waiter, whose features she left firmly in the here and now and whose service had been impeccable. She was feeling very tired, suddenly, as her long day was finally catching up with her, but, as she walked back to the flat, the warm air helped keep her attention and a gradual excitement started to envelope her at the prospect of the next three weeks in Berlin.

The flat was as cool as a sea breeze when she got in and she lay on the bed and basked in the welcome climate. She had no doubt in her mind that she was going to like it here and she got up and opened the curtains slightly that she'd closed before leaving to get a glimpse of life outside again. It was something she often did at home just before she went to bed as it just reminded her that, though she was alone in a building, there was still plenty of life to be had out there. She looked across to the hotel opposite her with its large, completely transparent windows that were more reminiscent of a department store. It seemed to be showing off its opulence, inviting guests to an experience that went beyond average comfort, one for which two hours at the very least should be put aside for using the restaurant. People walked discreetly into the foyer, singly or in couples, and a suited member of staff waltzed elegantly and purposefully towards or away from the desk, according to what was required. Everything, apart from the building itself, had the appearance of recent renovation and new decoration. It was the result, she mused, of a Western make-over, a before and after, where after is always supposed better, even though, presumably, it could be enjoyed by only a few.

She closed the curtains again, which fell from the ceiling to the floor and were so light and delicate they danced across the entire front of the flat, past the front door and as they reached her, she noticed a note on the ground she hadn't previously seen. She picked it up and saw almost immediately that it was from Herr Bayer. She read the perfect English.

"Dear Mrs Thompson, I'm sorry I had to leave so suddenly. I hope you don't think me rude. I hope also that everything in the flat is as you wish and that you've settled in OK. If you'd like to have a cup of coffee with us sometime during your stay, you'd be very welcome. Please don't hesitate to knock on our door, best wishes, Peter Bayer."

She smiled. It was a very sweet note, though she was slightly surprised at his need to write it, and surprised, too, at the invitation for coffee. She put it down on the table by the sofa. It reminded her that she should ring Margot first thing in the morning to let them know she'd arrived and was it still OK for next Tuesday?

3

The last thing Helen said to Stephen was, "Can you get some matches?" It was their daughter Emma's eighteenth birthday the following day. Nearly a year ago. She'd arranged for the cake to be made weeks before by a woman recommended by a friend whose praise of the caterer seemed to know no bounds. The woman had asked for photos of Emma and a list of her interests. When Helen collected the cake she saw an edible model of Emma sitting on top of a large iced sponge cake, watching TV, even *Friends* transcribed on the screen, with a phone in her hand, surrounded by clothes and books. She journeyed home with this work of art in the boot of her car, convinced all the while that someone would run into the back of her. They didn't and, after showing it to Stephen, she hid it in a cupboard she knew Emma never visited. The candles were already in place, but there wasn't one match in the house.

The first thing she said to him was, "Hello, are you Stephen Thompson?"

He graciously replied, "Yes, I am," during which moment she read "Stephen Thompson" on a label on his shirt. It had often been her dubious blessing in life that she spoke before putting in the research. They were both at a legal conference and she was looking for a new secretarial post, following the early retirement of her old boss who'd taken this path quite unexpectedly after a holiday romance in Spain where he was off to live. One of the other partner's secretaries said she'd heard something about Thompson and Partners needing a new secretary and maybe she should seek them out at that conference she was going to. She told Stephen she was looking for work. He didn't need anyone, but he knew one of his partners soon would. He went over to a nearby table and brought her a glass of wine. She forgot to say thank you. The last time she spoke to him, the day of the candles, she forgot to say please, relying on well-established intimacy as an excuse for omitting a politeness that's just standard practice elsewhere.

Their getting together was a long while coming during which time they routinely crossed paths, enjoyed jokes at office parties and were introduced to one another's dates. It was because she'd made a mess of an urgent document and was working late re-typing it that they accidentally, really, ended up having a drink together. The Dog and Duck near Leicester Square. That was one hell of an evening.

She woke unusually refreshed. Her first thought was Stephen. It always was. Her second was her children and her third, how comfy the bed was. She got out of bed and made her way to the kitchen area. She'd brought some tea bags with her and some powdered milk. Not perfect, but it would do till she got to the shops. Herr Bayer had given her directions to the nearest ones.

Her phone buzzed. It was a text from her daughter, Emma, thanking her for the text she'd sent last night saying she'd arrived safely.

"Hav a gr8 time." It ended, "Ur gonna b ok."

They lived over a hundred miles apart and before Stephen died, they'd seen her about once a month and his death hadn't altered anything particularly, apart from the first couple of months when she thought Emma had perhaps felt an obligation to see her a bit more, but the trouble was neither knew what to say to the other face to face. She thought it came down to the fact they were both frightened of seeing each other's tears, which was odd because they did plenty of crying on the phone. It was as if watching the tears made both of them feel a burden of expectation that was too heavy to bear and was one that could easily end in failure. But it was also the nature of their relationship. In less grave times, they had always got on better on the phone. They were a funny lot. She mostly heard what her son, James, was up to through Emma. And she didn't want to do Facebook. She was too old, with what now seemed like very old-fashioned views of privacy. Emails were her limit.

She sipped her tea. How English.

"Hello. Is that Margot? Hi Margot, it's Helen... Yes, I'm fine, thanks. Got here about six last night... No, no, that's very kind, but I went out and had a pizza. It was good getting some fresh air after all the travelling. I was just ringing about Tuesday. Is that OK still?"

She laughed at Margot's enthusiasm. Of course it was OK, more than OK, they'd had it on the calendar for months. What was she going to do in the next couple of days? Did she want to come round before then? Well, she must make sure she goes to the Reichstag and the Tiergarten; they would be lovely on a day like today.

She gave Helen the same instructions as she'd emailed and said that Hans would be at the bus stop, and just to let them know when she thought she'd get there. Was she still sure she didn't want Hans to come and collect her? Well, he'll obviously take her home. She was really looking forward to Tuesday.

She tried to make herself another cup of tea, but the kettle didn't seem to be doing anything. She went to the bathroom and switched on the light, which also did nothing. Bugger. And everything was going so well. She tried a few more things, which were equally uncooperative. She'd have to ring Herr Bayer's door after all. It was something Stephen would've done and she'd have carried on getting ready.

4

It was very annoying, what had happened to Mrs Thompson, Herr Bayer thought. Luckily, she'd been a lot calmer than the couple from Hanover who'd threatened no payment for the whole week. The electrician had mumbled something about a poor job having been done last time but seemed to quickly forget this when Herr Bayer reminded him it was his firm who'd done it and the bill presented was roughly the same as last time. Herr Bayer could have quibbled, but Elsa had woken up and it was all too much of a bother to make a fuss. Still, by the time he'd seen to Elsa and gone round with the money to Mrs Thompson, fatigue had mingled with relief to successfully blot out any remaining irritation he felt towards the electric company.

He started to look for a book he seemed to have mislaid when the doorbell rang. He tried not to leap straight to despair at the thought of possibly more trouble. He remained a little disconcerted when it was Mrs Thompson's face he saw, but she was smiling.

"Hello, Herr Bayer, sorry to bother you, but I thought you might like these." She gave him a bottle of wine and some chocolates. He was slightly stunned as she continued. "Just to say thank you for sorting things out so quickly. You know, you really shouldn't have given me that money. I don't need any compensation."

At last he found his voice. "No, no, Mrs Thompson. It was an inconvenience for you."

"Well, very kind of you, even so."

He took his gift and thanked her, saying what a lovely surprise it was and how much he would enjoy both. Gently tapping the chocolates, he said, "Why don't I open these now and we could have some with a coffee?"

Mrs Thompson looked at her watch. "Well, I…"

"It won't take long to make," he reassured.

"Ok, well yes, thank you, that would be nice."

Mrs Thompson seemed a bit reluctant and he hoped he hadn't pushed her into staying. He stretched out his left arm slightly, directing her towards the living room where Elsa would, as usual, be staring out of the window. Introducing her had become easier over time and necessary, really, if he weren't to become completely isolated from the outside world.

"Elsa, wir haben Besuch." Elsa looked confused and a bit cross. Herr Bayer turned to his guest. "You'll have to excuse me while I explain things to Elsa. I'm afraid she doesn't know English." Mrs Thompson smiled. "It's Helen, isn't it? I just know from the paperwork for the flat. Do you mind me calling you Helen? I'm Peter and this is Elsa."

His wife was still confused. "Wir wollen kein Besuch."

Peter couldn't disguise the tone of anger in Elsa's voice, but he didn't have to tell his guest that she'd said she didn't want visitors for it wasn't true of him. "I'm sorry, Mrs… Helen. Elsa, she has dementia. She gets very cross these days, I'm sorry. This isn't my wife, she's not like this; she's the most sweet-natured…"

Helen felt she'd done completely the wrong thing in coming here and fervently wished she could just get herself out of the flat as quickly as possible. She'd intruded on something very personal and something that had nothing to do with her. The invitation for coffee was just one of those things people say and her coming here had obviously caused problems. It was like the moments, and to be fair they weren't that often but they were always the most memorable, when giving a client a beauty treatment or a therapy, she'd asked one question too far or got the wrong end of a particular stick and she was very grateful when they'd handed over the money and walked out of the room. Like the time when she'd said to a client that she hoped her new puppy would settle down soon only to be told they didn't have a dog but they did have a baby daughter. She'd unfortunately lost her concentration halfway through giving the poor woman a foot massage, but honestly, who does call their child Princess?

"It's OK," was all she could think of saying. "Please don't apologise."

He had his back to Helen and was trying to help Elsa calm down. She'd been aimlessly circling around the living room and now she was sitting down, worn out with it all and crying. He leant over and reached for her hanky, which was just behind a cushion where she'd left it about an hour or so earlier. He dried her face with it and then wiped her nose. He could have given up but instead turned to Helen.

"How do you take your coffee?" he asked.

Though she wanted to run, Helen had rarely felt such an urge to oblige.

"Just milk, thank you."

He nodded and put the television on for Elsa.

"Maybe you'd like to follow me into the—"

At which point Elsa stamped her feet.

"Ich gehe gerade in die Küche mit Helen." He looked at the TV. "Schau mal, du magst diese Sendung." Elsa smiled into his eyes. He held her hands tightly, asking for release. She withdrew hers and gently patted his knuckles. "You can imagine, Helen, how confusing another language is for her. Maybe you'd like to join me in the kitchen." He was tired and needed to make coffee as much for himself as his visitor.

"How long have you lived here?"

He listened to her question while thinking how long it had been since he'd heard someone talk in his house. Like a song you haven't heard for some time, it had a strange yet welcome resonance and took him back to times that seemed a lot easier.

"We're a bit boring, I'm afraid. In ten weeks we'll have lived here thirty-four years – 30th November 1972." He smiled. "It was mainly because I'd got a teaching job at the school down the road. Have you seen it?"

"Oh, the one by the supermarket?"

"Yes."

She seemed genuinely interested. An immaculate woman who obviously took time with her appearance, he wagered she was a businesswoman or lawyer.

"What did you teach?"

He laughed. "English."

"Wasn't it a bit close for comfort, living so nearby?"

"Yes, that was a consideration initially, but we just loved the house. I bet you find that hard to believe."

"No, it's…"

"Not what it was. Please, you don't have to be polite." He poured the coffee for both of them. "Elsa's just had a drink. I have to be there with her, she likes warm chocolate." He swallowed some coffee and found himself struggling with this more than he'd imagined. It was a long time since he'd been in the position of talking to someone new and the experience was difficult because he'd almost forgotten the rules. When it was the doctor or Inge or a neighbour or such, he already knew them well and the conversation, more often than not, was about Elsa, how she was, how he was coping, and they'd look at him sympathetically while all time he knew they were thinking, *Thank heavens that's not me*. And they'd walk away feeling relieved and he, well, he'd just feel flat. But here there were things to be found out and he was interested in the answers, though he didn't want to appear too inquisitive.

He asked her if she had a job in England.

She told him she was a complementary therapist, that she was widowed and that it had become necessary to build up a business that had previously relied on friends and word of mouth because, while she was married, her income hadn't been essential. Which was a hell of a lot more than she was used to saying to people she didn't know. Being out of the country seemed to have cut her usual inhibitions in half.

Peter could see she wasn't used to talking about herself. Her dark eyes saddened at times, but she nervously recovered with a broad smile. Everything else was perfectly controlled. Her dark, short hair, falling just above pearl earrings, beautifully manicured hands and smart clothing that matched so well, he couldn't imagine any of part of her life being uncoordinated.

"Weg von mir. Wer sind Sie?" *Who was he?* Elsa was asking. It troubled her greatly that he had any interaction with others and, when he thought about it sympathetically, he understood that this scene must indeed be very troubling for her, given that she may, fleetingly, have only an idea that she knew at least one person, but then hold the frightening thought that she knew no one. When, on the other hand, his mood was less generous, he just thought her childish need for attention was unreasonable and unkind. Didn't she realise he had to talk normally and not engage in the daft, weird ramblings that had become her sole means of communication? As to who he was, he had no idea these days. How did they both look to this English woman? Did she think at all that at one time Elsa's eyes were the bright blue of a kingfisher's feathers and that she would take them and skip down a country lane as if life had an airy quality that just required knowing a few light steps?

"Er ist abgehauen, hat mich im Stich gelassen, weisst du."

"She says that I've gone and left her, but as you can see, Helen, I'm here."

He looked at his wife and held both her hands for what

must have been about a minute, which seemed enough time to placate her. He then looked at her.

"I'll go and get the coffee."

His face was so tired and she wasn't sure whether she should stay. But to leave seemed rude and she could feel an almost urgent need from him for conversation undisturbed by disorder.

She smiled at Elsa who wasn't pleased at all by this and responded with a glare that seemed to say, "How dare you," so she sat as still as she could and glanced around the room without appearing to do so. It had a weary intelligence about it and was predominantly brown, with bookshelves on one side as high as the ceiling and wallpaper on the other that probably used to be fashionable. In one corner there was a table with drawers on either side and papers strewn across the top.

On another, more centrally placed table she saw flowers, past their best but not thrown away, sitting next to a pile of books that had been lovingly read and marked in various places for a return visit.

On a shelf in one corner there were photos of a couple she presumed was Peter and Elsa, young and enthusiastic, and a larger school photo in which Peter was probably one of the adults in the front row. An old black and white photo of a boy was sitting in the middle of these, his thick, blond, curly hair beautifully in place considering its natural extravagance and a look of steely determination and responsibility more reminiscent of a company director than a boy of no more than ten years.

"I was a lot slimmer in those days," Peter laughed as he came in with the drinks.

"Elsa looks very happy in them," said his guest.

"Yes. Yes, she does. I miss that," he replied.

5

It was very peculiar, Helen thought, sitting on a boat and listening to the guide describe the destruction caused during the war and knowing it was your country that was responsible. A disturbing vision of history in which you are the perpetrator, even though you and the others on the boat were so familiar with the reasons. It made her uncomfortable, a feeling heightened by his bland presentation, which was devoid of all malice or self-pity.

Her complacent view of history was being nudged a little, awakening more than perhaps was intended and she shuddered, feeling slightly ashamed of who she was. She thought of the war-damaged church she'd seen only that morning, with its broken spire displaying a courage and determination that renovation work would have simply removed, depriving passers-by of the reminders of war. Instead, its imperfection was startling and the clock, telling the correct time, showed anyone who cared to see, a similar optimism to daffodils whose will to survive brisk springs, she felt, should always be applauded, as their bright coloured heads nodded "so what?" to wind and rain. It was an image that was more memorable than anything perfection could offer.

When the wall came down she'd taken Emma to play in the park. Europe was changing, but the swings were more important and when they returned she had settled herself in front of the TV, mug of tea in hand, and simultaneously watched her daughter draw pictures of sky and flowers and the footage of the wall coming down from the evening before.

It was how she'd always received world news, against the background of her child's life. The shouting, the relief, the singing and excitement and Emma saying, "Look, Mummy," at a stick man who had a smiley face.

And then she remembered the stories of others, who'd either come to Berlin soon after the wall had fallen and who'd brought back a bit of it or who had a piece from someone who knew someone who'd brought it back, grey pieces of concrete, with the odd bit of colour, taken from this letter or that, messages of anger and desperation. Now, when she passed the gift shops, there were still small pieces, presented in almost equally small plastic bags, that you could buy with your postcards, a tiny bit of freedom perfectly packaged and ready for sale.

In another life, of course, she'd be saying all this to Stephen and the conversation about the war and the wall would somehow confirm a shared view of the world and they would agree how odd it could be to get a former adversary's perspective; then this discussion would gradually merge into what they would do next or where they'd eat. So it was very different, to say the least, to share your view with yourself and have a completely selfish stand on where your evening meal should come from. It wasn't all that appealing but nor was it as upsetting as she thought it might be.

She smiled to herself. The guide was still talking, but she momentarily stopped listening and thought of what she'd said to Peter about her evening in Brecht's restaurant. How it was very good food but the waiter was a bit sullen in a way that seemed deliberate almost to the point of being provocative. It was as if he was adopting the restaurant's history and former owner, taking it as his own and rehearsing a part, she'd said, to which Peter had laughed out loud. He'd said he'd once taken a class to see *The Threepenny Opera*. He wasn't sure they'd fully grasped the satire and thought, perhaps, the songs had got in the way. He just remembered them humming the tunes in class afterwards, mainly in an effort to distract him from setting them work. "But, sir," they'd moaned when he'd asked them to stop, "it's Brecht." He said he hadn't had the heart to say, "Actually, it's Weill."

She closed her eyes and let the breeze waft across her face and influence her mood. It didn't surprise her particularly; it lifted her level of optimism, as the combination of sun and a slight wind often did, and she heard Stephen's suggestion of an Indian meal, which suited her down to the ground. As the guide abandoned his microphone for a few minutes while he spoke with his colleague who was steering the boat, she reached for a letter she carried around with her, one she'd had in every handbag for several years now, written by her father, when he was stationed in Bermuda during the war and was written hopeful that the war would soon end.

It was a letter composed on light blue airmail paper, so thin it was barely more than the finest tissue and every time she opened it, she was reacquainted with her father's familiar hand that had an upright confidence not entirely shared with its owner. He could be a nervous man whose anxieties ran through him in little tics – a slight stutter; a tap of the fingers on a table – that she strongly suspected, rather than having some genetic imprint, came from a father who'd been on Belgian battlefields and an incurable virus of slight anger and terror had run through her grandfather from that time on. A brave man, it turned out, who'd taken a hit in the back rather than see his poor horse die and who'd had innocuous little bets on the Brighton races ever since. But a man who'd preceded post-traumatic stress disorder because it wasn't a generally held belief then and who was at sea when it came to handling such memories, so instead adopted a stricter demeanour than a man without a war in his blood might have. A sad fact for his children who only really saw the more compassionate man in their adulthood when perhaps old age had worn their father down and he relaxed his defences a little.

She took the letter out of its envelope, as she had many times previously. It had danced between handbags and the top drawer of a cabinet at home for many years and as time went on, so the ink had faded, making her type a copy just in case the ink finally dissolved into the paper. But she could still read the Bermuda postmark today and she could imagine her father stationed there and see, in her mind's eye, the photo of him in his RAF uniform.

BERMUDA. THURSDAY, 8TH JUNE 1944

Dear Mum and Dad,

On Tuesday morning about ten to seven I was woken from my slumbers by several voices talking hurriedly outside in the corridor. The gist of their conversation made me get up and see what was happening. The sun was streaming in through the window as I sat on the bed, still half asleep, feeling with my feet for carpet slippers, where I'd kicked them off eight hours before, although then it seemed only five minutes previously.

I eventually slid my feet into my slippers and shuffled outside into the corridor. The chaps were still talking and I soon gathered that landings in France had been made. I couldn't quite believe what I'd heard but was convinced a few minutes later when I heard it over the wireless. The reception was bad that time of morning but nevertheless heard it OK. Well, that's how I heard the beginning of D-Day but even then could hardly believe the momentous news!

How did you hear it over there? I hope that everything is OK with you as I guess Brighton must really be a front-line town today.

I couldn't sleep again; I went down to breakfast at half-past seven and lo and behold there were about ten blokes already having breakfast, whereas generally there's no one there till eight at the earliest.

She looked up from the letter. It was as if she could practically smell the eggs cooking from all those years ago.

6

Elsa pressed her lips against the glass, kissed the boy in the photo several times, then rubbed the glass clean with her wrist. She kissed it again, told the boy she loved him and rubbed the glass clean. Peter looked away and picked up his newspaper. This was a daily ritual of Elsa's. The only thing he could confidently predict she would do. He got his glasses out of their case and began reading the reports of war and corruption, her voice all the while in his ear, "I love you, I love you," directed not at him but at the boy in the photo, and then the intermittent sound of kissing. Her mutterings persisted, breaking his concentration and irritating him more than usual, so that anyone aware of him, and Elsa wasn't, would've heard the unusually noisy turning of the pages or the odd loud slap to flatten them out a bit.

He started to think about an ex-pupil of his and was sorry he hadn't been able to speak to Karl for longer when they'd bumped into him the other day. What a good bloke he'd turned out to be. So reliable and trustworthy. It wasn't surprising, though. With the exception of one or two poorly judged pranks, which, Peter suspected, he'd more than likely been coerced into by one or two more dubious sorts, he'd been pretty much the same as a boy. His eagerness to learn was unfortunately his downfall and eventually study had become a poor second to survival. But wistful as he was of Karl the graduate, he couldn't deny he'd benefited hugely from his pupil's expertise with the old shop. If it hadn't been for Karl and his team of builders he'd have been sorely tempted to throw in the towel a long time ago, but Herr Muller, an old friend of his mother's, had been determined he should have it and putting it up for sale, Peter knew, would've broken his heart. But thanks to Karl's hard work and terrific imagination, the shop had been completely transformed into the holiday flat where Helen was now staying. Herr Muller would've surely known that with recent competition, the shop would've almost certainly gone to pieces. No, he felt quite certain Herr Muller, the gentlest man you could wish to meet, would've been pleased so many holidaymakers were benefiting from its new role.

He looked at Elsa, whose hands were clasped so firmly to the photo her knuckles were white. He stroked her curly, grey hair and quietly suggested taking the photo from her.

"Let me put that back," he softly suggested.

"No, no," she barked at him and her knuckles, like four little mountain peaks, showed a grim determination he didn't have the will to fight.

Instead, he tried to plump up the cushions behind her, but she responded to this by momentarily relinquishing the photo with her right hand and using it to pinch his arm with such ferocity, he could only yell, "Stop, stop, Elsa, stop, you're hurting me."

He managed to pull away and he walked into the kitchen to calm himself. He was going to get ill. He knew that. He knew that at some point there would come a day when he wouldn't be able to get out of bed. His doctor had told him as much, but he wasn't going to put her away somewhere. How could he do that? These bloody medics were good at dishing out the advice, but what did they know? They didn't. They didn't know his daily life, the turmoil in his head. And what would people like Karl think if he dumped Elsa in a home, because that would be what it would feel like, like he was putting her out with the rubbish? He wished he still smoked.

Right now, a cigarette would be the next best thing to, well, he would say heaven, but it wasn't a concept he believed in, so a cigarette would be the next best thing to a fine classical piece of music. It was just as inaccessible as heaven, as Elsa nowadays often hated him listening to music unless he invited her to join in. Maybe he'd buy a packet the next time he was in the supermarket, go to the nearby park and make his way through each and every one of them in the allotted quarter of an hour he gave himself to leave Elsa alone. He rubbed his face with his hands, as if beckoning a new start, and returned to the living room, where Elsa was staring into space, unaware, most probably, of what had just happened and certainly oblivious of his presence. If she was calm, he wouldn't do anything to alter that, so he just plonked himself back in his chair and reached for a nearby book. He was hot and clammy, which wasn't just the result of his bumping up against Elsa's fragility but a climate outside that was humid. It was as if the weather felt sick and needed to vomit up a storm.

He opened one of his cherished poetry books and saw an English poem that celebrated the end of the First World War. "Everyone suddenly burst out singing," he read and smiled to himself ironically, not because of the sentiment of the poet, but because singing was something that seemed quite alien to him now when Elsa pursed her lips against the soup he tried to put in her mouth – couldn't she possibly realise how long it had taken him to make it? – or when she seemed to prefer that wretched photo over him.

"And I was filled with such delight/ As prisoned birds must find in freedom." He looked out of the window and remembered when he'd first learnt these lines from Sassoon's poem "Everyone Sang". He was fifteen and hungry for the words of their recent adversary, even then, and despite everything, appreciating the sometime comfort of being part of a losing side. He'd wanted to understand what the Americans were saying every bit as much as the English. They had a confidence he'd envied, laughing and jostling one another, as if the streets were theirs. Such flair made a strong impression and he'd devoured the language with an enthusiasm he hadn't had for his other studies.

"How can you like that bloody language?" some of his mates had said and as he'd moved towards university with English books under his arms, he'd heard the whispers of his mother's friends. "Do you like him doing this? How can he? Who killed his father?" Actually… he still wanted to answer that one but hadn't done so to this day. "Why English? Doesn't he remember 22nd November?" He did. It was a Monday and two days before he'd celebrated his tenth birthday. He was feeling quite grown up and excited that at last he'd reached double figures.

"Herr Muller said we'll be all right tonight." His mother dropped the shopping basket, filled with ration goods from his shop, on the hallway floor and shook the rain from her hair. She undid her dripping coat and put it on the coat stand. "It's terrible out there. Herr Muller says we can't possibly have a raid tonight. The weather's too bad. Visibility's too poor, he said. Peter, can you take the shopping through?" Peter's Auntie Gerda, who was standing next to him, thanked God for the rain and the fact they could look forward to a peaceful evening together.

"What did you manage to get?" she asked and his mother gave them the news that fish and potatoes were for supper followed by apples, which she'd been very lucky to get as, apparently, they'd only just got to Herr Muller's. Auntie Gerda left Peter and his mother to unload the shopping, then reappeared a few minutes later with the stripy towel from the bathroom. "Come here," she said to his mother and rubbed her head hard. They all laughed when she emerged from Auntie Gerda's vigorous rubbing, her hair looking more dishevelled than during the last air raid, when they'd both crouched, fully clothed, in the bathtub.

"Better this," his mother had whispered, "than flying splinters from the furniture," and when they'd heard the drone, she'd folded herself over him where, goodness knows how, they'd remained for nearly an hour.

He played excitedly with the toy train Auntie Gerda had given him for his birthday while she and his mother prepared their meal. It was only years later he learnt the train belonged to his cousin who was serving in France. He could never really hear what they said when they were huddled in the kitchen. For much of the time Auntie Gerda and his mother spoke in hushed tones. They were all glad of their fish and potatoes on such a horrible night and his mother had mashed the potatoes to perfection, particularly good as she had no butter or milk. He finished and felt, as he often did, that he'd have welcomed seconds if they'd had any.

As his mother picked up their plates to take to the kitchen, they heard the siren. "Surely not," and she limply let go of one of the plates. Auntie Gerda took control, for his mother couldn't seem to move.

"Come on," she shouted, gathering him in her arms and practically shoving his mother towards the cupboard under the stairs. "Run!" As they obeyed her they heard the first bomb explode. The noise pierced his ears and his mother calculated it could have been only a street away, an utterance she seemed to regret as she immediately said sorry to him and pulled him towards her. He felt her lips on his head, her breath blowing gently on his hair. Another one fell. So close to their house it shook. Then another. And a crash, this time somewhere in the house, followed, as if triangles had joined cymbals, by what seemed like a mountain of glass shattering on the floor. He'd shook as much before only when he'd had that fever and he was clammy with a temperature of 103. His mother was hugging him so tightly now he was sure he would bruise and none of them speaking, thinking, probably, that if they did, the bombers may hear them.

The bombs didn't stop that night. Usually, they came in waves – the drone, the quiet, the drone, the quiet – and each period of quiet they'd learnt to take deep breaths, in relief and preparation. But that night, there was an unrelenting drone, a determination by their enemy to offer nothing in the way of respite. So they had to tolerate the combined sound of droning, crashing and the eerie crumbling of houses around them for over an hour, imagining, or trying not to, what they would see of their city when they could go out again.

After about an hour, he remembered, it did go quiet for a while, but the all-clear didn't sound and they braced themselves for another bombcarpet, as Berliners had begun to call them, Peter defying his mother by daring to go out of the cupboard for a few minutes as his legs couldn't keep still any longer. Then the droning started again and he flew into their arms, where he stayed for what seemed like a lifetime. The all-clear came at 10pm, an hour after his bedtime, but no one was ready for sleep.

They crawled out of the cupboard, their bones weary from the task of saving their lives. The telephone rang almost straight away. It was Herr Muller, checking to see if they were all right and apologising for his erroneous prediction. "Who'd have thought it, on a night like this?" his mother reassured, then put the phone down and reported Herr Muller's words to them that the danger, he'd been told, was now a rising wind, which would be sure to make a fire storm in a few hours' time. "The fires of hell," she said and they all looked into the living room, which they could do now as the door had blown off its hinges.

After they'd cleared up as much as they could, and Peter was pleased to see his train had also survived, they gingerly opened the front door and it was only when they saw that nothing before them was recognisable that they began to realise how lucky they'd been. His mother began crying and Auntie Gerda thrust him protectively into her stomach in a tardy attempt to stop him seeing the devastation. He could still hear his mother sobbing and he started to cry himself as hearing her like this was the thing he couldn't bear the most. His tears soaked Auntie Gerda's lavender-scented skirt, a smell he could still just detect underneath the stronger waft of smoke and an odd stench in the burning fires. He remembered he hadn't cried since he'd been very cross with a friend who had come to tea but who wouldn't let him play with his own toy plane. He'd got so cross he'd lashed out at and hit his friend. His father had come in and told Peter he was extremely disappointed in him. Somehow, coming from his father whom he loved beyond anything, disappointment was worse than anger and he'd gone to his room and cried until he was sure there were no tears left.

Nobody said anything until he could hear his mother and aunt, in almost whispers, utter expected condemnations. Then, slowly, he heard them try to piece together what had been lost and he ran into the house because he didn't want to know. They followed in quickly, frightened for his safety in what was now a fragile place to be.

"Stop," his mother shouted for there were no lights and it wasn't long before they knew they didn't have a phone anymore and nor had they water or heat.

He stayed in the hallway with Auntie Gerda while she looked for candles in a drawer in a cupboard in the lounge where he liked to keep his pencils. She lit a match and he could now see her tear-stained face.

"Be careful of the glass," she advised them both and they followed her in, every crunch of broken glass under their feet seeming to lay their past to rest.

Soberly, they sat and counted their good fortune and his mother found a small bottle of brandy. It was his first introduction to alcohol and he remembered he loved the warmth it gave his mouth and his tummy. Despite protests from Auntie Gerda and her son, his mother went upstairs and minutes later returned with pillows and blankets. They started to settle for the night. It felt important to at least try to do something normal, though the eerie sound of crumbling buildings did much to shake this attempt. He lay between them, wondering if it was possible that their hearts were beating as hard as his.

When morning came, both adults tried to do usual things, his mother saying she must go out and try to find more food, but her quandary lay in whether Peter and Auntie Gerda should go with her. The fear of what would happen if they let anyone out of their sight won the day and they all ventured out but were immediately stopped in their tracks by a cloud of smoke pushing its way past them as they opened the door. They immediately shut it again and Auntie Gerda said something about wet towels for their faces.

"There's no water," reminded his mother, but Auntie Gerda said she'd thought of something. She emerged from upstairs carrying sodden towels, telling them as she did so with a slight self-congratulatory smile that she'd filled the sink in the bathroom just before the bombing.

"I was going to wash my face to wake myself up a bit," she said, glad that her weariness had had such a positive outcome.

"Cover your face as much as you can, Peter," his mother instructed him by demonstration, as she often did, a technique he'd always found useful in his teaching, and he could now see only her bright green eyes, which winked encouragement to do the same. He opened up the bundle of wet cloth and saw it was the same towel Auntie Gerda had used on his mother's hair the day before. He put the icy towel against his skin and followed them outside. He wanted to know what had happened to his friends, to Friedrich and Gerhard – what would they be doing now? Where were they? – but didn't ask, instead letting his imagination go to places he didn't like and thinking of all the stories he'd read where heroes had ended up in sticky situations.

It was horrible outside. He couldn't recognise anything and he began to feel cross at his mother for letting him see such things. He couldn't see the shops or the streets and most houses were a pile of rubble. He wanted to go back in the house where he could still see things he saw yesterday and hoped beyond hope they wouldn't be out for long.

It was difficult to walk on the piles of bricks and glass, but with his flat shoes he coped a little better than his mother and aunt who on various occasions nearly twisted their ankles with their heels. He felt frightened of everyone's charcoal faces, which, along with the faces covered with scarves, looked like monsters from another planet and even though some raised their hands in greeting and said, "Hello, Peter," he recognised none.

No one stopped to talk, which was unusual in itself. Many a time, he'd stood patiently by his mother while she exchanged news with someone or other, so enraptured would the adults be that the only concession to his being there was a pat on the head by one of them. Now all he could hear was coughing. So much of it. And the odd car horn. Negotiating anything with hands pressed firmly against the wet towels was hard and as the once cold water gradually warmed and the initial relief lessened, they had to come to the miserable conclusion there was nowhere to get anything and they would have to rely on the mediocre provisions in the house. But complaining was not only not an option but was something none of them wanted to do and they turned round to face the same rubble and dust and the sound of firemen calling for people and trying to extricate them from buildings.

Just before they reached their house, they saw a small group of women huddled round something that Peter didn't quite see as Auntie Gerda had pulled his towel over his eyes and with a warm but firm hand kept it there despite his protests. What he didn't see but what Herr Muller told him about years later was that his mother had joined the group and together they gathered around an English pilot, shot down hours before but in the chaos still where he'd landed, and stayed with him until his inevitable death, talking to him even though the one's understanding of the other's language was probably negligible. Nevertheless, they remained with him until he died.

7

Helen concentrated as hard as any predator, hungry for the right stop and determined that nothing should tempt her away from her task. She felt exhilarated, excited by the connection she was about to have with a past Stephen had talked of so often and comforted that there was a reason he should be brought into a conversation. She'd noticed she'd begun to feel less anxious and was beginning to celebrate the unfamiliarity of her surroundings, feeling less intimidated by them and more excited by the white or cream houses with their red or orange roofs, the billboards whose meanings she could only guess at and the conversations she didn't understand. She enjoyed being on the other side of the road; it jostled with her mind a little, if only to challenge an instinct to call it the wrong side. Her mind was taken up with the other guest Margot and Hans had invited to the lunch who, they said, had been insistent on seeing her, but they had given her nothing else, so her anticipation leant more towards anxiety than excitement as withdrawal of information, in her experience, generally seemed to mean something was wrong.

After about half an hour or so, she got off where Hans had told her to and she immediately rang him, also as he'd instructed. "I'll be with you in a couple of minutes," he said in a rushed but nevertheless pleased tone and she felt a sudden jolt to be hearing a voice she'd last heard when Stephen was alive. It reminded her how much she'd been striving to avoid this, how she'd tried to live away from him somehow, ensuring that she spent as much time as she could with people who hadn't known him because those who did didn't seem to know how to be around her and the mutual discomfort was not only something she could hardly bear but something that also made her angry because she'd found that she'd allowed the situation to engineer itself in such a way that she'd invariably try to relieve their awkwardness. She'd always hated the troubled minds of others; it was a difficulty of who she was that their ease took priority over what was attempting to unscramble itself in her own head, but this irritated her about herself no end.

When Hans walked towards her, she felt both sorrow and contentment. It was a confusion she supposed she would have to get used to for the rest of the day but one she ultimately welcomed. She could see the last five years had served him well. He was no different from the Hans she remembered: tall, a little portly with a thick head of hair where grey and blond strands seemed to be in conversation with one another.

He held out his arms. "Helen, how good to see you." There was a tidy formality about Hans that took his involvement with people to concern but not a step further. He knew what he was supposed to do and he did it beautifully. She allowed him to hold her and for a few seconds there was a silence in which all she let herself feel was relief that she'd arrived at her destination. "I'm so sorry about Stephen," she heard him say. "It's too young."

She gently pulled away. "It's really good to see you, Hans. How's Margot?"

"Swearing amongst a lot of steam in the kitchen," he laughed.

"I hope she hasn't gone to too much trouble."

"Not at all. She's been very excited about seeing you again. She's just such a perfectionist, never thinks the food will be good enough."

She remembered that about Margot, the attention to detail

and a slight apology never far from her lips, which told anyone who did feel something she was responsible for was less than perfect that she was the first to realise the error. It was almost as if her fear was that of being taken by surprise.

She told Hans she was famished, so anything Margot had made would be eaten with relish.

Hans smiled. "You look very well, Helen, considering what you've been through. I hope you don't mind me asking what happened."

She did mind, but she didn't tell him that and as Stephen was going to come up quite a lot in conversation, she thought she might as well get used to it. So she told him how Stephen had gone out for petrol, how he'd been a long time, but she'd thought perhaps he was at the supermarket. She'd asked him to get some matches and maybe the petrol station didn't have any. But it had got late and every time she phoned him, it had rung out, then gone to answerphone. She'd said to Emma she should go and look for him. And that was when their phone had rung.

Hans listened with polite attention; he had no wish to venture further and as ever Helen was happy to accommodate this standard social normality. It came as no surprise to her; Hans wasn't naturally empathetic. But he still had an attractiveness that was drawn, she'd always felt, from a good helping of self-confidence rather than attributes that may have required a greater humility. Stephen's friendship with Hans had intrigued her because there had never been anything brash about her husband who was surely too shy and cautious for the man who was walking alongside her now.

They carried on walking for what must've been another five minutes or so, with Hans asking her what she'd seen in Berlin and canvassing her opinion of his city, to which he was obviously expecting favourable replies and to which, she suspected, he would have slightly mocked anything to the contrary. But no such controversy emerged and he was pleased his city had walking around it another satisfied customer. After turning into the street he declared was his and passing three or four houses similar to the ones she'd seen from the bus, they turned left onto the gravel forecourt of his and Margot's house. She smiled as she looked at it: detached and cream, as the others they'd passed but grander in size and appearance, as if everything was meant to lead to this one.

As their feet crunched their way through the gravel, the large, panelled front door opened and Margot, ever the enthusiastic hostess, came running towards them with outstretched arms and Helen knew that being bundled into her arms was all but inevitable. How lovely it was to see one another was both articulated and meant; there was a genuine warmth between the two women who'd been thrown into one another's company and obliged to get on.

"But Hans tells me you've been stressing in the kitchen," said Helen.

"What did you tell her that for?" She shook her head. "Come on in."

Margot seemed to have got older than Hans, Helen thought, as if both she and time had fallen out and either time had reduced its favours or Margot had stopped accepting them. It was disconcerting to see a friend after an interval of some time because in witnessing a friend's ageing, it somehow made you see your own mortality more clearly. In that sense, far more comforting to see your friend in your mind's eye.

Margot carried on holding her tightly round her waist, as she showed Helen through the front door and into their house. She expressed her condolences and said how fond she was of Stephen.

"We were so sorry to have missed his funeral," she said and Helen detected a regret in Margot's voice she immediately felt obliged to reassure because her absence from Stephen's funeral had clearly caused Margot great concern. So she told her friend that she mustn't worry, that Stephen always avoided funerals where he possibly could and that she knew they were thinking of her. Then, without a moment's pause, she changed the subject to that of their house, which was taking her breath away, so grand and imposing was it with its high ceilings that created a slight echo when everyone spoke, so that Helen felt she was in a home a guide might be taking her through, rather than one a friend inhabited. Margot smiled at her raptures, taking Helen's raincoat that she'd needlessly brought with her and put it in what seemed like a room underneath the stairs. Then they both showed her through to the dining room.

They had prepared everything beautifully. Helen was guided into a large room with French windows, which, half-opened, invited the eye into an oval-shaped princess of a garden, prettily groomed and not one that expected to look after itself very much. The brown oak table, polished and seeming to serve as a reflecting river for the swan-shaped napkins that glided across it, was laden with silver, a white dinner service and a platter hosting a pyramid of lemons.

She shuddered slightly to think now what Margot must've thought of their haphazard dinner party when, if she remembered rightly, Emma had dangled a pair of muddy trainers over Margot's lap, asking her mother what she should do with them. This, on the other hand, was exquisite and whether it was the trouble they'd taken or that she suddenly felt Stephen's presence more strongly than she had for quite some time, she suddenly felt overwhelmed.

It was noticing that four places had been set that brought her back from some kind of collapse and she remembered her friends emailing her a while ago about someone they knew who was very keen to meet her. It confused her and made her feel silly that this had somehow completely slipped her mind. She tried hard to think what the email had said, but all she could recall was that it was a young woman. She was sure there was nothing more, though how sure she could be of anything had just lost ground somewhat.

"Helen, can I get you a drink?" She turned round to face Hans who was standing next to a silver tray filled with decanters of different drinks, all alcohol from what she could see and any she chose would've gone down a treat, but she played it safe and sent him to the kitchen for a sparkling water, which he handed her with not a small degree of amusement. Margot then apologised and said she'd have to return to the kitchen, waving aside all offers of help because Brigitte, her housekeeper cum everything else, had done most of the work this morning.

"I expect Hans forgot to tell you that when he was trying to portray me as overworked and stressed."

"She likes it when I do," he protested as she walked out of the room. "You're probably curious about who wants to meet you," he continued.

She felt her stomach lurch a bit as Hans was doing nothing to steer her away from the idea that he had bad news for her, though what that could be she couldn't quite imagine.

"She's a young woman who works for Margot at the museum. Her name is Rosa."

Helen knew Margot worked as an administrator and had started only fairly recently. She'd been surprised when Margot had emailed her to tell her. She'd never thought of her as a woman who went to work somehow and had always associated both Margot and her beautifully lacquered hair with the world of ladies who lunched and dined for charity, though she had hinted at missing the children when they left home and for all her glamour and seeming worldliness, Helen could see Margot was a woman for whom an empty home wouldn't be easy.

"She has two small children," Hans continued, "so works

for Margot just a couple of days a week, but they seem to have struck up quite a friendship. We've known of her for quite a while and I think Margot felt a bit awkward about appointing her, but she wasn't the only person on the interviewing panel and, according to Margot, she was streets ahead of the rest. From the very first day she started, both she and Margot seem to have got on like a house on fire, and we've got to know her really well." He paused and took a sip from his whiskey glass. "You see, Rosa's father, Erich, was one of the fifty-seven. I don't know how much Stephen ever talked about it, but that's why she wants to meet you."

The doorbell rang and, as Hans excused himself to go to the door, Helen looked out onto their garden again. A small bird flew out of a silver birch and she almost envied its freedom because right now all she wanted to do was to sit on a Cornish beach. Stephen hadn't really talked to her much at all about his life in Berlin; he tended to cut short her queries and said he was too tired or asked her what was on the telly that evening. He'd invariably had a long day, as if there were more hours in his, so she'd got the point and talked, instead, about things that were acceptable to him like how the children were getting on at school or where they should go on holiday. She'd heard snippets of conversation between her husband and Hans when she and Margot were supposed to be engaging in women's talk, something about a Tunnel 57, but by then she was too weary about the whole subject of Berlin to find out anything.

"I'll go," she heard Margot shout and Hans re-entered the room and took another sip of his drink. As Margot greeted her colleague, they entered into a kind of social purgatory in which neither seemed to think it appropriate to talk anymore about Rosa or to begin another topic. But they didn't have to maintain this for long as Margot, enjoying her role as hostess, ushered Rosa in and introduced everyone with confidence and grace. Rosa was a petite woman, her straight brown hair pulled back tightly from her face and placed in a neat bun at the back of her head, revealing pale skin and bright blue eyes. She had the perfect posture for a ballerina, Helen thought, and was as careful and as graceful, though her dark-rimmed glasses, of a type Helen had often thought of for herself but had never had the courage to buy, gave her the appearance of a librarian or, indeed, someone who worked in a museum. There was definitely gravity about her, but it didn't lack warmth. Her fine, bony hand shook Helen's and she said how pleased she was to meet her. She apologised for her English, but it seemed pretty good to Helen, who found it embarrassing that anyone should apologise to an English person for their inadequate language skills. But for the first ten minutes or so Rosa didn't put her English to the test, preferring to answer questions with tentative smiles and quick conformations, leaving the bulk of the conversation to everyone else, so it was therefore established that Margot and Rosa had been working together for about eighteen months, that Rosa's two children were called Katja and Jakob and that Rosa was particularly interested in how German artists had been influenced by the French Impressionists, at which point she began to talk more fluently and said how Monet was perhaps her favourite artist and that although she loved the famous ones of his, she particularly liked 'The Red Cape', a painting of his wife, Camille, passing by a window on a snowy day. She liked the fact it was winter, a season often neglected, she thought, and the passing nature of Camille, because this was how we saw most other people, fleeting past us, with only our curiosity to wonder who they were. She'd had a little help from the others with her English but had managed most on her own, so Helen didn't think there was too much for her to worry about with her English.

"Have Margot and Hans said why I wanted to see you?"

Helen was surprised at this question, which seemed sudden

and unexpected. She thought they were going to continue inconsequential chitchat for quite a while longer during which she would carry on quietly applauding Rosa's English and Margot's food. Her surprise rendered her speechless, so Rosa continued.

"My father was saved by Hans and your husband, Mrs Thompson. Before that, his life was very grim." She looked at Helen with a slight query on her face, as if expecting some reassurance that she'd chosen the right word, so Helen just nodded and smiled.

Hans joined in. "Erich was cut off from the rest of his family when the wall was built. He hadn't seen any of them for three years."

Margot saw a brief silence between them as an opportunity to invite them to sit at the table so she could bring in the first course, so they took their places while holding on to what had been said with an almost religious reverence. Helen looked at this young woman as she delicately and politely sat where Hans had suggested, a stranger to her, yet someone who spoke of Stephen as if she knew him; her husband, the man who made her tea and toast every Sunday morning, who'd helped her with nappy changing and who burped at the end of every meal, then apologised and said he really shouldn't do that, seemed to be something of a hero in this room. She settled into her chair while Rosa squealed with delight at the swan serviettes, her enthusiasm prompting what sounded like a congratulatory remark in her own language. She was as obviously in awe as Helen was at such attention to detail and Helen took comfort in that, assuming Rosa's home life was just as casual as hers was.

"Brigitte and Margot did them." Hans was answering what must have been a question about the serviettes. "Apparently, it's easy."

"What's easy?" Margot appeared from the kitchen carrying a large tray. Her husband got up and relieved her of her burden.

"Making swan serviettes," he answered as he did so.

"Oh yes, anyone can do it." Margot dismissed her achievement with an ease Helen envied, though she wasn't sure how comfortable her friend would be if her prediction was correct. Margot's sense of self, it seemed to Helen, depended very much on others not having the same skills as she had, which was not to say this was a dislikeable trait but that both her and Hans's sense of being relied quite heavily on their separateness and a feeling that they had accomplished things that were beyond the reach of anyone else.

So when Margot put down the tray and declared this was to be a European meal starting with French onion soup, Helen smiled to herself as she looked at the delicious-looking offering with its appetising aroma and contented herself with the thought that what she was about to eat could probably not be produced so well in most of the Berlin restaurants. It didn't disappoint and Margot basked in the compliments as everyone took their first sips. But it wasn't long before Rosa returned to Stephen with Helen insisting she call him that and not Mr Thompson. Such formality seemed unnecessary and not true to her husband's nature who eschewed titles and always insisted on his first name. She told everyone that he hadn't really told her much about his life in Berlin and it was a part of his life that had remained quite a mystery to her. She felt it was a brave thing to admit, especially to someone who until today was a stranger to her. It wasn't easy to admit she was in the dark about something when she had been the one who'd spent so much of her life with Stephen.

"So he didn't tell me about the actual workings of the escape," she concluded, searching for everyone's reaction, but if they were making some private judgement about the state of her marriage, they didn't let it show and Hans was only too pleased to recount the operation. He was telling the story of one of the most important times in his life. He looked at Rosa who understood what he was thinking and said she would let him know if there was anything she didn't understand. He took the last couple of spoonfuls of his soup and wiped his mouth with the now dismantled swan.

"Stephen and I were, as you know, at university here together. Stephen was studying German and I was law. We were part of a group that was passionately opposed to the wall and to the division of Germany. It was a terrible time. Families divided with no way of knowing when they'd see each other again. We wanted to do something."

Margot offered Rosa and Helen more bread and Hans sipped his wine before continuing.

"A man, Fuchs, who'd recently managed to escape with his wife and child, wanted the same freedom for others. He raised money and gathered anyone who was interested, knowing he could get quite a few of us from the university. He had a plan for a tunnel. It was nothing new. Two years before, a student at the university had been responsible for organising a tunnel. He and his team got the escapers through, even though they were plagued with doubts about a couple of people. The Stasi, you understand, were beginning to infiltrate these projects. But his downfall wasn't betrayal. Their suspicions were right and they outwitted the informers, but a water pipe cracked and filled the tunnel. What he did do, which was truly inspirational, was involve the media who actually filmed the escape."

He stopped and said something to Rosa. She nodded, as if to acknowledge she'd understood what he was saying.

"What Fuchs did was to continue the tradition of involving the media and managed to get donations from journalists and newspapers all over Europe. In fact, Rosa's father, Erich, joined *Die Welt* soon after his escape and became quite a respectable journalist."

Rosa laughed. "A very respectable one, thank you."

Hans smiled. He was just making sure she understood.

Margot collected the soup bowls and seemed to give Hans a bit of a ticking off for having left some. She said she hoped they didn't mind but she'd carry on with the meal; she knew the story and she didn't want anyone to go hungry during the telling of it. Everyone thanked her again for such a delicious soup and asked if she wanted any help. She didn't, so Hans continued.

"We began work on a tunnel in April '64. Stephen was in his second year, I think."

"It was in the French sector, a bakery cellar, near the Bernauerstrasse, to the bathroom of a flat in Strelitzerstrasse," said Rosa, as if she'd learnt this by rote.

"It stretched for about a hundred and fifty metres," added Hans, slightly wincing at the memory of the back-breaking work.

"How long were you digging?" asked Helen, who was beginning to feel oddly displaced by such a dangerous and brave story. She had no knowledge of such a life, but it was also that they were talking about her husband and she couldn't place him in these situations. It was disturbing to have him unravelled in such a way, not only because it made him a different person to the one she knew but she started to think it would change so many perceptions of their lives together.

"Seven months," came the reply. Stephen and Hans had never talked much about their university days when they were all together, probably in deference to both she and Margot, and Stephen had had the habit of compartmentalising his life, putting up a brick wall of his own whenever she asked about Berlin, so when they were dating she'd got to a point where she felt that by continuing to probe and pick away at his life there she could seriously jeopardise a possible life with him. So by his monosyllabic answers and her desire to protect their relationship, it had been laid to rest and hadn't been resurrected during the course of their marriage.

"My father," said Rosa, keen to take up the story, "had decided to live in East Berlin. He preferred it there. He liked the fact that it had many artists and writers. He left home and got a flat there."

"He left his girlfriend in the West," interjected Margot who was bringing in a serving bowl with the main course.

"He did," agreed Rosa. "He said if he could get a good life, a good job, she should join him. She said she would. They were heartbroken, but I suppose it was something he felt he had to do. He wanted to write and he found the thinking inspirational there. He enjoyed the Bohemian life in the East. Is that what you say?"

They all nodded and Margot announced a dish of pickled pork chops, a German dish she called Kassler Rippen. Berlin, said Hans, was famous for it. They all joked about not having to eat again until tomorrow and Margot reminded them to leave enough room for pudding, at which there was a friendly groan.

Hans asked people to help themselves to the chops and vegetables, after Margot had brought them in, and said he hoped Rosa didn't mind him saying but her father's decision was perhaps the arrogance of youth, leaving it as a question in the air, but Rosa agreed wholeheartedly, saying she thought her father had, in his mind, an idea that he would become a big novelist or playwright. He'd told her it was fifteen years before he settled happily into writing for a newspaper.

"So he left his girlfriend and family and on that terrible night in August 1961 he was sitting with his friends drinking and talking. Most of them liked the Communists, you understand, and my father, well, he wasn't sure but generally trusted them. So, that Sunday evening, when he watched many Westerners go home, he, well, he didn't believe it wouldn't be possible to do that afterwards."

"What happened to him?" asked Helen.

"He said when it was clear what the wall had done it was plain to him where he wanted to be and he joined the many who wanted to escape."

She paused and seemed to need a rest.

"The opening in the bathroom was hidden by a packing case," said Hans. "I can see it now, a beaten old leather thing with gold initials on it. I couldn't remember a more glorious sight than that bathroom. Seven months of back-breaking work. Stephen and I just laughed uncontrollably. It was…" He puffed with his lips. He looked at Rosa. "Your father received one of our telegrams. 'Dear Erich…'"

"Aunt Gretel dead. Stop. Please come immediately. Stop. Hanna," said Rosa. "I've seen it. My father put it in a frame. It was on a wall in our house."

"Escapers had a password," explained Hans.

"My father's was 'sunlight', which seems very appropriate." Rosa smiled.

"They gave the word to a courier who took them to Strelitzerstrasse. Then it was a question of waiting to go into the flat where the tunnel was without being seen. Stephen and I weren't involved with that side of things."

"No, you did the hard work," Rosa said quite emphatically. Helen found this oddly amusing. Her Stephen, the Stephen she'd known all those years, would, she was sure, have preferred to be a courier rather than a digger, but maybe the tunnel had put him off manual work thereafter because he'd always been more willing to pay someone than do jobs in the house himself. She couldn't stay amused. This was a serious conversation. But she made a note to herself that this was probably the first time she'd felt like sniggering about her husband, certainly in the company of others, since his death.

"If Stephen and Hans hadn't dug the tunnel," she could hear Rosa saying, "I wouldn't be here." For some odd reason, because she wasn't prone to do this sort of thing, she touched

Rosa's right hand, who seemed to appreciate the gesture and squeezed Helen's hand, her fingers so delicate it reminded Helen of Emma's tiny hands in hers when they both walked to her school, noises coming out of the top of her daughter's head as she chatted away, fighting the noise of passing lorries.

"Fifty-seven people escaped through the tunnel, giving it its name." Hans's journalistic tone by-passed Rosa's emotional attachment to the story. "But the tunnel was betrayed. It was going to happen eventually." And Margot just thought about the fact that it was the last time people escaping had to pay to do so.

Hans looked around at everyone, reprieved by the conversation of the others, and contemplated his very good fortune. This was his life and he loved it; opening his house to great company, good conversation, he enjoyed every minute. It was sad Stephen couldn't be among them, but his untimely death had hugely surprised him. Stephen was a man who, despite what he decided to show, had always seemed to have that tragic element that deprived him of the sort of happiness he had known. Contentment, that was it. Stephen harked back. That was never a good way to live.

But this, to sit here, with all this wonderful food and company, well, it couldn't be topped. And Helen seemed to be doing OK, better than he would've anticipated. She seemed very well indeed.

He looked at Margot. My god, he'd struck lucky with her. Wonderful wife, wonderful mother and damned fine cook. Unflappable Margot. He knew he was the envy of others and when friends told him so he could only agree. He'd always worked long hours, hadn't been around much for the children and had cancelled arrangements he'd made with her more times than he could remember. And for what? For some meeting or another that had rarely been as important as it had promised. But stoicism had been one of the many qualities he adored about Margot. And a smile that could be appreciated from the other side of the room.

He savoured another delicious bite, then picked up his glass of wine and, before taking a sip, offered a private toast. To life, he said to himself, and to Margot. For not one jot of it could he have done without her. He swallowed the wine, which washed down his last piece of pork splendidly.

This time, they all ignored Margot's protests and helped her take things back into the kitchen. They were still talking about how they'd enjoyed the meal when they got into the kitchen and laughed with despair as they saw a trifle on the table, with Margot declaring what they could all see: an English trifle.

When they returned to the table, along with the trifle, the conversation seemed to have slowed down somewhat; maybe they were all getting a bit sleepy, Helen thought, and as she sat back she could see that Hans and Margot had found a way to work in complete harmony, complementing each other's roles, passing plates, the one prompting the other, exchanging actor and stage-hand beautifully so that they danced in step to the perfection that surrounded them. Rosa was quiet for a while too, content to be another member of the audience watching a couple entertain. They both listened, then, to their hosts talk about their children and how Stephan was spending a year in Thailand and Petra was just finishing her doctorate in philosophy. It was like they danced together, quickstepping through things best forgotten when children are silly or forget things while their achievements were met with a slow waltz, one they didn't seem to want to finish.

Then, as if coming out of a reverie, and when they had all had coffee, Hans suggested he take Rosa and Helen to the site of the bakery and smiled at Margot as if this was a pre-arranged idea they'd had and she'd excluded herself from. Helen said she wasn't sure, it was a bit sudden, and Margot, ever the accommodating hostess, put blame firmly in their corner and said this was something she and Hans should've thought of, but Rosa, who'd been before, seemed very keen to see the bakery, as if this would somehow complete the circle of their day together. So, feeling a bit reluctant because she wasn't sure she should become any more involved in a life Stephen had been unwilling to talk about, she agreed to go.

The goodbyes took a while, as these things often do, with everyone remembering something important they'd forgotten to say because goodbyes are invariably difficult, even if they are only *au revoirs*. Margot and Rosa remembered something important about the museum and fell into German to discuss it; Hans remembered to ask Margot to ring the gardener about tomorrow; Rosa remembered she'd left her glasses on the dining room table; and Margot remembered Stephen's funeral, whispered in Helen's ear how sorry she was to have missed it and hugged her as if she really was. "Let's meet up for a coffee," she suggested and Helen said she would ring her. Finally, Hans opened the front door, they walked towards his car and poured themselves in. Once it was moving, Rosa and Helen turned their heads from the back seat and waved to Margot till they could see her no more.

As they both thanked Hans again for a lovely time, Helen was processing the shock of realising how little she knew about the young Stephen Thompson and how knowing didn't really help her much; in fact, it hindered because there was nothing she could do with the information. She wasn't even sure she wanted to tell her children, as the question on their lips would be why hadn't he told their mother? – and any questions she had would have to remain unanswered.

Rosa distracted her by fumbling around for something in her bag. She picked out a purse, then produced an old photo, which she showed to Helen and said it was her father. "Erich," she declared proudly and Helen looked at a man as he would've been years after Stephen had helped him escape. A slim face with fine bone structure, it showed determination or stubbornness, she wasn't quite sure which, tempered by a smile in his eyes that accepted he wasn't always right but more often than not he was. She liked the look of him, not an easy man perhaps, but an interested one, a man who looked around him and wondered why. She said what a lovely man he seemed to her companion and Rosa told her how he'd discussed politics with her as long as she could remember and how once, when she just wanted to be young and carefree, she'd dared to tell him she wasn't interested, to which his stormy reply had been, how could she not be, she was politics, she was a human being.

"Just a minute," Helen said and after her own grappling with belongings, as if to reply in kind, she showed Rosa a photo of Stephen.

In contrast to Erich, Helen could see an uncertainty in this face, and more conservation in spirit, as if challenging was not something that caused it much comfort or reassurance. She realised she hadn't quite seen this before. His legal persona had always struck her as being very sure of itself, but, she supposed, it was within boundaries written and fought for long before, established thought that he just had to ensure was carried out.

When Rosa and Hans told her they'd arrived at the place where the tunnel was, she felt surrounded by the monochrome world of all the films she'd watched about the East, with its eerie menace and a claustrophobic heaviness that barely allowed you to breathe. Government buildings flanked one side and faced a bleak-looking park, mostly stone and dry mud, where a few teenagers played football and shouted frantically at one another, as if missing the ball was almost as desperate as anything previous generations had felt. The bakery was no longer there. Hans and Rosa could produce only a tacky newsagent's, but that didn't matter. They all stood there for a few minutes without saying a word; then Hans suggested they go to the café over the road. It seemed a good plan.

8

Audrey couldn't remember the last time Kenneth looked at her as if he was pleased to see her. She wasn't a fool. She knew romance went out of the window to a lesser or greater degree over the years and she wasn't expecting any grand gestures or anything. Leaping up the wisteria and declaring his love through their bedroom window would put his knee out and that kind of stuff had always seemed pretty desperate, even to her more romantic way of thinking. No, she wasn't wanting that sort of thing; it was just that when he said "lovely to see you" after he'd been out seeing to the car or whatever else he'd been doing, she wasn't really sure how exactly lovely it was for him. She often suspected it was lovely for him to see the garage mechanic or the woman behind the till in the supermarket, as they were a freedom she couldn't give him, so, unlike the time he spent in the house, he'd probably merrily chat away to them to his heart's content. And she wondered if he put "the" instead of "my" in front of "wife" whenever he talked about her like those blokes do on TV quiz shows.

"So, Len, what will you do with the money if you win?"

"Oh, that's nothing to do with me, Kevin; the wife's got plans for it."

Ha bloody ha. Why not just be honest and say the marmite jar's got plans for the two grand?

Before she was sixty, she'd gone to work a bit, doing this and that. In fact, she used to be the woman behind the till, so she damned well knew what the buggers used to say. How many times had she heard that *the* wife had sent them out shopping, but they'd probably got it all wrong and she'd see them again before long? "Hopefully not," she'd reply, smiling politely and they'd laugh, while never really catching on to what she was saying. Oh well. Thank goodness for friends. Over the years they'd been a real godsend, although one or two had waned off. She didn't really see Gloria much these days, even though she was only a few miles away, mainly because Gloria was offering what seemed to be like residential care to her grandchildren a lot of the time. Poor kids, they never seemed to see their parents, from what she could gather, but Gloria was always saying that people need two incomes nowadays. Well, personally, she was never quite sure about that one and had said as much to her friend the last time she saw her, who seemed to be almost passing out with fatigue on that particular afternoon. And so, over a cup of tea and against screaming children in the background, they'd debated how their generation had accepted you had to be a bit more frugal when children came into the world whereas nobody seemed to want to give anything up in this day and age. It was all about the stuff, as Gloria put it, and to her friend she'd agreed as Gloria had a very attentive husband whose needs, she could see, would be a pleasure to meet and preferable to trekking out to work every day, but, on the other hand, she didn't think many women these days would put up with being called "the" anything.

Like Helen, for instance. She wasn't all that younger than her, but they could've been born a million years apart because she would look at her and think that that woman had a different kind of life altogether. Or she had done until Stephen had died and then, instead of slightly envying her, she'd found herself in that tricky position you find yourself in where somebody's tragedy has made you appreciate what you have all the more. Even if that was Kenneth. There was nothing like a death, she was finding ever more increasingly in recent years, to make her want to cook Kenneth's tea more than she did the day before. And then she'd feel a bit lousy.

She missed Helen and Stephen, which was strange because there was nothing that particularly bound them, apart from the fact they were neighbours, so maybe that was it. A shared interest in the street they all lived in and the comings and goings. Sometimes, she supposed, it doesn't have to be any more than that. But she was surprised how she found herself gradually becoming more concerned about them and they'd shown her and Kenneth one or two kindnesses over the years, like the time her husband had been rushed into hospital with a suspected heart attack. They'd given her lifts to the hospital a couple of times – why oh why had she never learnt to drive? – and Helen had popped round after Kenneth had come home.

It hadn't been his heart, just a problematic digestive system, which had made her a bit cross with him because she was always telling him off about the way he devoured too many biscuits and liked rather too many brandies. It had been embarrassing telling their neighbours what it actually was, after all they'd done, but they'd been very gracious and said no problem, they were glad he was OK. She was sure, though, with their busy timetables – they were forever rushing in and out of their cars – that it had caused them considerable inconvenience.

She particularly remembered conversations they'd all had about the house opposite, which, after old Sally had died, had remained empty for years. Stephen, being a lawyer, assumed there had been some kind of family dispute; then she and Helen had speculated on this, but really it was all thin air because neither had got to know Sally well enough to know with any degree of certainty whether this was the case. But what they did know was that a lot of building work went on year after year, without much sign of progression. All Kenneth said on the matter was that the family were mad not selling it and putting the money in the bank. Her own conclusion was that it was probably a bit similar to her not being able to take her mother's scarves to the charity shop after she'd died. She loved to open the plastic bag she kept them in and smell her mum's perfume.

Yes, she was sorry when Helen and Stephen had decided to move and sorrier still that they'd lived in their new house only eighteen months before he'd died.

9

She couldn't understand why Stephen hadn't talked about his bravery and she hated not understanding people's motivations and actions, if they were dissimilar to the ones she would've chosen. It was frustrating but also demanding because it required a tolerance of something she couldn't quite relate to and that had to be one of the most difficult things asked of anyone. But when it came to someone so close, it indicated some sort of blemish, a tear, perhaps, in the piece of paper that was their marriage licence, and she didn't even know of the mark or realise the paper was cut. So any pride she might have felt was scarred itself by an anger she couldn't quite articulate yet. Time had to help her do that and, hopefully, would one day offer either understanding or peace of mind.

She was walking towards Peter's door because she just wanted to see if he was about. She'd had a lot to process and felt like having an English conversation with someone who hadn't known Stephen. As she got closer to his door she could hear muffled sounds and was relieved he was in, but, although she knocked several times, no one answered. She quickly got a little piece of paper from her handbag, found a pen right at the bottom and wrote a little note, just saying how much she was enjoying the flat and his city. It was an odd thing to do, a reminder to herself, perhaps, that she was unused to holidaying alone. After bending to reach underneath the door, she slipped it inside his house and walked away.

★

Elsa quite often looked at Peter and said, "Who are you?" because being roughly twenty-eight or nine, she had no idea who the old man was standing in front of her. The man she'd married only a few years ago looked nothing like this old codger who, for some reason best known to him, insisted he was her husband, which was an unbelievable cheek.

So Peter could see, quite obviously, why getting his wife ready for bed was less than easy. He saw it only too well the first time he understood that her demented mind had rolled itself back nearly fifty years and he'd carried on understanding it for a good long time. But there was only so much understanding within any one individual, wasn't there, or did others have an infinitesimal amount, because now, for him, it was tedious. He wanted to fix it like he fixed his TV or computer, or at least he wanted to take her to someone who could fix it. But there was no medical equivalent of an engineer or IT expert. The illness had foxed everyone and it remained, like cancer, on their to-do list.

Yet again, she'd hit him and hit him hard. Why wouldn't she, given the circumstances in her mind, engulfed as they were in a story in which a strange man was trying to undress her? What about him, though? He almost dared not ask that question, even if it was only him who heard it because of its selfishness. It was there, though, and he found himself crying a little because he was in a lot of physical pain, but he'd also raised this question.

He held the pain that was the side of his face with his right hand and looked at Elsa, his attacker. Her eyes were full, watery pools that understood something sad had happened to Peter, so that amongst the maelstrom, all the jumble, all the re-arranged memories, a spark of something received had torn a little at her. But she could do nothing about it for nothing in her mind could organise itself well enough for her to help in any way. She was exhausted and, with it, calmer now, but in a private world of grief no one fully understood, least of all her.

There was silence for a minute or two while they just stared, both at each other and into space, as if the one had no more meaning than the other. There was often silence these days. He'd had to learn to get used to it, which wasn't easy for someone who enjoyed the sound of music, but he'd been told by their doctor to limit noise as much as he could as this was confusing for Elsa. So whereas he used to leave the TV on while he went to make some coffee, now he put it off as the noises from the kitchen merging with those of the TV could send her into a panic. It was all change and none of it for the better. He took a deep breath and, while still holding his face, he took the brave step of asking her to take off her cardigan. It was more of a plea because he wasn't sure if he could cope with another refusal. He then said nothing. She had to think about this simple request without being bombarded with any other conversation. Instead, he thought again about his face and how it smarted. Then slowly, Elsa began to unbutton her cardigan, sweet as anything, like the most contrite of his former pupils who'd caused mayhem in the classroom and who was beginning to realise that everyone was fed up with them because nobody was laughing anymore. He smiled at her and she did too because this was obviously the right thing to do and she wanted to do the right thing.

When Elsa was asleep and he was turning off all the lights, he passed by the front door and noticed a piece of paper. He picked it up, then unfolded it. "Oh God," he said wearily when he'd read the English hand.

10

Helen went to the museum because finding out more about the wall had become something of a priority since it offered clues to a dead husband. It wasn't that she felt betrayed exactly. He had a right, of course, to a former life, but she wasn't sure if he had a right to one he never wanted to talk about. It confused her and she'd started to think about the things she hadn't told him, like the sleazy colleagues who thought working with someone meant sleeping with them and though she wasn't sure if you could liken this to international politics, she began to think there'd been times when an equivalent bravery had been required. But she didn't think Stephen would've been particularly inquisitive, once she'd told him. He certainly wouldn't have been interested in staring at them across a crowded room and quietly analysing them. But she was. So she found herself, amongst many others, gazing into Stephen's past and a wall that had been built and had fallen. Photos of distress and misery abounded, with two in particular gnawing away at her and making her think about a life beyond the quiet neighbourhoods that had always been her experience, where a careless word was merely embarrassing.

One was a photo of a man and a woman, each holding a small child high above them, both only a few months old. Maybe they were twins. Behind them, a woman was standing on a chair, seeing if this would allow her to see over the wall. She had her hands on her waist, inquisitive yet defiant. Her hair was in a bun and she wore a smart skirt and cardigan but comfy slippers adorned her feet. A man in an overall seemed to be having a conversation with the woman on the stool...

"Can you see anything?"

"Not much, oh there's Frau Trenkner. Frau Trenkner! Frau Trenkner! Frau Trenkner!"

"Stop waving like that. You're going to get into trouble."

"No, I'm not. We're OK here."

"But Frau…"

"Frau Trenkner! What's happening? She can't hear me. She's knocking on Herr Kielberg's door by the look of it. They seem to be doing something at the end of the road, but I can't see what. Let's hope they're not going to pull down Herr Miller's shop. Bastards."

"Shut up, Petra."

The young man, his child still held high above him, turned to the woman who was loftier than any of them.

"Can you see a young woman, about my age?" He smiled nervously. *"Actually, she looks very like me. It's my sister. She wants to see the children and we said we'd be here now. It is eleven, isn't it?"* He indicated that it would be dangerous for him to look at his watch. Instead, the woman consulted hers and nodded that it was ten-past.

"There's someone walking towards the wall who could be her."

"That's my sister. Always a bit late. Well, if it is her," he added, not wanting to judge a stranger in any way.

"What's her name?"

"Anna."

"Hey, Anna! Anna! They're here," and she pointed across to the children, who were only a little lower than she was.

The woman broke into a run and started waving frantically. *"Siegfried! Martha!"*

"She's coming," and the woman smiled at the couple who now completely straightened their arms so the children were as far as they could possibly go.

"Is that you, Siegfried?"

"Yes, hello. Can you see them?"

"I can. I can. They're beautiful. They look so like you, Martha. Which is a good job! How are you both?"

"We're OK. We haven't had much sleep with these two, but we're managing. How about you?"

"I'm OK. It's OK." And she repeated she was OK, a little more quietly the second time.

The man and woman looked at one another and lowered the children. They walked right up to the wall and touched it with the hand that was free.

Helen walked towards another photo. It was of two soldiers.

"What did you really want to be?"

"You mean apart from being a soldier?" and his mate laughed.

Bernd smiled. "Oh, I dunno. My dad wanted me to be a lawyer, but I never did well enough. I think he was upset about my results, but he didn't show it." Bernd stared through the wire and readjusted his rifle.

"What's that?" His mate turned to look in the same direction as Bernd. They could see someone loitering a few metres away.

His mate sounded stern. "I could swear I've seen him before. Troublemaker. Hey, you! Yes, you! One more move and I shoot." He cocked his rifle. The man ran. "Well, that's probably the most excitement we'll see on this duty." He grinned.

Bernd smiled. "Yeah, usually, it's so…"

"Boring?" suggested his mate.

Bernd only half smiled. He never knew who he could truly trust.

She gathered around a group watching the TV. It was footage showing people jumping from the windows of their apartment blocks down onto the street below. Many had their arms outstretched, trying to catch those who were crawling down the walls of the apartments. Many were crying. Many yelling. She vaguely remembered seeing this years ago in the comfort of her home. She reached for a board, which was lying on one of the benches, that described what was happening in English. It was Bernauerstrasse. The street she'd visited with Hans and Rosa. The place where Stephen had helped dig a tunnel.

11

Peter thought about what the electrician had said the other day, how people these days couldn't seem to be able to live a minute without being connected up to something or another, as if they'd die if they couldn't put the telly on or get the internet. He'd pointed out that what his tenant had wanted was hot water, not so much of a luxury, but it got him thinking. The electrician was right. People could live without more than they realised.

Immediately after the war, there was always a joke in their house that Freddy, the English soldier, fraternised. It was the only time he heard his aunt use an English word and it was Freddy himself who started the joke.

When Freddy was with them, he got them all to say it as quickly as they could to see who'd say it the most times without tripping up. Peter remembered he usually won, though looking back he suspected they let him, and a great cheer would go up accompanied by much clapping. Freddy was running quite a risk, because without a wall or windows on one side of their house they could probably be heard at least a few metres down the road.

He was a gentle man and when he was older Peter always wondered how on earth Freddy had ever got through the war to be so emotionally intact. And physically it must've been a struggle for he was slight and not very tall. He had a kind face that smiled a lot and winked at Peter when he was joking, using mime rather than a raised voice to overcome the language barrier. He would smuggle in a bit of extra soup or whatever was going that day and there wasn't much. It didn't matter they didn't understand what he was saying. Such a gesture was common language enough.

"You know, Frau Gunther said they're calling our windows 'sparrows' delight'." His mother looked thin and weary. "Though God knows what sparrow…" She seemed surprised to see him standing next to her. "Hello, my fine young man. And when did you wake up?"

He didn't say the same time he started to hear her walk about, which was probably about 5.30. This was when she told his aunt she usually woke. The cold did it. No matter how many rugs and blankets they tucked around their bodies and pulled over their faces, the howling wind and chilly night air disturbed them all intermittently throughout the night and after 5.30 it was only rarely possible to catch any more sleep. But he didn't tell his mother that. He liked her to think he felt better than he did. None of this was her fault and he was frightened by the fear in her face every time she stepped out of their living space to begin the exhausting hunt for food. Nothing would have induced him to add to what had become, to him, her permanent look of anxiety.

Sometimes, he would've given the world to let out a good moan about the lack of food. He could hardly remember a time when he didn't feel slightly hungry and since the end of the war it had become just hungry; there was no slightly anymore. His mother would say, "Peter, food is scarce and hard to come by," again and again, so by now, apart from being bored by her saying this, he felt they were being punished, which he thought was hugely unfair as he'd never killed anyone in his life and never wanted to. And his mother and aunt had always tried to save the lives of the tiniest of insects; this was true even now, when there were so many of them it was tempting to tread on the lot.

She hugged him. "We have some milk."

He squeezed her hand because he could feel how happy she was. That they had milk was a great achievement. Yesterday, they hadn't managed to get any and he'd heard his mother complain to her friend Heike, something about her ration card having the lowest grade possible.

"Housewives," she groaned. "In the pecking order we apparently have the same grade as Nazis." He heard her asking Heike about working in the American canteens, but Heike had replied that that wasn't much good if she was trying to get food for Peter because she'd heard somewhere that they resented German women taking any food away with them, but what did they expect? It's a woman's instinct, isn't it? How could you enjoy feeling well fed when your children were starving? And the state of a lot of children she'd seen recently was... and he didn't catch Heike's next words for she'd lowered her voice into a whisper, but he'd guessed them anyway. Exactly how old did Heike think he was?

"Good Germans, bad Germans, we're all the same," Auntie Gerda had added. Well, he'd heard that from some of his friends often enough and it was true; the people who were in charge now didn't seem to know the difference. They were all bad in the eyes of their old enemies. Sometimes he felt like he did at school when a teacher gloated over his innocent stumblings, as if the moral triumph was always theirs for the taking. Which was why Freddy was so special.

The Russians got to them first and they didn't see any other soldiers for weeks. Both his mother and aunt started to look tenser than they ever had during the war. And if they went out, they were always with a group of friends. That was when she and Auntie Gerda got to know Heike.

Once, they came back and his mother asked him for his bicycle. It was a strange question because she liked walking better, but he thought it was probably difficult underfoot, so he got his prized possession, which had survived everything, from beside his bed and gave it to her. His father had given it to him just before the start of the war and had lived for only another eight days, so Peter had done everything in his power to look after it. His mother knew how much it meant to him and had said that the best place to put it during the war was in the cupboard under the stairs.

His mother was crying when he passed it over and disappeared outside with it. When she came back she was still crying and she didn't have his bicycle. Despite her protests he rushed onto the street and saw a Russian soldier cycling on it, pleased with his new acquisition and showing it off to his comrades.

At that moment he was so angry with her he thought he could never forgive her. He hated her and that felt very odd because he couldn't imagine his life without her. He heard a German voice behind him. It was saying, "Never mind." Peter shrugged and turned round. A man, probably only a few years older than him, offered a consoling look. He looked dirty and smelt foul. He touched Peter's shoulder. "Never mind," he said again and gave Peter a sad smile. Peter burst out crying. Once he started he couldn't stop and the man offered his arm to Peter's face. Peter rubbed his snotty nose up and down the grey flannel sleeve, said thank you and walked away from his bedraggled comforter.

It was doubly painful because he'd have to walk everywhere. There were no buses and no trains, so on top of his mother not feeding him properly he would only be able to go to places he could walk to. He didn't speak to her or Auntie Gerda for two days afterwards and his mother, he was almost glad to see, couldn't have spoken to him anyway because she spent all the time crying. That night he wanted dark to come more than anything because then he wouldn't have to look at her; they'd run out of candles, and he could think about his father, who would never have betrayed him like this.

After what seemed like a very long time, other soldiers came to Berlin and Peter got to know Freddy.

His mother had warned him that one day, when they were out walking, he might see some horrible things. Really horrible. And she squeezed his arms so hard, he could only respond with, "Ow, you're hurting me," and didn't really hear what she said next. He couldn't understand why she was saying this. They'd seen almost nothing but horrible things when they went out of their house in the last few years – houses blown to pieces; people crying; soldiers shouting – and only yesterday he'd helped her clear the rubble of a house while the person who, he supposed, had lived there stood by and wailed. And then he'd seen that bastard of a soldier ride off on his beloved bicycle.

"Peter," she implored, "when we walk past these things, these photographs, I'll tell you to close your eyes and you must hold my hand."

Inwardly, he felt annoyed that, like Heike, his mother didn't seem to understand he was growing up and that he would much prefer to see something horrible than face the humiliation of holding her hand in public.

So it was when he was disobeying her and looking at a photograph of what seemed to be a tractor ploughing something that Freddy said, "Hello," and he turned, before understanding the photograph, to hear an English word spoken by an English person. He felt a tingle of excitement, but his mother looked worried and pulled him towards her.

Frankly, he was getting a bit sick of her doing this. The war was over. Life was hard, but it was about time she let him stand up for himself a bit more. He smiled back at the man. He liked the look of him, but his mother said, "Come on," and he was forced to walk away. "Don't talk to foreign soldiers," she said. "They don't like us and they're not supposed to talk to us." But he didn't care. He was fed up with his mother and

Auntie Gerda being the only adults he had anything much to do with, so when she wasn't looking he turned and waved at the soldier, who waved his right hand a little and waved back.

They saw him again about a week later when they were helping clear another lot of rubble.

"You make us clean up what you caused," he heard the grumbles and whispers amongst the women.

★

Freddy was helping to organise the operation. God, this must be back-breaking work and he felt sorry for the sad-looking women; most of them had probably lost their husbands, spending most of their day with bent backs, carrying loads that would've defied the strength of a well-fed bloke. What a bloody mess this all was. A world gone mad. Arthur had said this was nothing compared to Dresden; you wouldn't think it was a city, he'd said, so much history just plain wiped out. None of us like them, he'd said, but… and there he'd been lost for words. Freddy wasn't sure he didn't like them. Seemed all right a lot of the time. Well, considering.

There was that boy again with his mum. Freddy felt a bit choked up because he was the image of his Johnny back home. Jean had said he was doing well in her last letter. He'd had scarlet fever, which had been a terrible worry and had occupied his mind most of the time over the last couple of weeks, but he was slowly getting back to normal and that had been a fine old day when the letter had come from Jean saying the doctor had given him the all-clear.

God, he missed him and he worried that Johnny wouldn't recognise him when he went home. How he'd gone over that reunion in his head. About a hundred times a day, he reckoned.

The boy seemed to recognise him, so he gave him a wave. Ridiculous, this not fraternising with the Germans, though he'd have to be careful, otherwise he might get his leave cancelled.

He wished he could speak German; he knew they weren't supposed to frat, but they had to give them instructions and it would make his life a whole lot simpler. But he probably wasn't clever enough. It took him all his time to read and write in his own language.

"Is that heavy?"

The boy gave him a quizzical look and his mum seemed to tell him off, probably telling him not to stop. She looked very frightened. Freddy smiled at the boy because he didn't want either of them to think they were in trouble, and mimed carrying something very heavy. The boy laughed, but his mum still seemed unsure.

He looked round; no one was watching. Freddy held out his hand.

"Freddy Butler," he said.

The boy shook his hand and said he was Peter Bayer.

★

The next time they went to the rubble Peter said "Hello" to Freddy in English. He was beginning to pick up a few words, hearing as he did the Americans as well. He knew "Hello", "Thank you", "My name is Peter", and "Hi".

He also knew his mother and aunt didn't like having the soldiers about and he didn't like the way they were living, but part of him was beginning to think it was a bit exciting. *Listening to conversations you don't understand must*, he thought, *be what it's like when you visit another country.* He couldn't wait to grow up when he'd be able to earn enough money to go abroad. He even began to think that maybe he wanted to travel more than he wanted a new bicycle.

Freddy shook his hand like he did the last time. He seemed

to like him, a feeling Peter hadn't got from a lot of the foreign soldiers, who still looked at him as if he were the enemy. They were particularly unfriendly near the photographs, which were by now inescapable. He'd insisted his mother tell him the meaning of them, but he couldn't really understand what she said and when he opened his mouth to ask a question she'd told him she had some pans to wash. It was Freddy who explained the photographs a few weeks later when they both had a little of one another's language, and Peter had to make the ghastly connection between them and the disappearance of their old neighbours, the Kleins. Every time he saw the photographs he watched the foreign soldiers as they passed by, looking sideways to see the Germans' reactions. They didn't have to say anything; the words under the photographs said it for them.

Diese Stadt ist schuldig. Sie sind schuldig. This city is guilty. You are guilty.

★

He was looking out of his living room window. It was like window shopping in a way, looking at things you couldn't have, but there was nevertheless a small pleasure in looking anyway. He used to be out there, scurrying around, laughing and joking. Now he was an onlooker. After another ten minutes or so, he saw Helen walking past. He rushed to their front door and opened it wide.

"Hello," he shouted and he beckoned her towards the house.

12

Earlier that day, Helen had bought a packet of cigarettes, which had simultaneously excited and appalled her. It was something she hadn't done for twenty-five years, giving up after watching the slow and inglorious death of her father from lung cancer. Nothing else would've done it because she loved smoking – it was good for her nerves – but when her poor old dad had succumbed to the disease, or rather when the horrible little blighter had got him, after only five or six a day, she'd told herself the undeniable pleasure wasn't worth it. So she gave them up, swapping them for worry and edginess. There was always wine; all was not lost.

The only time she'd been tempted back before was when she'd got it into her head that Stephen was having an affair. It was that vulnerable time when the children were young and there was no time for each other and he seemed to have gone into himself quite considerably. So she'd secretly had the odd cigarette and smoking them seemed to have convinced her that the only thing that was the matter with their relationship was sheer exhaustion and probably an unwilling acceptance that expectations hadn't been quite met.

The life she'd thought they would have together involved him in a legal firm in a relatively quiet market town where they would embrace predictability rather than view it with suspicion. And where she would do a part-time admin job while looking after the children. It hadn't exactly started out that way and life in London had journeyed with them through their courtship and into the early years of their marriage. But when children came the capital had felt hard work and hostile and they moved to what had always been her expectations: a market town she loved. A few years down the line, though, Stephen had become visibly restless in the small legal firm there and, though his apparent unhappiness completely contradicted her contentment, she supported his move to a London business, and he spent much of his time commuting there and abroad.

Thoughts of an affair became a TV programme she was always watching or a book she never put down, but the cigarettes converted them into mere adverts, forgotten as soon as seen, silly magazines that were only a contentment in a hairdresser's salon or a doctor's waiting room.

So here she was. Sitting on a Berlin wall, watching life go by and enjoying a smoke.

13

Audrey couldn't help remembering a particular afternoon. It was quite a while after she'd got to know Helen and Stephen and, by then, she'd grown fond of them, so it troubled her.

She first saw Stephen when he was getting out of his car after a day at the office. At least, that's what it looked like. They'd been away for the weekend. She tried to remember for a moment where they'd gone but couldn't place it. She knew they'd stayed the Sunday night as well for some reason. She could see, even though he was a little distance away, that Stephen was handsome, the sort that could have easily been a film star – tall; slim; dark hair; everything you'd want – and she had him down for a businessman of some sort, but Kenneth said he thought he was a solicitor and on this occasion he'd been right. He said the slightly old-fashioned briefcase with its straps and battered appearance didn't look slick enough for a businessman. A solicitor, though, was likely to be rather proud of his more weather-beaten holder. It was almost a requirement, he said, showed a history.

Stephen always smiled – there was nothing offhand about him – said "hello" and made some comment about the weather, particularly if it was doing something you wouldn't expect, but he didn't seem keen to engage in longer conversation. He was probably tired a lot of the time, she'd always said to herself. Helen was more inclined to stop and have a chat.

Their children were beautifully behaved, far better than the lot directly opposite, who seemed to be given more freedom of expression than was good for them, pestering her with far too many whys and wherefores whenever they caught her doing something in the front garden. Still, better that than silence, she supposed. Children weren't meant to be quiet. Even she knew that. She did prefer Emma and James, though. They talked just the right amount.

Stephen was extremely helpful when a task needed to be done. It was like he needed something to concentrate on if he was ever going to get a bit closer to you and the way he mowed their lawn on the odd occasion Kenneth's knees played him up was a godsend. Nowadays, they had to get a professional in.

It was odd. She'd only just realised the other day how much the same seasons did slightly different things to their garden each year. Take her birch tree, for instance. They'd had more winds last October than the year before, so there were far fewer golden leaves on the branches by the end of the month, as if the weather had said, "No, Audrey, you were far too nosey last year." She was. She couldn't stop looking at their glorious colour, especially when Mrs Hortham's cat next door set off her burglar light. It was as if they were floodlit on a stage. She'd taken a photo on her phone. It said the 31st. Then some children had come round and trick or treated Kenneth. It was peculiar how she noticed the leaves because she wouldn't have done when she was younger and busier. She sometimes thought she was becoming more in tune with the earth the nearer she got to being placed in it, but when she'd said that to Sean, their gardener, he'd told her to stop with the morbidity. Those were his exact words. And then she'd made them a cup of tea.

Stephen was one for preoccupied thought. When he ploughed up and down their lawn, he'd look as if he was miles away, so much so she would worry that he might have an accident because she could see his mind was nowhere near their garden. He perhaps found their garden a bit tedious. Kenneth often said he probably worked as much in his head at the weekend as he did at his desk during the week.

She hadn't really got to know him any better through her conversations with Helen either. During them, they were more likely to talk about her children, things in the news and, of course, the weather. When she asked about Stephen, all Helen offered was that he was fine, working hard and often she'd say he was away somewhere on business.

Both she and Kenneth were very sad when their neighbours told them they were moving and, as with these things in life, it was only then that she began to fully appreciate what she was going to miss.

On that particular afternoon, she was doing a bit of weeding at the front of the house. She did that from time to time, usually when Sean wasn't due for another few weeks. She saw Stephen get out of his car, so she went over to him. She knew he didn't like conversations much, but she was determined to say thank you for everything he'd done for them over the years. She probably went over too soon because he was still trying to gather up his work things from the back of the car. A photo had fallen out of his briefcase and she'd gone to pick it up, even though she risked doing her back in. He'd insisted, though, brusquely as it happened, on picking it up himself. But before he did, she'd caught a glimpse of it.

It was quite dated. The woman had a beehive hairdo, the sort Kenneth had guarded her against, and heavy mascara. The style had come around again in some circles, mostly pop stars, but this woman looked more soberly dressed. The photo seemed very dog-eared and looked as if it had been for a very long time.

14

Helen lay in bed, eyes wide open. It was as if it was first thing in the morning, rather than last thing at night because sleep felt a long way off. She was remembering something and she kept remembering it again and again, like she was trying to learn the lines from the particular scene, making sure they came back to her the same as they did the time before.

She was twenty-four, slimmer, bubblier and with more energy and naivety that were all bundled up together. There was an added confidence of having just started dating Stephen Thompson and thinking he might be falling for her, especially as she was pretty sure she was for him.

He was at some conference or another for work and had suggested she join him at the end of it, so she travelled to see him. It was the first time they were away together and it was all very new.

"Can you tell me Stephen Thompson's room number, please?"

"I'll call his room for you, madam. Could you give me your name, please?"

"Just say it's Helen. Thank you." A call was made.

"Room 210, madam. Just go to the top of the stairs, turn right and it's about the fifth door on the left. Room numbers are signposted."

"Thank you."

She walked up the grand stairway of the hotel, feeling quite tired from her journey. The carpet underfoot was plush and the handles on the doors round and gold. She walked along the corridor and counted until she reached five. Room 210, as the receptionist had predicted.

After putting her weekend bag on the ground, she banged the door with her knuckles as hard as she could.

"Hello, Helen. Good to see you." And for a few moments they hugged one another. "Let me have your bag." He bent down to pick up the bag from the ground. "Come on in."

It was a large, comfortable room with latticed windows. There was a cushioned window seat that spanned the width of the windows, two easy chairs and a spacious table. She fell into one of the chairs and kicked off her shoes. "At last," and she threw back her head. "Coffee, please, sir."

Stephen smiled. "Coming up."

She watched him make the drinks. Everything was done carefully and with great precision. He turned round and held up a small carton of milk. "One or two?"

"One, please."

Having regained some strength, she got up and walked round the room. On the corner of the table poking out from underneath a pile of law books she could see something glisten in the sunlight. She walked towards it and picked it up. It was a hair slide made of black velvet with three small diamonds in the centre. She held it in her hands and walked nearer to Stephen.

"Who is she?" she asked mischievously.

He turned from stirring her coffee and paused a second.

"It's for you, actually."

She said nothing.

"I thought you might like it."

She brought it towards her in a cupped hand and stroked it with the forefinger of the other.

"Turn round," and he took the slide from her hand. Gently, he gathered up a few locks of her hair and manoeuvred it into place. "Beautiful."

It's for you, actually. Beautiful.

★

She thought she must've drifted into a sleep as she felt heavy and disorientated. She could hear the same footsteps as she'd heard on other nights, the sharp but definite sound of a stiletto heel with its purposeful rhythm. They probably woke her. She got up and walked as quickly as her sleepy state would let her and slightly drew her curtains. She was intrigued by these feet. Walking towards the end of the street was a young woman scantily clad and in heels so high they would've challenged most women. Yet she walked fast and with confidence. Helen watched her turn into the next road and, as she did, saw from the woman's profile that she was probably about the same age as Emma.

She got back into bed and tossed the duvet off as she lay down, leaving her with just a sheet. It was another warm night and she could hear distant cars and an occasional ambulance. There was the odd conversation and, because she couldn't understand a word, they seemed less intrusive, leaving no queries behind them.

She thought about the conversation she'd had with Peter that afternoon. It was so good to have someone she could talk to in English apart from Margot and Hans. It felt like she'd made her own discovery in Peter, her own friend, and she didn't feel she was annoying him in any way. He said he was always excited to have the opportunity to speak her language and she had no reason to disbelieve him. There was an enjoyment in his face when he both spoke and listened that made it obvious he relished conversation. It was a rare gift, she thought, to enjoy being the narrator and audience in equal measure.

So she'd told him about Tunnel 57, about Stephen's bravery and how such courage in her husband had surprised her, not because she'd thought him a coward but because she'd never seen him as someone who'd be prepared to sacrifice everything for an ideology.

"It was a funny time," he'd replied. "A very frightening

time. Sometimes I feel as though being able to think for myself properly is something that's come very late in life. This restaurant here" – he'd pointed across the road to where she'd told herself she must go sometime – "has an interesting past. It was a place of" – he'd smiled – "shall we say, independent thought. Many cultural figures, people with opposing views, met and dined there, but it became too much for the Stasi, who had it closed." Pausing, he'd shook his head gently from side to side, uncomprehending such a violent reaction to the fear of conversation. "Elsa and I used to enjoy eating there and the atmosphere was, well, vibrant, exciting; it almost made you tingle but realise also, I suppose, what you were missing. This, after all, was what most people in Europe could experience all the time."

He'd then looked at his watch and it was only then that Helen saw how bruised his arm was.

"Would you like to come round for a meal tomorrow evening?" he'd ventured. His tone was uncertain; it was clear he didn't want to impose on her.

"Yes," she'd found herself answering and hours later, she wasn't regretting her answer.

15

Peter wiped his eye. At this moment, he just wished he could wear make-up because he could disguise himself and pretend Elsa was as sweet as she used to be. He felt nervous now about having invited Helen round on what had been something of a whim, he supposed, a moment of excitement that had excluded all his worries and woes and had placed him in a make-believe world where there was normal social interaction, where he invited people to his house to share food and tell stories. He'd loved telling her about the history of the restaurant; it was the same exhilaration he used to feel in front of an attentive class.

He looked at his face again. He knew these bruises. They usually took a week or so to clear properly. He took the towel from its rail and dried his face. He looked awful. There was a greyness in his face he hadn't noticed before. He dried his hands and placed one half of the towel over the rail and pulled it down so it met the other half. Helen was a polite woman, discreet enough not to mention anything she saw, either to him or others. He just had to be resolute, possess a determination to put everything aside for a few hours, convince himself, more than anything, that nothing was amiss. Then they could talk as they had done yesterday morning, pleasant exchanges in his beloved English. He stared at his face again and suddenly felt an overwhelming desire to cry but instead took a deep breath and swallowed so hard he hurt his throat. He must start cooking. She'd be here before he knew it.

Elsa had calmed down. Even when she'd struggled to break free so she could give him another hard slap, he'd managed to be quietly firm. "No, Elsa," he'd repeated softly several times and while they'd both fought for their competing desires, his mind had exchanged her slaps for her caresses and he could see the way she used to stroke his right cheek – it was always the right side of his face – after a bad day at school, then gently touch his nose with her left forefinger. "Forget them," she'd say. How could he? He had at least a couple of hours' marking ahead of him.

As often happened when things were difficult, he'd suggested a television programme, one that she often seemed to like, a quiz programme that had sometimes managed to elicit a correct answer from his wife, who drew on parts of her brain less damaged and quite in tune.

She smiled, giving her permission for him to pursue this idea, and they'd walked slowly into the lounge, until Elsa had found a seat she wanted. These days she didn't have a favourite chair, she had no memory from one hour to the next of what such a thing was, and in fact the chair they had taken as being hers, with its soft, velvet feel and its seat so frequently used it had only a fraction of its old depth, had been long abandoned by its owner, who frowned at its discomfort and shuffled in it whenever she did find herself there, as if it caused great offence. So it stayed in the corner of the room, an old relic, unused and, like a church without parishioners, only comforting the bones of the odd visitor, like Karl, who was young enough to care little about the varying degrees of comfort offered by chairs.

She'd settled into another with an obedience he could've expected only from his most nervous pupil and, catching the moment, he'd dared to tell her he had to go to the bathroom and, because the TV programme seemed to be pleasing her in some way, there had been no reaction.

Now, as he walked past her to the kitchen, there was laughter from the TV but not from Elsa, who looked at it with the face she now wore more often than not: free from expression, a dummy in a shop window. She was, and this had become a way of her life he would never get used to, holding her precious photo; it seemed to offer her more comfort than he could, and she stroked it as she might a teddy bear.

He went into the kitchen and reached for the chopping board. It was an old one, wooden and heavy, and, as he felt its weight, the task ahead of him seemed daunting, for he was beginning as he might end, with every drop of energy taken from him, but as he began to chop vegetables and his focus shifted, he began to feel revived and he began to look forward to the evening ahead of him.

When the doorbell rang a couple of hours later, he was pleased that he'd managed to get a casserole in the oven, where it bubbled contentedly, and a simple pudding of fruit salad, with various creams available should anyone wish. All this despite constant interruptions from Elsa, whose interest in the television had changed to something more disturbing when the quiz had finished and Elsa had panicked because she thought she was in the African jungle of the following programme. Even her photo had failed to offer much comfort on this occasion as she convinced herself her life was at risk.

"Hello, Helen, come on in," he greeted his guest who immediately offered him wine and chocolates.

"I wasn't sure if Elsa drank wine," she said, as if to explain the chocolates.

"That's so kind of you, you shouldn't have. Thank you. Elsa loves chocolates."

"I hope you haven't gone to too much trouble."

"Oh, it's just a casserole I've had bubbling away for a while. Not too much trouble at all. Just a question of chopping up a few vegetables. Have you had a good day? You've been very lucky with the weather."

"So lucky. Yes, I used the lovely weather to go to

Charlottenberg. It was beautiful walking round the gardens. And so close to the river."

"Oh, you chose the best day for that. It's lovely by the river there. Did you see the French paintings in the palace? Apparently, they're the largest eighteenth-century collection outside France."

"Yes, I did. I enjoyed—"

Elsa joined them. She gave a smile, a vacant sort of thing that hung on her lips reluctantly, as if not quite knowing what it was doing there. A look of vague recognition came Helen's way as she walked towards Elsa, but it didn't loiter for long and was followed by a lot of agitation and pulling of Peter's sleeve.

"Helen, I think you remember Elsa."

"Yes. Hello, Elsa."

He told her who Helen was and quickly ushered his guest towards the lounge, Elsa attached firmly to his right arm, the directions hopefully preventing Elsa's next question, which would, more than likely, relate to absolutely nothing.

He couldn't help thinking what a striking woman Helen was, but this had as much to do with him still, even after a decade or so being still struck by what he called the Western appearance, which seemed to sit comfortably with an affluence, a glamour if you like, that he didn't think Elsa, even if she were still well, would ever have done entirely, though of course he wasn't so stupid as to believe it brought with it no pressures, as Karl had reminded him once, saying his wife seemed to have less to discuss these days, since her weight and lines on her face seemed to be her main hobby.

Elsa, despite lacking all the riches the West had to offer, was such a beautiful woman, as true today as any other, but he missed the real beauty on Elsa's face, when she caught him out on a white lie, told only to save her from discovering a surprise, the stifled giggle when she was still finding something funny long after others did, or her beaming smile when she bumped into him somewhere quite unexpectedly, like that last day of term when he'd taken his class to the park. But Elsa never thought herself worthy of pampering and probably would've felt the same if she'd lived in the West.

Elsa made a noise at Helen's greeting and pulled at Peter's sleeve. He stroked her hand.

"Shall we all sit down?" he suggested and repeated himself in German to Elsa. "Supper will be ready in about half an hour, but would you like a drink?"

Helen said she was fine and could wait until the meal and when he mimed the idea to Elsa she just shrugged the idea away. He smiled nervously, preoccupied with his eye, which he'd seen she noticed. It would've been impossible not to, but the moment was fleeting and had passed, as he'd anticipated it would, without obvious shock and certainly no comment.

"Elsa will eat with us, then go to bed. She gets tired and likes to go to bed soon after she's eaten. Ich meine, du gehst wahrscheinlich schlafen nach dem Essen."

Elsa nodded and put her head to one side as if to demonstrate tiredness, then looked questioningly at Peter, as if asking him what they were discussing.

"Her evening meal seems to exhaust her."

Elsa giggled a bit and then responded to something Peter said to her. She smiled, got up, tousled the top of his head and walked towards their sideboard. She collected a photo, walked back to the sofa, took her place next to Peter again and hugged what was obviously a precious possession. It seemed like a well-rehearsed activity and she began to play with it, stroking it and engaging in a one-way conversation, as if it were a favourite doll.

"I'm really enjoying the flat," Helen ventured. He told her it was down to an old pupil of his, a chap called Karl, whose talent and commitment for renovation knew no bounds.

"It used to be a shop, one my mother and aunt used. The owner was a very nice man. So, what have you been doing today?"

She told him she'd been thinking more about the tunnel and Stephen's part in it, how strange it seemed to her. She found herself talking more about her husband than she had done for a long while. Elsa had demanded his attention from time to time, reminding her of half-finished conversations with friends when the children were young, but she felt, nevertheless, that she managed to say quite a lot, mainly because Elsa's photo seemed to be pleasing her so much.

Peter thought it was strange that her husband's past appeared to be such a surprise to Helen. He was reminded of something in Dickens – which novel was it? He'd always liked it – that even in marriage every human is a profound secret and mystery to every other.

"Everyone was very fearful," he said, "so suspicious of one another, you know, passing even what might be thought to be the most innocuous of remarks could result in strenuous questioning from the Stasi. To dig a tunnel therefore was, well…" He raised his hands in admiration. "That street where the tunnel ended up," he continued, "Strelitzer. Funnily enough, a colleague of mine, a fellow teacher, had lived in one of those flats there. Erhard. Taught German. One year, he had a couple of particularly bright pupils. Very talented. Potentially great writers, Erhard always said, and from the little I'd seen of them when I'd had occasion to teach them, I could see what he meant. But the problem was they were what the Stasi had labelled 'border crossers'. They were from families who'd previously worked in the West and as such were never considered to be proper East Germans. Worse still, they were regarded as untrustworthy. Consequently, these two boys were prevented from going to university and Erhard was, as you can imagine, furious." He paused, because he could see the pupils' faces very clearly. "Erhard was normally such a mild man, a teacher who had natural authority."

He paused. He'd always liked Erhard. Such an honest man. And a kind one.

"Our job was to encourage and nurture. You can imagine how undermining it was for us to have to witness talent like that curtailed. To be fair, if fair's the right word, Erhard was told they could apply for a course, but there were strings attached. They would've had to be puppets of the Stasi, basically, and neither the boys' families nor Erhard were interested." He got up. "Your husband was very brave, Helen. I'm sure I could never muster such courage."

By now, Elsa was glowering at him, wondering why this man had so much to say in a language that meant nothing to her. He knew she hated him giving others much attention, that in her diseased mind a jealousy took over and led her to anxiety or anger.

"I hope I haven't bored you and if I don't go back into the kitchen, I'll probably starve you as the food will have burnt. If you'll excuse me, it won't be long now. Please have a look at any of the books. The left-hand side is all English."

Elsa was up too, still puzzled and cross but ready to follow Peter, her toy photo carefully placed where she'd been sitting.

"Komm, Elsa, schauen wir ob der Eintopf bald fertig ist."

"Welcher Eintopf?"

"Lass uns einfach schauen."

As Helen watched them disappear into the kitchen, Elsa clinging to his arm with as much tenacity as if she were about to fall off a cliff, she wasn't so sure about Peter's lack of bravery. It was confined in so many minds as something set against a backdrop of a wider, adversarial situation, but looking at him now, the way he listened to her talk about nothing in particular and with an injured face she was sure Elsa had caused and which she hoped she hadn't looked as if she'd noticed, she felt as though this was as terrifying a situation as any.

She turned round and looked at all the books, venturing towards the shelves he'd suggested and being slightly overwhelmed by the sheer number of volumes they held. There was a small, wooden stepladder for those books that seemed to be nearly on the ceiling, but she wasn't going to attempt to get on it. Her record for the untried and untested wasn't great and usually resulted in something breaking.

His interests largely lay in the works of Dickens, Forster and Shakespeare, *Hamlet* obviously favoured if the number of texts relating to that play were anything to go by. There were many books about Britain. She picked out an expensive-looking guide to its coastline and smiled when she saw the familiar. It was funny how near the images felt, how actual distance did little to diminish an attachment to what felt one's own. She opened the book and saw there was an inscription in English:

Dear Herr Bayer,
Thank you for believing in me. I know you wanted more for me, but I am happy. I hope you and Frau Bayer can go here one day.
Karl

"Here we are." Peter came in with a large pot in his hands, followed by Elsa who had seen the sense in not getting too close and had put two or three steps between them. She put the book back on the shelf quickly, wrongly feeling she was prying where she shouldn't.

He invited her to sit at a table at the end of the room, near enough to one of the book shelves that she could still read many of the titles, and quickly put the pot on a tablemat, which along with others had been placed in an orderly fashion, but with none of the flair of Margot's swans. A table lamp, perched at one corner of the table, which probably normally rested elsewhere because it looked distinctly uncomfortable where it was, had been placed there, she suspected, to offer warmth and enough light to ensure nothing harsher needed to be used.

The consuming of the meal, though delicious and hot, was an uncomfortable affair, eaten as it was beside Peter's swollen eye and Elsa's indecision about whether she wanted to eat it. But later, when she remembered this part of the evening, it wasn't either of these that left a lasting impression but the memory of Peter carefully placing a crisp, cotton napkin on her lap and asking her if the temperature of the room was all right.

One by one, he put little portions from the casserole dish onto Elsa's plate – she didn't like it getting cold – and fed her, saying reassuring words as he did this, asking her if she was ready for more and having to put up with her sometimes firmly closing her lips and turning her head away.

"She says she doesn't like it. It's one of her favourites," he informed their guest. "Last week it had a very good review," and he smiled, exasperated at the inconsistency of his wife, which could usually be relied upon to foil any of his attempts at perfection. During the administering of one spoonful, his English commentary for Helen meant he forgot to blow on one spoonful and this omission caused Elsa to shriek, shout at him and slap him firmly on the wrist.

He wanted to join in and shriek as well but couldn't because of their company. It was all so embarrassing and he regretted his inability to fully accept the limitation of his life, which, in truth, couldn't accommodate outsiders for any length of time. He didn't really know why he bothered to try to change the tedium when he knew he would invariably end up being told off by Elsa, but conversation was a compelling thing, the prospect of which would always be his downfall. He was now feeling remorseful, though, of having drawn Helen more closely into this situation and vowed not to repeat it.

Pudding passed without incident; it was fruit salad after all, a favourite of Elsa's, though conversations were rarely finished and never properly explored. Elsa, with Peter's help, said goodbye to Helen by asking her who she was and Helen, with Peter's help, said goodnight and hoped Elsa would sleep well. He excused both of them, saying he would try not to be too long putting Elsa to bed and Helen didn't lie when she said she was perfectly fine looking at the books because there was little she liked better than to be left alone to do something while knowing she wasn't completely alone. It was a state of mind and being she'd always enjoyed when they'd been a family.

"She's quite tired tonight," Peter said as he entered the room again. "We did quite a bit of walking today, well quite a bit for Elsa, and I think it's made her sleepy. Goodness knows where she goes to in her dreams."

"You're very patient."

"Well, you have to be, don't you? I suppose you're given something. You don't have a choice."

He paused and looked out of the window. She thought he seemed tired.

"I think a real test of character," he continued, "is when you do have a choice." He turned to Helen and smiled. "Like your husband, for instance."

She looked at his poor, worn-out face. "I really think I should be going. Elsa can't be the only one who's tired."

"No. No, don't go. Please stay." Peter immediately felt embarrassed at such imploring and tried to recover. "Please stay. I don't have many conversations these days. I miss them. You're right. I am tired. But I'm tired because I'm bored." He felt choked. In a thousand years, he would never have thought he would've been bored with Elsa's company.

She smiled reassuringly as she felt the tedium that hung around him and the sense that nothing could change for the better. Looking at all the books on all the walls, she strongly suspected there wasn't a thought or an idea in any of them Peter didn't know.

"I'd love a coffee," she said.

They went into the kitchen and he put two heaped spoonfuls of coffee into a percolator, which looked like an old friend, scratchy glass and a plastic top that had suffered a burn at some point because a small part of it had melted into a distorted shape.

"You know, I was thinking about your colleague and his pupils and what a sheltered life I've led," she said as he poured boiling water into the percolator.

"Keep your innocence," he replied. "Be at peace with it."

"I've taken it for granted."

"Freedom of expression's invariably treasured most by those who don't have it. When I was teaching I often had that desire, you know that feeling when you just want to put your hand on a hot plate to see what happens, even though you know exactly what'll happen. Perhaps it's about wanting to check you're alive. Anyway, I often felt like shouting, sorry but, 'F you, bastard Stasi' in a park or any public place. But I never did. That burnt hand was just too painful a prospect and personal security, even of the sort offered in the East, was, at the end of the day, something to hold on to. The problem was that everything – art; literature; history – had to have a socialist message. And the East German addiction to paperwork – it's a wonder any of us had the time to take a bath."

He asked her a lot about England. He always wanted information about the country he loved. She told him she lived in an area of London that was considered quite fashionable nowadays but wasn't so much when they moved there.

"There's a park nearby; it's lovely, you can see London's skyline. It really blows the cobwebs away."

He smiled and thought of all the times since the wall had

come down that he'd promised himself he must go to England and how often he'd discussed it with Elsa, who'd patiently listened to him extol its virtues and agreed they must go; he suspected this was probably so he would shut up and stop endlessly talking about it. She knew, of course, it had much to do with Freddy, whose interest in him during such terrible times had never left him and was almost entirely responsible for his love affair with the country. He imagined blue and green whenever he thought of England, a place full of gardens, surrounded by sea. He couldn't begin to think what it would be like to see the sea every day and when Helen shrugged and said you take it for granted when you live by it, he laughed and replied, take the sea for granted? No, he could never do that. Something so powerful and exciting? And its different emotions. Watch the sea, he said, and it's like observing ourselves.

She noticed that Peter bore no particular expression when he listened, almost as if his mind was a blank page on which anything could be written because he'd cleared it completely. He must've been a good teacher, sharing his passion for a subject and country that had been a foe, while genuinely interested in his students' ideas.

"So coming to Berlin was…?" Peter poured her another coffee.

"I don't know. A way of… I suppose it was a way of connecting with" – and she thought about it for a few seconds, trying to work it out for herself as much as attempting to explain it to someone else – "the person Stephen was before I met him. I'd often been curious about his time here and had suggested we come, but he never seemed very keen on the idea and the friends we knew here, the ones I saw the other night, well, Hans's business frequently brought him to England, so we used to see them there."

"And you've remained curious. Your curiosity, as you say, got the better of you?"

"Yes, I suppose it did. Grief, also, that sometimes seems to determine your journeys. You know, feeling closer again to someone by treading the same ground, seeing the same people. But it must seem odd to you. There are plenty of places in England where I can do both of those things."

"But not where he went to university. No, it doesn't seem odd. After all, it's the unanswered questions, isn't it?"

She laughed. "It's the 'none of my business' questions."

"When someone dies, it's natural to think more about their past, to wonder why they did this or didn't do that."

"Our relationship became so much about the children."

"That's not unusual. I'm sure it's the same for many couples, though I wouldn't know." He paused. "We could never have children."

She didn't reply but instead took another sip of coffee.

"We've had a good life, but I suppose there's a pang, a curiosity, if you like; you see curiosity, it's a powerful thing. Working with children, it was a mixed blessing, really. Sometimes it filled a gap and, to be honest, gave me a sense of relief that I didn't have to put up with this kind of behaviour and, let's face it, probably worse, when I got home, but then it also made me ache for my own children and there were some days when I could hardly cope with the pain. It sounds horrible, I know, but the times when I had to talk to parents who I could see weren't interested, who were there on sufferance, well, you can't help but think life seems a little unfair."

"But you got a lot of satisfaction from teaching?"

"Oh yes, no doubt about that. And there are difficult times in all jobs. No, the teaching of English, well, it was something I wanted to do at university and I can honestly say something I've never strayed from. And when you get a class or even one child who is truly gripped by what you're telling them, well, I doubt if working in an office would've given me anywhere near such exhilaration. I'd come home and Elsa would almost smell the excitement. 'You've had a good day, I can tell,' she'd say. 'You know Greta?' I'd reply. 'She came up to me in the corridor and said, "Herr Bayer," – her eyes alight – "you didn't tell us how scary *Wuthering Heights* was. I had to put it down at ten o'clock, otherwise I wouldn't have slept. But I love it."' Then Elsa would tell me it was stew and dumplings for supper and I could only think I was the luckiest man alive."

They must have carried on talking for another hour or so. It was one of those evenings when the exchanging of stories is more interesting than the passing of time and two people, unlikely to meet in everyday circumstance, found no need to look at a clock or consider how tired they were.

He was about to tell her what they were doing when the wall came down, how they first knew when they were watching TV in a bar and the newscaster announced that East Berliners could travel wherever they wanted. Everyone wondered if this was some kind of joke as it was difficult to conceive such a notion, but they all knew the newscaster, who delivered the words as seriously as usual; they all decided to go outside, not quite ready to cheer yet but forming a collective movement towards Bornholmerstrasse to test this truth and how, then, Elsa and he became two of the first East Berliners to cross to the West. And what had struck him most were the soldiers' faces, once formidable and frightening, now laughing and jesting with those who, a day before, they would've easily shot. And how, crossing that bridge, completely overwhelmed and lost for words as the shock of what they'd just done took over, they reclaimed what had been theirs but what they thought they'd left behind for good. As they hugged each other and it gradually sank in, memories of his young life came flooding back and that, in many ways, was as difficult as the presence of the wall had been.

But she didn't hear that because Elsa came down, as agitated and shaky as he'd ever seen. She came up to him and started tugging at his sleeve.

"Was tust du? Er ist spät? Wir mussen einkaufen gehen. Warum ist sie noch da? Wer ist sie? Wer ist sie?"

"I should be going," Helen said and got up from the sofa.

"No, you mustn't feel you've got to go. Elsa will be all right in a few minutes. This often happens. She wakes out of a sleep and gets very frightened. It'll be OK. Please sit down. I'll get her photo. That, er, that usually helps."

He walked towards the sideboard where the photo was, trying to block out Elsa's questions and protests and something she said again and again. He hated getting the photo, but he was enjoying this conversation too much for moral dilemmas to start tampering with his enjoyment.

Helen stood where she was and although she felt she really should push the point about going, particularly as she was having serious misgivings about staying and witnessing Elsa's distress, it somehow just seemed voyeuristic; she could see how keen Peter still was for company, so she decided to stay and made this clear by sitting down again. She remembered later how she thought it had little to do with mere politeness, which was normally her motivation, because she was always very guided by what seemed right.

Elsa became more distressed, the photo held firmly in one hand but the other flying all over the place, occasionally knocking against Peter.

"Warum ist sie immer noch da? Warum? Sie ist eine beschissene Engländerin. Weisst du was sie tun, die Engländer?"

"Elsa, Elsa, ist OK. Ich bin da, Liebchen. Bitte beruhige dich. Es ist OK." Peter kissed the top of Elsa's head, but she pushed him away.

"Die Engländer. Die Engländer. Ich hasse die Engländer."

Helen got up from her seat. "I think it's me being here, Peter. I really should go."

"Die beschissene Engländer."

"What's she saying?"

"It's nothing. She's not herself. This isn't Elsa, this isn't—"

"Sprich Deutsch. Sprich Deutsch. Du bist keine Engländerin. Nicht Englisch. Nicht Englisch."

"Beruhige dich. Bitte, Elsa, sei ruhig. Ich werde ihr sagen, dass sie gehen muss. Ich sag's ihr. Bitte beruhige dich."

"Sag ihr, warum ich sie hasse. Sag es."

"Nein, Elsa, nein. Es hat keinen Sinn. Sie ist nicht schuld."

"Doch, doch. Sie ist Engländerin. Die Schlampe ist Engländerin."

"Elsa!"

"Sag's ihr. Sag's ihr. Sag ihr, dass die englischen Scheisspiloten meinen kleinen Bruder umgebracht haben. Sag's ihr!"

Helen reached for her bag. She had to get out of the house because her being there was obviously awful for Elsa. She was obviously saying something about her Peter didn't want her to hear, but his protests dimmed as Elsa's shouting grew louder; there was a determination and sharpness in her voice that weren't going to be told to stop. She turned to Helen and started walking towards her, still shouting, still screaming. It didn't matter that Helen didn't understand the words because, compared to her level of anger, they seemed irrelevant. Then Helen was in pain, there was an acute pain on the right cheek of her face and she cradled it and yelled.

"Elsa! Elsa! Nein! Nein!" she could hear Peter shouting. Then he said, "Sorry, sorry, I'm so, so sorry."

"Sag ihr, dass englischen Scheisspiloten meinen kleinen Bruder umgebracht haben. Jene Scheisspiloten haben den kleinen Heunrich getötet. Meinen kleinen Bruder."

"What's she saying?" Tears were now falling down Helen's face.

"It's nothing. It's the illness. She doesn't know what she's saying. She—"

"Peter, what did she say?"

"I really don't want—"

"Peter. Your wife's just hit me. Please."

He looked at the floor and hated himself for wanting something more, for wanting a conversation with someone. She had a right to know. She had a right to know why his wife had been so abusive.

"She said…" He stopped and looked straight at Helen. It was the least he could do. "She said those bastard English pilots killed her little brother."

Helen said nothing because she had no idea how to respond when the shock of what had just happened was making her whole body shake. It was as if she were no longer part of her own life as she'd experienced something that was so alien to her she could barely understand it. Maybe if she could have extended some sympathy for Elsa, she may have felt better, but that was impossible.

Peter left the room with Elsa following closely behind. He, too, seemed to understand that language couldn't yet remedy anything and though she was tempted to leave, she didn't, partly because a paralysis seemed to have taken over, and waited for what she took to be his imminent return. A few seconds later he did come back, holding a wet towel. He pressed it gently against the side of her face Elsa had slapped, while Elsa, like a discordant note, accompanied this with, "Nein, nein, nein."

"I'm going now," Helen said and put her own hand on the towel. Then Peter let his go.

She shut Peter's door behind her and walked, dazed, towards the flat, holding the towel against her face. It still hurt and tears were still falling down her face. But the fresh air was soothing and the fact that the street was quiet helped. Only one man walked purposefully and soberly on the other side. She could hear what sounded like a woman's footsteps behind her. They struck the ground hard and loud and she could hear their pace quicken. Then she felt a tap on her shoulder. She shrieked and started shaking, now more than ever.

"Es tut mir Leid. Ich wolte nur sehen, wie es geht."

She wasn't sure, and just now she couldn't be sure of anything, but it seemed like the young woman she'd seen at night-time from her flat window. Only this time walking the other way. Home, perhaps.

The woman spoke again and pointed to the towel that remained inseparable from Helen's face. She could hear concern in the woman's voice.

"Danke," she replied. "Ich bin Engländerin."

Behind all the make-up the woman had a kind face and though Helen felt vulnerable she wasn't fearful. She assumed the woman was asking if she was all right, so she smiled and held her left thumb upwards, lying without saying a word.

"I don't speak English much," the woman said, "but your home?"

Helen pointed to where the flat was so the woman could see she didn't have far to go.

"We walk?" she said.

Helen nodded. The woman put her hand in her bag and produced a tissue. Helen wiped her face and said sorry. The woman smiled, mumbled something sympathetically, then took Helen's arm, ready to escort her the last few steps.

When they got to the door she waited for Helen to find her keys, which she struggled to do, as she was shaking so much. The keys felt strange in her hand; they felt hostile now. She didn't really want to go in.

She showed the woman the keys.

"Will you be OK?" she asked.

"Yes," Helen replied, while tears rolled down her cheeks. The woman took the keys from her without any resistance from Helen and opened the door.

Years later she would still remember this woman with a

greater clarity than others she'd known for many years. She'd remember that the woman, whose feet were all but vertical in her very high heels, walked with noisy footsteps around the flat, putting the kettle on, finding tea bags, finding milk.

They had no conversation for one another, but as Helen had nothing to offer and no ability to listen, a silent companion was just what was required. So she took the mug of hot tea, sipping it with more gratitude than she'd felt in a long while, and let the woman sit with her and hold her hand.

16

Margot picked a single tissue out of the square cardboard box decorated with pink roses and carefully pressed her painted lips onto it, removing any excess of the Strawberry Surprise shade. Luise had done her hair very well this time. She'd been wary of the new colours, but Luise was right. They were softer and she didn't look pale now. She opened her jewellery box and lifted out various brooches, holding them against her dress one by one until she chose the pearl clusters Hans had bought her for their last anniversary. It was only lunch at the new gallery, but nevertheless, she was going to be the sole representative of the museum and it was impossible, on these occasions, to overdress. She stood up and walked towards the bedroom door, collecting her beaded clutch bag on the way out, which she held tightly, as if it were the arm of a friend whose support she needed.

As she opened the car door a few minutes later and bent to put the bag on the passenger seat beside her, she suddenly found herself thinking about Rosa's life and its seeming simplicity. How straightforward the lives of others. How Rosa, for instance, was less concerned than she was about who she was in the eyes of others. There was an inner confidence in her Margot had rarely found. She'd always shown an outward assurance. Living with Hans it was required, a performance if you like, but she was becoming very tired of the show; there was nothing more it could tell her.

The gallery was splendid, bright with high ceilings and unquestionable cleanliness, where visitors would be able to breathe in the same way they might on a country walk because it had somehow magically conveyed more space than it actually had.

She saw many faces she knew, all suitably coiffed or suited. They knew the rules and those who didn't were excused their lack of dress code on the grounds of artistic brilliance or eccentricity. There was nothing unusual about the small talk, focusing, as it so often did on these occasions, on work and children. Well, she could strut her stuff as well as anyone; she had a job at the museum and children predictably performing, as was required, at different universities. It was a fanning of feathers, with only the odd remark here and there about the paintings.

"It is with great pleasure, therefore, that I declare the gallery open." Margot smiled and clapped. She liked the look of this director. She'd already been introduced a few months ago to her by an old friend of theirs who made it his business to put considerable amounts of money into as many artistic ventures in Berlin as he could lay his hands on, which in turn, over the years, had given him more respectability amongst this community than perhaps he deserved. He bought culture. It wasn't in his veins. This director, though, was impressive and passionate. In that sense, he'd invested well.

She congratulated those who should have been congratulated, promoted the museum where she could and where seemed appropriate, and told others she didn't want to see again that she and they should meet up for a coffee sometime, then picked up a third glass of wine on her way out, which she finished just before she was able to leave it on the last small table before the entrance. She didn't particularly want to go home straightaway, so she made for the first café she saw and ordered an English tea. The girl said, "Milk", with a question on her face; "No, no, no, lemon," and turned towards the street and saw her reflection in the window. She squinted to see more clearly and touched her lips. She'd managed to go through an entire afternoon without re-applying lipstick and she could just about see that she needed to put some on, but she couldn't be bothered.

She thought about the lunch with Helen. Hans could be such a hypocrite with all that heroic nonsense. She always ended up going along with it somehow and it depressed her that her desire for a certain standard of living had seemed to deprive her all these years of a sense of greater morality she was now looking for. It had been so easy to collude because the house was beautiful, her clothes exquisite and the food they ate expensive and delicious. She wished, though, and this had everything to do with her determination to think differently, they'd let sleeping dogs lie, that they'd told Rosa they didn't really have any contact with Helen anymore and their English friend would never have known any different. It was dangerous bringing it to Helen's attention because she couldn't ask the one person she would anything about what happened and she doubted Stephen had ever told his wife about the girl. That was Hans, though: as long as he had the attention, it was irrelevant what debris fell in his wake.

It was about an hour later when she got home. No one was in. She walked into the lounge and picked up an ornament from the mantelpiece. It was a small glass her daughter had bought her on a school trip and had "mum" engraved around the top. She took it upstairs and walked into her clothes cupboard. Underneath her dresses and behind her shoes was one of her suitcases, so she opened the zip and carefully placed the glass next to a few scarves, making sure it settled safely there. After quickly popping downstairs, she returned and put a rose she'd kept pressed between the pages of an old encyclopaedia into the suitcase as well. It was pink, which could still be recognised, even though it was thirty years old. Hans had picked it out of someone's garden on his way to see her. He didn't have much money then. He'd cut his finger on one of the thorns, an occupational hazard without the paper, tissue and careful arranging of a florist's hand. It was their first date, which was just a walk by The Spree. Just. She smiled. His unwavering attention and enthusiasm for everything she uttered was enchanting and his idealism completely seduced her because she hadn't ever witnessed such a vivid example of it. He belonged to a group of friends whose hatred for the status quo and their desire to bring about change in Germany and unite it again occupied most thoughts and nearly every sentence. The other topic they touched upon was love and one of the first conversations she'd had with Hans was about his English friend Stephen and how he'd fallen hopelessly in love with a woman called Christa.

She placed the rose in a paper bag, which she'd first filled with a piece of card to keep the rose straight, then folded over the top of the bag and placed it carefully into one of the side pockets of the case. Then she closed it and put it back in the corner of the wardrobe where it had been for some weeks.

She went downstairs again and opened the front door. She was wearing her tracksuit bottoms, a T-shirt she usually reserved for gardening and her face was as naked as it was when, aged fourteen, she'd tentatively picked up her mother's lipstick to paint her lips for the very first time. Her stomach churned over for, in all her adult life, she'd never dared go out like this. Everyone knew Margot as having the most careful of dress and make-up regimes.

She clasped her house keys, then put one key in the door, turned it round and did the same with a second key. She was due to meet Rosa who'd never seen her in such attire, though she'd seen Margot's appearance spiral downwards a little recently and had barely concealed her surprise the first time Margot had entered the museum in trousers and flat shoes. Hans hadn't seemed to notice that anything was different about his wife. Maybe when he looked back and thought about it, but she couldn't be sure he'd do either.

She turned ninety degrees and stared for a few moments at the ceramic pot filled with geraniums under which they kept the spare keys. They were still thriving, thanks to a summer that refused to give up. She touched her lips. They were dry without gloss. A bird sang, prompting her to turn in the direction she wanted to go.

17

Dear Helen,

I'm writing to apologise from the bottom of my heart for what Elsa did to you last night and I hold myself to blame for thinking I could invite a guest into our situation.

In normal circumstances I would obviously say, without hesitation, that her behaviour was inexcusable, but I hope, shocked and distraught though you must be, you will find you can forgive her for truly it's the illness and not Elsa that did this terrible thing to you.

If you had known Elsa, you'd have seen one of the gentlest women you'd ever be likely to come across, who would've welcomed you into our home with great generosity and warmth. It is me you must blame for gambling with your life, risking something happening that has occurred many times before, but I've only ever seen her lose her temper with me and I genuinely, though now I can see stupidly, never thought she would raise her voice to anyone else, let alone strike them. But of course, it's the old Elsa I speak of.

My only defence, pathetic and entirely inadequate though it is, is how much I've enjoyed our meetings, the extent of which is now difficult to put on paper.

You're obviously a very kind and loving woman who's spent time with a couple of old people while on holiday in one of the most exciting cities in Europe. And I can't tell you what a complete and utter delight it is for me to have the opportunity to speak English with an English person. That excitement within me will never die.

There was an Englishman, a soldier. What can I say?

That man, Freddy, he saved our lives in many ways. I got to know him at the end of the war, when I was thirteen; he was part of the allied forces in Berlin. And, clichéd though it may sound, he did become my ally, my friend. It was Freddy who started to teach me English and it's to him I owe my enthusiasm and love of the language, and to him I owe my living.

You must be wondering why on earth I've enclosed an old English chocolate bar wrapper in this letter. I'd like, if I may, to tell you about other Englishmen. Pilots. Ones to whom we owe our lives.

I expect you've heard of the Berlin Airlift. It was three years after the war and in Berlin we were facing yet another crisis. The Soviets were trying to block access to Western Berlin. Gas and electricity had been cut off to Western sectors and what was particularly worrying was the shortage of milk. There was a very real fear babies' lives would be lost. As you probably know, what followed was the airlift. For nearly a year our food and fuel supplies were dropped at two airports by English and American pilots.

I remember one particular day I stood with a large group of people watching one plane flying past us very low. It seemed to be the only thing we could see that was intact. All around us were remnants of buildings bombed during the war and our group stood on a pile of rubble, looking up at this noisy object; it was similar to the buzzing we'd heard only a few years before and might've instilled fear, had it not been for the knowledge that on the plane was our food. You can't imagine. An angel in our midst.

I stood behind a little girl and boy, brother and sister, I think, dressed smartly in their school uniforms. The little girl, her hair tied up in ribbons, was clutching a briefcase, which almost seemed the same size as its owner. They started jumping up and down. "Roisenbombers! Roisenbombers!" They could hardly contain their excitement. Their mother, beside them, tried to tell them to calm down but with no success. I knew the word. Friends told me about the airmen who were dropping sweets and chocolate, usually wrapped in handkerchiefs, for the children. They were nicknamed "roisenbombers", raisin bombers. The bombs this time, you see, were to save us. It was, I suppose, the first time we'd felt cared for in a long while.

I looked up. It was a beautiful day, much like the weather we've been having recently. We knew the plane was English because we were near Gatow, where the English planes landed. The young boy and girl were still shouting, jumping higher and higher the nearer the plane got, as if they were trying to reach the very hands of the chocolate magicians. Sure enough, they weren't to be disappointed. As it flew overhead, small packages fell out of the plane and all us children (though I'd have hated to call myself a child by then and, if I remember right, I had some anxiety about whether I too should run and whether this would make me look silly) ran to where the packages were landing. I managed to find one. I still have the handkerchief and, as you can see, I've kept the wrapper. You probably know the make.

The airmen became our heroes. They were mobbed when they walked down the streets and were presented with flowers. The last recipients of such a gesture had been the hierarchy of the Nazi party, but, as with the sweet packets, the flowers were now symbols of something so much more hopeful.

I just wanted you to know this story. I do hope you don't mind and thank you for reading it.

May I once again say how sorry I am that you had to suffer like you did and I'm so sorry I didn't have the foresight to prevent it happening. Elsa, as I say, was such a kind woman and, though it's hard, I have to let her stay in her house, though others have tried to persuade me to put her somewhere else. But how could I live with myself?

Please, please enjoy the rest of your stay in the flat and if there's anything I can help you with, please don't hesitate to let me know.

With very best wishes,
Peter

Helen looked across the room and saw the letter from Peter, which was sitting on the table by the sofa next to a half-finished cup of coffee and a plate with orange peel on it. She returned to her book and read page twenty-four for what must have been as many times, but still she had no idea what was on that page. She looked out of the window and acknowledged to herself that this holiday had been a mistake, that attempting to know more about a person after their death was perhaps wrong when it was someone so close. Stephen had revealed all that he'd wanted to reveal and that was his right. This search she'd embarked on was, in sympathetic terms, a grieving process, an unwillingness to accept what she'd have to, that he wasn't lingering somewhere around the next corner, waiting for her in a cosy part of Berlin, and in less generous terms, it was the action of someone who's merely grovelling around for information that isn't hers to know. In short, she was nothing more than a nosey parker and, for her punishment, she had a slap in the face from a woman she barely knew and had very little inclination to know any further.

She felt alone, floating in a vacuum with no support and wanted to ring someone in England, but there were various reasons why she hadn't, from not wanting to worry her children to feeling uncomfortable about bothering her friends. There was also the problem of wise silences down the phone from those who'd advised her not to go to Berlin. Let the past be the past. Get away from it all. Go somewhere that has nothing to do with anyone's past. The truth was as well that she didn't have much experience of being upset with friends. She didn't like the thought of it because it would always be there in their minds, no matter how many good times were had afterwards. It made her slightly cringe. She'd always been taught such outpourings were self-indulgent. It was a view she'd learnt to embrace and live by. Even when Stephen died, she'd managed to keep things to herself and was proud of not having given in when the children were around.

She went across to the sofa and put her feet up. Peter's letter stared at her and she picked it up and read the last couple of paragraphs again. "Please, please enjoy the rest of your stay in the flat and if there's *anything* I can help you with, please don't hesitate to let me know." She threw the letter back on the table and picked up her address book, angry that she'd put herself in such a vulnerable position and even angrier that she now seemed to need someone to talk to. This was so unlike her and she began to feel a bit frightened.

Then she saw the name of a woman she couldn't really call a friend, an old neighbour, and for some reason, maybe precisely because she wasn't a close friend, she thought, on and off but for quite a while, this could be the very person to ring. An hour or so later she started pressing the numbers on her mobile.

"Is that Audrey? You may not remember me."

Audrey did. Helen said she was sorry to bother her. It was so silly really. She was in Berlin. Yes, she was on her own. Did she know Stephen had died? Thank you. Yes, anyway, she was here because this was where Stephen had studied and she'd seen some friends of theirs, well his, really, and there was her landlord and... she missed Stephen so much, no one could possibly understand.

18

Audrey put the phone down, shocked by different things. Shocked that it was her old neighbour Helen who was sobbing on the other end because it wasn't the sort of thing she did; shocked by her own ability to deal with the situation with a not inconsiderable amount of calm, which had, in turn, eventually helped stop Helen crying; shocked by some of the things she'd said – that Helen would be surprised by the number of people who did understand her pain; it just wouldn't feel like it at the moment; take her, for instance, but at this point Helen said she knew really it was just that she felt so lonely, to which she'd agreed it must be very difficult; and then she'd listened for a while about this incident with her landlord's wife. It all sounded a bit involved and she couldn't quite make head or tail of it, but dementia seemed to be in the mix somewhere amidst the sobbing, so she said it wasn't personal because Mrs Brown down the road could be very unpredictable. She had the same thing. Then Audrey was very shocked at herself because in the middle of all this she'd offered to go and see Helen. To be fair, Helen kept saying no, she shouldn't, that it was very kind of her, but she shouldn't go to such trouble, no, she really shouldn't, and to her surprise Audrey had kept insisting, saying she could do with a break and that Kenneth was only going to be spending the next couple of weeks mending something in the garage, she couldn't remember what exactly, at which point she'd managed to get a little laugh from her old neighbour, who then said it would be lovely to see her.

This had been enough to convince Audrey. It had been a long while since anyone had told her it would be lovely to see her. Now, in the quiet of their living room she was processing what had just happened and after a few minutes, she laughed and punched the air just like all those sportspeople do on the telly.

She went straight upstairs to look in her wardrobe and sort out stuff she should take. As she was going through things to take or not take, putting them in different piles, Kenneth came through the front door, back from his daily walk to get the evening paper and shouted, "I'm back," upstairs and some comment she didn't quite hear; it was probably about the weather.

She heard his footsteps on the stairs; they were always laboured and were usually accompanied by heavy breathing and sighs. She thought he overdid it a bit, some kind of need for attention.

"I've got the paper," he said, throwing it on the bed. "Seems like they are going to build that new supermarket after all. Just what we need. Another supermarket." He sat on the bed and got his breath back. "What the heck are you doing?" He paused for a few seconds. "You're not leaving me, are you?"

She smiled because she was touched that he seemed so worried.

"Only for a few days," she replied and explained the conversation she'd had with Helen.

He helped her book a flight and a hotel, being quite handy on the computer these days, but he was perplexed. He wasn't really sure why his wife was rushing off to Berlin to see Helen; they'd never seemed that close when they were neighbours, but what did he know? Maybe Audrey just needed a break or, more to the point, a break from him. He could be a miserable old sod sometimes and he wasn't all that good at showing her his appreciation.

So, roughly thirty-six hours later, when they'd had the chat about the contents of the freezer and what he'd find easy to cook, a lot more than she thought and not all of it was in the freezer, there were one or two things he thought he might try, and when she'd packed the final things and he'd driven her to the airport, negotiating various road closures on the way, he found himself waving at her plane, in the vain hope she may have seen him.

Audrey had done this only once before and that was to Wigan when her sister was very ill. Kenneth had offered to drive her there, but she was so upset she said she'd prefer to go on her own. Years down the line, she often thought he'd been hurt by her decision, but it was something they hadn't discussed because they both knew she was the only one who could start a conversation about Jean.

She looked down at the airport below and shuddered slightly as her hasty decision to travel began to sink in, but even so, she still managed to congratulate that part of her that hadn't wavered and as the houses and roads disappeared and clouds replaced them, she welcomed a different reality: the possibility of her first cup of tea in the sky without the company of anyone she knew.

19

Peter felt about as far away from the day when he went to the World Cup match with Karl in the summer as he could possibly imagine. That day, he'd felt excitement he'd completely forgotten. What was this? A glee in his body that almost made him want to jump. It had meant he'd found a way of being around Elsa in the weeks leading up to it that had been more affable, almost not minding their situation, comparing himself more positively with others. Things could be a lot worse.

He'd looked forward to the World Cup for months. It was good to have it in his united country, an excuse to talk to Karl a bit more often about their shared passion. How they'd always exchanged views, taunt one another, he chiding his old pupil for supporting Leverkusen – what did he do that for? What about a Berlin team? "What Berlin team?" would be Karl's retort. "Yours? They'll never reach the Bundesliga." And so it would rattle on, like an old lorry trying to get to a destination it never would, and Elsa would say, "For God's sake, give the poor boy a rest," and they'd both laugh because they knew this was their rest, this was exactly what they wanted to do. "Don't worry, Elsa, I love talking to Peter about football, especially as I'm always with the winning team," and Peter would make a gesture for him to stop, partly in fun, but also because he knew the so-and-so was right.

They'd managed, or rather Karl had managed, to get tickets for Germany v Ecuador at the Olympiastadion; he was waving them in his hand when Peter opened the door. Peter couldn't quite believe it. Karl had said he would get tickets, but he knew how difficult these things could be. He wasn't sure how many times he'd thanked Karl that afternoon, but it was probably about as many times as Elsa had insisted on another piece of cake because she couldn't remember having the last slice.

"They're on me," Karl had insisted, no matter how many times he'd argued the point. "I really want to do this, you've done so much for me," and Peter had known to stop then.

"Thank you, it's wonderful," and Peter had thought it was just one of those moments that are too good to be true, like the day he'd bought his first record, after weeks of saving up, and put it on the record player. It was Beethoven's *Piano Sonata No. 14*.

"Don't worry about Elsa. We'll sort it out," and that was exactly what both he and his wife, Ingrid, did. Unusually, everything worked out perfectly that day; Ingrid arranged for the children to spend the day with her mother, "They always love spending the day with their granny, she spoils them rotten and never seems to tell them off", and she looked after Elsa, who had no memory of her, so they had a couple of practice runs with both of them going over to Karl and Ingrid's. The lead up to the day, despite his excitement, had torn his nerves in shreds because so often he'd tried to leave her with someone like Alke and Elsa had kicked up such a fuss he'd had to abandon his plans or he'd had to rush back from somewhere because she was crying her eyes out and was calling his name incessantly or had filled up her pad and stunk to high heaven.

He didn't know what it was about that day; maybe an occasion so vast disallowed private consideration, but he always thought this would be the one day that would be uninterrupted and they'd be able to watch the entire match. It was easier to lose oneself in crowds, he thought, the contrast to normal life so marked that everyday worries dissipated, spreading themselves so thinly it was as if they barely existed.

Since Elsa had been diagnosed, he couldn't remember a time when he'd been able to relax into a situation in which she wasn't by his side and very few when she was, but there was something about Ingrid's assurances, her ability to think of as many possible situations as she could that might occur and prepare for them that left him full of confidence that this would be a great day out.

They walked most of the way to the stadium. It was so enjoyable walking at a good pace with Karl, watching buildings pass him so much more quickly than they could with Elsa, whose concern about where they were prevented any attempt at speed.

"How are your parents, Karl? Have they decided to move yet?"

"No, they haven't. They can't agree on where they might go. Dad definitely wants to leave Berlin and move to the country, but Mum's dragging her feet a bit. I think she's worried she's going to miss her friends too much. To be honest, I think she's worried about having him around her feet twenty-four-seven without any excuse to get out and see anyone else."

"She's very sociable, though, isn't she? She'd make new friends. I remember her at parent evenings. We always had a good chat and she seemed to know a lot of the other parents quite well."

"That's just it. She made good friends with some of the other parents and they're all mostly still here. Did you know Friedrich's dad died?"

"No, I didn't. He must've been young."

"Yeah, he was only sixty-three. Heart attack."

"So, how's Friedrich?"

"As you'd expect. Pretty devastated. He and his dad were very close. I saw him a few weeks ago. We went out for a pint. He's not brilliant, but I did manage to get a smile out of him."

Peter gently slapped Karl on his left shoulder. He wasn't surprised that Karl could make someone's grief easier. Unlike many, he seemed to have little fear of it and therefore had no need to steer the stricken person towards a false contentment merely to oblige their own sensitivities.

"He's lucky to have you as a friend."

Karl smiled but was unable to reply. An excited group of about seven or eight people came from nowhere, faces painted in the national colours, some with brightly coloured wigs, jostling for attention and shouting "Deutschland!" at them as if expecting a reply. Karl shouted back and Peter, older and more astonished, just laughed. Then more and more crowds were walking with them, chanting and singing, so that Peter found private thoughts disintegrating, wafting off somewhere because there was no place for them here. Here he was no longer Peter the teacher insisting on quiet, Peter the husband making soup that would be thrown on the floor, Peter the carer caught in a claustrophobic intimacy, Peter the worrier rooted to the spot or Peter the prisoner looking at an outside world.

"Deutschland!" he shouted and this time it was Karl who laughed. This was his quiet and thoughtful teacher who, in Karl's experience, had never shouted to get the attention of his class.

Peter found himself bellowing the name of his country over and over again, sometimes in a straightforward way, sometimes in a sing-song way, but it was almost as if he couldn't stop himself, a contagion he had to sneeze out of his system, but it was the most liberating thing he'd done in a very long while and he didn't want to stop. Karl joined in, both loving being part of it, taking pride in something that could be influenced by the support you were giving.

They found their way to their seats. It had been such a long time since he'd been anywhere so vast.

"I can't believe I'm here," he said to Karl.

"Yeah, it's great," replied his younger friend, his face no different in its expression to anything Peter was used to seeing. It was a youthful acknowledgement, Peter thought, one that, having gone past the pure excitement of childhood, had not yet caught up with that childhood exhilaration again in older age but instead was firmly planted in the middle somewhere, probably because everyday life was more eventful anyway, but it also came with a desire to show that childhood was no longer their domain and that something so much more grown-up had happened.

Peter looked around the stadium of over 70,000 people. It had been many years since he'd been in here, thirty-three he thought it was the other day. He'd forgotten how loud and overwhelming crowds were on the individual, whose own truth could easily be lost amongst such simplistic chants. He looked at his phone before the match started. There was no message for him.

He took in a deep breath and enjoyed the fresh air.

Then there was a roar. "Here they come," Karl said and Peter's stomach churned with the thrill of anticipation. This was going to be good.

20

Audrey knew that many Germans had some knowledge of English, a view that had been confirmed by the woman behind the counter in the chemists, and this was a thought that was helping her during the flight, especially when she glanced to her right and failed to see the person who was most familiar to her.

When she had to put her seatbelt on again because they were preparing for landing, Audrey was nervous but was relieved that the initial part of her visit, the greatest ordeal, was about to begin. She knew that as soon as she'd found her hotel and had met up with Helen, she would begin to feel more settled. They'd agreed that Helen stay at the same hotel while she was in Berlin.

After gathering her things with a new level of concentration, needed because of Kenneth's absence, she walked towards the exit door and thanked the airline staff who smiled politely and said goodbye with a degree of cheer she almost regretted leaving, as if the umbilical cord they offered was hard to break and the air outside unwelcoming.

She waited at the conveyor belt for her suitcase, a turquoise one with five pink flower stickers on the lid to avoid the possibility of taking another passenger's, something that had happened in the past when she had a black suitcase, a popular choice, and she'd opened what she thought was hers in a hotel room in Barcelona only to find a lot of children's clothes and a couple of teddy bears. The inconvenience of the lack of clothing was easily resolved in such a busy city and she'd quite enjoyed an unscheduled shop, but it was the sight of the teddy bears that had left Kenneth with a lot of hard work to do before she returned to some sort of normality a day or so later.

She'd always found the waiting game for the suitcase a tricky business since then, so she searched in her bag for her phone and used the time to contact Helen.

Her old neighbour sounded upset still and they agreed to meet in the foyer of Audrey's hotel later on and, as these things do when you least expect them and when you certainly don't invite them, as she put the phone back in her bag, Audrey found herself thinking about the day she and Jean were in a shop and were each trying to convince the other that they really didn't want the last size fourteen jacket in navy blue.

"I've got plenty of jackets," Jean had said.

"But you've got the wedding to think of." This was for Jean's friend Julie and a man Jean secretly didn't approve of. "You said you wanted to wear navy."

"Audrey, it looks much better on you. We both know it." Actually, they didn't. Jean had always been prettier than her and, as soon as she put it on, Audrey thought she could have modelled it for a magazine.

It was a good three hours later when former neighbours and present friends Helen and Audrey hugged and said hello in a slightly formal fashion that came as no surprise to Audrey in its restraint but which came as a slight surprise to Helen in its warmth from her own side. But she was, on seeing her old neighbour, perhaps genuinely overwhelmed by such a generous gesture on Audrey's part as it was disproportionate to the quality of their friendship, which had never been one of great intimacy. Helen, though, had no quibble with this as she was desperately in need of a familiar face. That that face was Audrey's was unexpected.

"My dear, what on earth's going on?" asked Audrey, as a face-to-face reiteration of what had already been spoken was perhaps the best way to start and would hopefully overrule any initial hesitation or discomfort.

Helen started to cry, something Audrey hadn't bargained for quite so quickly, so she said they were to go back to her room where they could talk in private. Keeping Helen by her side, she went to the reception desk and asked if tea could be brought to their room.

"Come on, we'll get the lift," she said softly and put her arms round Helen's waist.

That evening, they talked of many things mainly, but not exclusively, relating to Helen. She learnt from her old neighbour that there was nothing unusual in the way she'd met Stephen, it was all a bit of a cliché, really, as simple as she was a secretary, he was a solicitor and they both worked for the same firm. Her initial impression of him was that he was very unassuming in an environment where many were not. Unlike some of his colleagues, things had to be teased out of him. It was as if he felt that anything he had to say wasn't worth listening to or would, in some way, alienate him from his listener rather than bring them closer. Over the years, she'd begun to realise that this may have been the point because he was someone who kept a distance that was safe enough for him to be able to have some kind of relationship with others but that didn't involve any kind of intimacy he might find disconcerting.

But his reserve, his shyness, she supposed, was very appealing, especially as before him, she'd been out with a terrible show-off and was tired of all that.

When it came to having children, they both wanted them and there was a silent agreement that she would stay at home while they were young, something she had never regretted, even when she was bored or tired or both. Of course, she got tetchy and fed up. Emma and James were pretty good on the whole, but they were bright and always needed things to do and there's no recognition of the work you do. It was harder than being at work. Concentration was required all the time and she was invariably on her feet, something as a secretary she of course wasn't used to.

Stephen was good with them, there was no denying that; she sometimes just wished he'd had them for more hours in the week, but then they'd made the decision for her to stay at home. She did go back to work part-time when James, the youngest, went to primary school, something she'd found very enjoyable. All those sentences she could finally finish without either Emma or James or the child of a friend wanting something or the answer to something. The times she'd gone home after seeing someone and wondered where it was they had gone out that day.

She didn't work in Stephen's office and was, by then, glad she could do something that was completely away from the family. It was somewhere she could not only make her own friendships but also where she had time to process what was happening at home so she could go home and say to one of them, "I was thinking about what you said, your homework, what so-and-so said to you the other day."

She also began to see more clearly that there were many things Stephen and she didn't talk about because she heard what others said to partners. Yes, there was a lot they didn't say; too often, she didn't ask him what was bothering him when he was quiet and, this was hard, but sometimes she didn't feel he was that interested in finding out what was troubling her.

Nevertheless, theirs had been a workable marriage and the children, they all, missed him terribly. In fact, she thought she'd neglected them recently. Yes, they were grown up now, but she hadn't been able to express much interest in what they were doing and she couldn't help feeling guilty about it. And this trip, well, it was just another way, she was feeling now, of her being a bit self-indulgent, even though they'd supported her coming here and perhaps thought it was about time she spread her wings a bit. She was trying to find something, she didn't know quite what, but she found herself wanting to know more about the person she'd married because he had always been so reluctant to impart any information.

She spoke of Hans and Margot and everything they'd told her. Audrey was as astounded as her friend had been and they both talked about what courage that required. In fact, Helen talked a lot about courage and how she felt she didn't have any.

"Nonsense," Audrey had interjected. "What rot," and she said that, from her point of view, having not had children, being a mother, for one thing, required a huge amount of it, not to mention the fact she'd come here on her own and without any German. She didn't speak German, did she? No, she didn't.

Yes, but being a mother was what so many did; if it was courageous, it was everyday courage. What Stephen had done was exceptional. Audrey pointed out that befriending a couple where there's illness in the house is something not many holidaymakers would do and, for the first time, her friend smiled a little and they agreed they needed to ring down for another pot. While they waited, Helen told her again about what had happened at Peter's and Audrey thought that sometimes horrible things happen for a reason. It didn't mean that perhaps this Peter shouldn't have been a little more aware of what could happen, but still, sometimes, life has a way of sorting itself out. She thought this because it had been the only way, on many occasions, she felt she could survive.

The tea came and they were both grateful for those first sips. Audrey looked at her friend, whose eyes were full with tears. This had been a struggle and she said to Helen that what she'd just done took courage. She of course didn't say anything about the photo that had fallen out of Stephen's briefcase all those years ago. Instead, she told her about Jean and that they'd found this navy blue jacket they both fancied. And how she'd worn it to Kenneth's retirement party.

21

Margot knocked on Rosa's door and as she heard her colleague's footsteps coming towards her, she thought how empty they sounded, unaccompanied by the usual sounds of her children, either telling her frantically that there was someone ringing the doorbell or asking her to tie a shoelace. Normally, when they had things to talk about and they wanted to get away from the museum, Margot came here because Rosa wouldn't have to find childcare, but she'd asked this time if it was possible for them to be on their own.

"I'm sorry, I know I look a sight," she said apologetically, almost before Rosa had finished opening the door properly. She caught a badly disguised look of surprise but had gone too far into a state of crisis to let it worry her.

"Come on in. Be careful of the toys at the bottom of the stairs. I asked them to put everything away, but you know how these things are. Can I get you a coffee?"

"A coffee would be great. How are the children?" Margot quickly glanced at the untidy mixture of boys and girls toys cascading down the last two or three steps of their staircase with slightly amused curiosity.

"They're fine," replied Rosa, in that warm yet resigned way she'd got used to hearing when she asked about the children. "I think Katja could be coming down with something. He really had it about him this morning. He was being a right pain."

"Where are they?"

"Rudi's taken them to the park."

"I hope Katja's well enough to be there. I'm sorry I asked if we could be alone. Will he be OK?"

"Oh, sure, don't worry. He was a lot 'better'" – and she made quotation marks with her forefingers – "when he was promised an ice-cream and even if he is coming down with something, a bit of fresh air isn't going to do him any harm."

Without being invited, because it was what she'd come to do when she visited Rosa, she sat at what she felt was her usual seat in the kitchen, which faced the garden, while Rosa put the coffee on. There were children's clothes hanging on the washing line waving in the slight breeze and causing a tiny bird a bit of a problem in its efforts to try to eat as much birdseed as it could, which was nestling in a feeder at the end of the line.

"Would you like milk?"

"Just a drop. Thank you."

Rosa put the mugs of coffee on the table and sat in a chair with her back to the garden.

"I'm so glad we appointed you as my assistant, Rosa. You know, you've been a real asset to the museum."

"Thank you. I try my best."

"Well, you've done brilliantly. You must know that."

Rosa smiled. She had been pleased with the way she'd managed the new post and caring for the children. She'd coped better than she thought she was going to.

"I had an instinct about you. No matter how many official hoops you have to go through, we should never underestimate instinct. It was the first time I'd followed my instinct so clearly for a long time. And I was right." She took a sip of her drink. "That's very good coffee."

"It's from a new shop round the corner."

"Well, it's excellent." Margot paused and looked at the bird again, who seemed to have had enough and was looking around wondering where to fly off to next. "Did you enjoy the lunch the other day?"

"Oh yes, I'm so sorry, yes, I did, thank you. The food was delicious, Margot. You'd obviously gone to a lot of trouble."

Margot waved her hand, as if brushing her efforts aside. "Thank you, but I wasn't saying it for that. I just wondered if you enjoyed meeting Helen."

"Oh, absolutely. I'd so wanted to meet her. It would've been great to meet Stephen, but..."

"Yes, his death was very sad. So young." Margot was thinking about the first few minutes she saw Helen the other day and how surprised she'd been to see Helen managing as well as she was. It was that difficulty of always seeing someone as part of something, one half of an entity, not all of another, so she wasn't used to seeing how Helen was around others away from Stephen. It had been the four of them. She and Helen had never taken the opportunity to get to know one another away from the men. "Actually," she continued, "Helen seems to have proved to be something of a catalyst."

Rosa's face was quizzical, but she said nothing. Helen carried on, determined to fulfil the purpose of her visit, particularly as a child, possibly poorly, had been whisked off to the park on her account.

"She wrote to us saying she was coming to Berlin and asked if she could come and see us. I was initially uncertain about it because I thought it might be very difficult for Hans, Stephen having recently died. They were such close friends at university. At least, that was what Hans always told me and I had no reason to disbelieve him because they got on so well when the four of us met up. But he seemed to be pretty indifferent to Helen's request. 'Yeah, tell her to come if she wants to' kind of thing. It's funny, isn't it, how the slightest thing can set you thinking. And it wasn't as if it was a new thought; it was just a thought that had lain buried within me somewhere because I was too frightened to bring it out, I suppose."

She shuffled slightly and took another sip of coffee.

"You see, Rosa, Hans is, well, he's a very… artificial man."

She looked at the garden; the bird had gone and the clothes hung still and vertically. The wind must have dropped. Her face was burning, as if it understood her anger and felt both her embarrassment and guilt at this flagrant departure from all the loyalty to husband and family she'd held dear.

"In that moment I could see that Stephen, their friendship, their life together, didn't seem to matter somehow. It was the first time I openly accepted to myself that it wasn't that Hans was someone who felt things but found it difficult to talk about them, it was simply that he didn't feel them. The material world was so much more to him than I'd ever suspected. It wasn't more, it was everything." She stopped and began to cry and it was only when Rosa bent forwards and took her hand that Margot found herself, even now, defending him with the remark, "He wasn't always like that. When I first knew him…" but she didn't want to continue down a path of reminiscences that weren't relevant to this conversation.

She took a hanky out of her trouser pocket and wiped her nose.

"You know, Rosa, our generation, we spent so much time convincing ourselves we wouldn't have been part of all that in the thirties, we wouldn't have joined the party, we were cleansed and we cleansed ourselves, hardly daring to ask questions of our families; who had done what to who was unbearable and secrets abounded. There were always whispers, of course, but no one ever wanted to start an argument because we all knew that the one thing we didn't know was that our own family was completely clean, the obvious question being that if they were, would they still be alive? And for decades we knew visitors here looked at us. What did he do? Was she involved? There was a dirt you carried round with you that couldn't be scrubbed off.

"So I suppose I wanted a hero, someone my children

could never wonder about; I'd done enough wondering myself and swore this wouldn't be a legacy for them. Hans seemed the perfect man, with a genuine passion for Western freedom and his desire to ensure as many people as possible could experience it. So his involvement in the escapes was very attractive." She paused and then sneered. "Hans my hero. No one's going to look at him and question anything. His credentials are impeccable."

Rosa shuffled slightly, then asked Margot if she wanted another coffee.

"No. Thank you," Margot replied and drank the rest of the coffee she already had. "What I didn't understand about Hans was that he wasn't an idealist. He was someone who wanted to make a lot of money. And, of course, I didn't complain. I had a big house, all the clothes and jewellery I could possibly wish for and holidays most can only dream of. A very desirable life, you might say.

"The trouble was, it was all a bit more complicated than that. That's an overused word, isn't it? It's almost as if something being complicated lets us off the hook, somehow.

"Hans did help Germans like your father, Rosa, and at first his work, certainly when he was with Stephen, was exemplary, but then Stephen left for England and from that point things seemed to change. You see, Hans began to charge for his efforts. He saw a business opportunity, if you like. At first, not much, a tip almost, but he knew he was on to something and that people, and especially their families in the West, were willing to pay vast amounts to ensure their relatives' freedom. It became very successful and Hans seemed to revel in his entrepreneurial luck.

"I suppose I did the classic thing of not asking too many questions and I kidded myself that these people could afford what was being asked. And on top of that Hans was being a businessman in the mainstream world, working in property, which always seemed to me to be legitimate, and for Hans it even tied in with his work with escapees as a few bought properties from him. What I didn't know then, though I'm not saying it's an excuse, was that Hans became completely unscrupulous in his dealings with people who were desperate to get out of their difficult and, more often than not, frightening lives. Knowing this fear, knowing their desperation, Hans started to charge exorbitantly for his services. He knew he could do this; people in the West would do anything to see members of their families they hadn't seen for years and even if they couldn't immediately pay him, he entered into a loan with them.

"But not long ago I discovered he'd become something of a loan shark, demanding cruel rates of interest that apparently turned him into a bully when they weren't paid. Funnily enough, I found this out from a volunteer who came to the museum. She didn't know who my husband was and began to talk about this man who'd helped her sister's family over from the East, and the description she gave of him and the circumstances, well, I knew it was Hans, but it wasn't the Hans I knew or for that matter the man our friends knew. I can't imagine the picture I was given is the one you have of him. Or Helen, for that matter. I tried to think it wasn't my husband, but then the woman said her brother-in-law had followed him home one night. Just to see what kind of a home he had. She said this man had threatened them when they had difficulty paying the money to him.

"I thought that was bad enough, but then she said, despite what the man had done and the way he behaved, they asked him to help them get their cousin out. He agreed but reneged on his promise when they missed a payment, though they gave good reason – an illness making it impossible for her brother-in-law to work that particular month – and their cousin was shot climbing the wall."

22

Freddy tapped the pockets on the front of his jacket, watched by Peter's enquiring eyes. They were standing in front of one of those notices that nobody wanted to talk about but that made Peter want to be sick. Freddy seemed to have found what he was looking for – a crumpled piece of paper and a pencil – and it looked to Peter as if he was copying down the words on the notice. *I can read*, Peter thought. *And I don't need you to tell me I'm guilty. I've read it a hundred times.* He started to walk away from the person he had thought was his friend. *How nasty of him to write it out like that, shoving it in my face. I'm only twelve.*

He could hear Freddy shouting his name, so he quickened his footsteps, frightened in case Freddy was going to fight any resistance he might put up. They were both running now and Peter could hear Freddy's pleas for him to stop. His German was pathetic, but he caught the word "friend". *That's what you've been taught to say; you don't mean it.* But it did make him stop and turn round. He stared at the British soldier. Freddy caught up and breathless – something Peter was pleased about because it served him right – offered Peter a piece of paper. Reluctantly, he almost snatched it, throwing the soldier a contemptuous look. "You're not guilty, Peter," he read and he smiled, not because he was deemed innocent but because Freddy couldn't even get that sentence right.

★

"I'll murder you." Elsa was standing over him. He must've dozed off. "I'll murder you," she repeated, as if condemning him once wasn't enough, and he wondered what part of her mind reached for that sentence. Had the illness infected her with those dark words in a way it might, with a different ailment, infect her with spots? Or had she always felt this anger towards him and it had remained dormant all these years, caught in a web of polite social normality, even with her husband? Whatever it was, she was very angry. In his few minutes of reverie, he'd abandoned her and his care of her was the only thing that could matter to Elsa.

He felt disorientated. His nap had taken him elsewhere and he wasn't quite sure of himself. He'd always disliked sleeping in the daytime. It left him in a strange reality that had no truth to it for a while afterwards. As if to guide himself back to the day as much as anything, he took Elsa's hand and walked her to the kitchen where he began to make coffee. She started one of her five main stories, the one about having gone with her husband to the posh hotel over the road for a meal.

"It wasn't like that years ago, you know."

He said he knew. He always said he knew.

The other stories ran like this:

Her grandfather had been in Ypres in the First World War. Did he know her grandfather? No, he didn't. He learnt some French there, you know.

Her husband was an English teacher. The headmaster said he was one of the most popular teachers in the school. He smiled at this one but gave no response.

One day, she'd gone out with Peter and halfway through the day she realised she didn't have any knickers on. As this was a story she seemed to often leave for company, his response ran something like he was sure the waitress didn't want to know, to which the confused, angry look on his wife's face suggested why not?

Her father was a very kind man. He always thought of others. "You are my beautiful little girl, aren't you, Elsa? Such a wonderful smile." Oh, yes, such a lovely man. Yes, he'd reply because she didn't understand argument. But it would churn him up no end.

He took their drinks and they both sat down on their easy chairs. She went with her husband to the posh hotel over the road for a meal once. It wasn't like that years ago, you know.

He put Beethoven's *Fifth* in his mind, deliberately and loudly so that each instrument was reaching its full potential, a crescendo, bright and clear to try to erase the posh restaurant, which he was beginning to loathe; there they were, those beautiful notes, so lively in his mind that what was happening in the room mattered less.

She went with her husband to the posh hotel over the road for a meal once. It wasn't like that years ago, you know. Then she gave up talking, exhausted with her own efforts and just looked at him with the vacant expression of someone wanting something but not quite knowing what that something was. It was as if someone he didn't know was sitting opposite him. The confusion was mutual. It felt as if they were both on a ghastly fairground ride that had nothing to offer but fear and there was no getting off. They couldn't even face it together. There was a chasm between them, belying their physical proximity and serving as a punishment for both.

★

Peter could see Freddy patting the dog. It was one of a regular group that wandered aimlessly, scratching around for anything that was going, worn out, their bedraggled coats dusty and knotted. Most wore collars and some had names, but without owners they no longer knew who they were and had no purpose. They were both standing on a pair of railings, Freddy looking around, probably waiting to stop any trouble, the dog just looking around. The last time Peter had seen him, Freddy seemed to know a bit more German. It wasn't good, but it wasn't all that bad and he was pleased that he was teaching himself a bit of English. It was his secret, his life that he kept quiet about because he was fed up of trying to share it with his mum and his aunt, who were stuck in their anti-English and -American chitchat. They seemed blind to the fact that some of them, like Freddy, were good blokes, but they just kept telling him he shouldn't make a friend of an English soldier.

But he enjoyed learning another language and he liked the world he'd made for himself around it. Now the bombs had stopped he walked about more, even though his mum talked endlessly about the danger of looters, rabid dogs and rubble – though what the danger of rubble was she didn't say – and made sure he found enough reasons to escape what could only loosely be described as home. So on this Tuesday afternoon he'd walked across the rubble and through indistinct streets to where Freddy often was and as he got nearer he could see his English friend, feet slightly apart, standing straight, and he felt a similar reassurance he'd felt when he was with his father, a thought that brought a melancholy comfort because it could never be retrieved, lost on the night when, unbeknown to his mother, he'd got out of bed and watched two men put his father in a car, though he didn't think for a moment then that this would be his last sight of him.

His aunt generally referred to his father afterwards as brave and stupid, a confusing concept for a boy used to adults referring to you as one or the other. The trouble was that nobody seemed to want to talk to him about his anger towards someone so close to him and so important, who'd apparently abandoned him without even bothering to say goodbye.

That afternoon, in broken languages, he and Freddy talked a bit about music and football, both lending themselves to a certain amount of mime, and Freddy picked up an old tin from the rubble and they kicked it around for what must've been half an hour or so. Then Freddy said he was sorry to tell him that he would be leaving Berlin the following week. He had to go back to England. But at least they could have a few more games before he left.

23

Margot tried to imagine what it would be like not to turn the double lock of the front door, not to have to pull it towards her and turn the key harder when it rained. She tried to imagine not putting the keys on the small octagonal table in the left-hand corner of the hallway and not putting her coat in the cupboard under the stairs. Not placing it on the third hook on the right. The first one was Hans's, the second and third had belonged to the children and she had been the fourth but had moved up one after they had left home, the hook next to Hans's left for visitors. It was easier to access. She tried to think what it would be like not to make coffee in the kitchen, go and sit down on the large sofa, kick off her shoes and wait for it to percolate. She could time that without reference to any watch or clock. She tried to imagine an evening when she was out and not returning here. The truth was she couldn't.

She sipped her favourite South American coffee, savouring every drop, and then started the business of writing a letter to Hans. She looked at the garden. It was as beautiful as the house and she'd miss it just as much. Had he ever really loved her? She thought about Helen and how Hans had always said it was the German girl who Stephen had truly loved. But these days she didn't believe much of what Hans said, so this was another story she couldn't be sure of, like the excuse he gave for them not attending Stephen's funeral. It had absolutely nothing to do with an illness in the family. Rather, a greedy deal her husband didn't want to miss.

She looked at the blank piece of paper and thought about

all the things she could have written – the amazing children they'd given one another; the lifestyle she'd had and how, despite everything, she'd enjoyed being able to write a cheque or draw money and never had to doubt it was there for her taking; the beautiful house where she thought she would live forever; all the memories only both of them knew – but feeling so awkward with Helen, knowing they should have been with her at Stephen's funeral was the last straw.

She wrote a note, not a letter. It read, "Hans, you're a bully and I can't be by your side any longer, Margot."

As she walked away from it and saw it lying on the table, she thought about Hans's response. Would he view it as a deal that hadn't quite come off?

He'd probably have a few drinks, then conclude it was life. There was always tomorrow.

24

Peter had been told by a nurse that there were certain colours people with dementia responded to. Many, like blue, would have probably already disappeared from Elsa's mind, she told him. Red, on the other hand, was one of the last to disappear and it was a good idea, for instance, to use red cutlery on a white tablecloth. Black was a hole, she said. "I hope you don't have a black toilet because she might be very frightened of using it if you have." They didn't, he replied; it was white.

Elsa was happy hugging her photo. She rocked herself like a child. It was hers and hers only. Well, he was more than happy for that to be the case. He was in his own world where he was still reeling from an argument he'd had an hour or so ago with Karl, who'd had the audacity to suggest that he couldn't go on looking after Elsa like this. It was a fine state of affairs when an old pupil was telling him how to lead his life. He just kept coming back to the point that Peter needed more respite. Respite. What was that? Worrying himself sick about Elsa somewhere else or worrying about her here because she was somewhere else? Didn't anyone understand there could be no respite, no rest, no peace of mind? These were all things that had deserted him long ago. Karl had said, what about the football match? Well OK, but that was a national event, something that he almost had an obligation to enjoy and he thought to himself there were the English conversations he'd had with Helen. But there, that was his point. They had ended in catastrophe. Karl said, "Peter, you need to look after yourself," but he had no idea and had raised his voice to tell

Karl so while Elsa asked who Karl was. He wanted to turn to his wife and say, "To be honest, I'm not sure," but such a thought was far too complex.

He had to grapple single-handed with the notion that Karl seemed to have changed from someone who was sympathetic to a person who was hectoring him to do something he had no intention of doing. He could only put together, "How dare you?" which in retrospect perhaps sounded a bit childish, but it came from the heart.

The last time he'd been anywhere near angry with Karl was when his pupil had rejected further study and university. Peter had said the usual things – he was bright; he'd be wasted leaving school now – but Karl had retorted that not everyone's passion lies in study, which, because it was said calmly and with great maturity, had felt particularly hurtful.

Why should anyone else care for Elsa? He wasn't ill, just a bit tired, that was all. Everyone gets tired. What about Elsa? How could he let his wife be looked after by strangers, washing and dressing her, seeing parts of her that were meant only for his eyes? He'd like to see them try.

He sighed, which was about where he and Karl had left it, at a point where there was an unspoken understanding that neither was going to change the other's point of view, but there was a tension, nevertheless, and Peter suspected both of them would be quite upset for another few hours.

It was when Karl had started talking about the flat that Peter found himself getting angrier as it felt this was outside of Karl's domain. There was such a history there that Karl couldn't possibly understand because he didn't have the information.

"You don't understand, Karl. I can't give up the flat. Anyway, I don't want to. That's the end of the matter and I shouldn't even feel I have to explain myself to you."

"But it would help pay for—"

"What exactly? A room in a strange home, surrounded by people she doesn't know?"

"Peter, she doesn't know—"

"Don't you dare say it. You must know, Karl, I couldn't do that. She's been my life. And what would people think? Local teacher can't even look after his wife. Anyway, the money from the flat, Elsa and I always said, oh, it's a long and complicated story. And actually, it's none of your business. But Elsa wouldn't want it used for her. I know that. It would, I don't know, it would humiliate her. She wouldn't want anyone else to suffer."

★

It was 1956 when his mother had died. She'd managed to survive only eleven years of peace and though cancer had caught her, Peter always thought she'd died of a broken heart, never really accepting life without his father, whose unwillingness to accept Hitler's regime had left them both with shortened lives, and as she wrapped widowhood around her like she might a comfy blanket, a dreariness seemed to occupy the air around her for nothing more optimistic could get through. Herr Muller was a perfect example, who often seemed to give his mother an odd grocery more than was strictly permitted, and, as a boy, Peter had felt fiercely protective of his father's memory when he thought Herr Muller talked to his mother more than he did the other women in his shop, but when the war ended and he wanted to start moving away from his mother slightly, Herr Muller's attentions could have proved helpful in this, but he grew to accept that Herr Muller wasn't going to make a mark on a woman whose anger at the war for having taken her husband was never going to allow him to offer any affection.

So it was strange when, just over ten years ago, Herr

Muller, an old man with no children but with quite a few nieces and nephews, had quite unexpectedly, without any prior knowledge of Peter's, left his grocery shop to the son of someone he must have had far deeper feelings for than Peter could ever have imagined. He didn't hear from the nieces and nephews, there were no grumblings, so perhaps Herr Muller had other assets no one knew about, and the shop was very rundown, but the solicitor had told Peter his client expressly wished Peter to have it because, he said, Peter would know what to do with it.

He'd been astonished when he'd first heard of what Herr Muller had done. There was only gratitude from both his mother and Peter towards Herr Muller, but by visiting the shop regularly for all his adult life perhaps he'd kept his mother's memory alive and that, for the shopkeeper, had been enough.

Peter, though, was uncomfortable with this additional wealth. It didn't sit well with him to own anything more than somewhere for both of them to live. Nor did they want to keep it as a shop, for though it had been excellent and well used in its day, it had begun to be something that had the past written all over it, and customers were few and far between. He mulled over it for weeks, but it was Elsa who finally came up with an idea.

She had, for many years, been something of a benevolent aunt, he supposed, to a young woman, Sofie, who had a son, Jorg. Jorg had cerebral palsy and Elsa had got to know them at a local community centre where she frequently went to see if there was anything she could do to help with this or that. It was her way of cleansing a past she didn't want anything to do with and disguising the fact she had no children to look after or, later on, think about and had time on her hands she hadn't expected. Elsa and Sofie became firm friends, with Elsa spending hours at Sofie's flat, helping feed the teenage

Jorg or changing his nappy. He remembered seeing Jorg's room once when he went over to collect Elsa. On his bed were five toys: two teddy bears, one panda, a multi-coloured patchwork clown and a zebra Sofie called Jorg's best friend because they could never go anywhere without him. It was a large bed for one person, with pine boards on all sides to stop Jorg falling out and pillows built high, like fluffy, white clouds. His changing mattress was at an almost perfect right-angle to his bed, making it possible for Sofie and Elsa to see outside and start nearly every conversation, according to Elsa, with comments about the state of Sofie's pot plants in her tiny, cemented yard she and Jorg called their garden.

"Peter, I have an idea," Elsa had said in that excited way she did sometimes, talking twice as quickly as usual, her face reddened with the joy of such a discovery.

He'd just walked through the door after a particularly arduous day at school when one of his more difficult classes had become disruptive while trying to grapple with idiosyncratic English spelling, for which he had a certain amount of sympathy but couldn't show that to this group as all might have been lost.

Elsa knew none of this, so continued. "Sofie's finding it difficult to pay her rent since that damned landlord hoicked up the price so much. She didn't want to talk about it, but I could see she was down, so asked her what the matter was and eventually got it out of her. So, it got me thinking, the flat."

"You mean we ask Sofie if she wants to live there. There's so much work that needs to be done. We need to ask Karl…"

"No, no, no. That was my first thought, but then Sofie was talking about how heartbreaking it would be to leave their flat because they loved it so much, especially Jorg, who just loves the dog next door." She stopped for a second or two. "Benno, that's it. That's the dog's name. If they want to stay there, why don't we tell Sofie we could pay her rent for her?"

Peter followed Elsa into the lounge, still wondering about English spelling, and put his briefcase and a bag full of unmarked essays on the table.

Elsa looked very pleased with herself.

"Don't you see?" she said, now getting just a tiny bit impatient with him for not understanding what she was trying to say.

"We could let out the flat and give the money we get to Sofie. Oh, I know she won't want to take it; you could explain to her that you don't want to make money from it, but nor do you want to sell it. You said yourself you'd find it hard to let it go because of Herr Muller. The solicitor told you that Herr Muller knew you'd find a good use for it. Well, this is it. We just need to persuade Sofie to let us do this."

"That's not going to be easy. She's proud. You've always noticed that about her. She won't want charity."

"Then we don't make it sound like charity. We tell her it's doing us a favour. Even if she just takes part of the money, then we can give the rest to charity. Please, Peter. I want to do this."

He knew she did. It came out of different things: a past she was ashamed of and a need to treat someone as her child. Sofie was like her daughter and her proposal just seemed to Elsa like the most natural thing in the world.

He told her he was fine with the plan, he didn't want Herr Muller's money, but she had to persuade Sofie. He wasn't getting involved with that side of things. Elsa squealed with delight and both of them knew her powers of persuasion. Somehow, she'd find a way.

Peter smiled to himself. Elsa certainly did find a way. Sofie agreed they could pay the increase that she was finding so difficult to meet and that she would treat it as a loan and pay them back when she was able. Elsa reluctantly had had to agree to this, which Peter had said to her was something of a victory as he'd been very unsure about whether Sofie would accept anything. Elsa, though, was not daunted and used other money from the flat to buy things Sofie needed and wouldn't take no for an answer.

They talked about the rest of the money and where it should go. Elsa wanted it to go to a charity for refugees and Peter agreed this was a good choice as it fitted in, he thought, with Herr Muller's awareness of the difficulties of others and his desire to try to make things better.

He looked at Elsa again. She was still at one with her photo. The revelation that the photo was still in their house was a shock to Peter because he'd always imagined the severance from her father was as complete for Elsa as it was for him. It had been a dull Sunday afternoon, one of those times when everything slows down a little, allowing thoughts to turn into the enemy who fights contentment and introduces every question mark possible, when he saw her with the damned thing. It was during the first stage of her illness and when he saw her looking at it with affection, he knew then that the Elsa he'd married had gone forever.

He tried to prise the photo from her gently, but she shouted at him. "No, no, no," she kept screaming and she held on to it with strength he couldn't remember her ever having, and all the time looking at him as if he was trying to cause her unimaginable pain. He stayed with her while this continued for about an hour, saying nothing now because nothing would work but just watching her incessant pacing; then she finally sat down, completely exhausted, her mission complete. She still had the photo in her possession.

He, too, was exhausted and maybe it was because of this and because he had no energy left even for contradictory thoughts that he picked up the phone and rang Sofie's number.

25

Helen showed Audrey Peter's letter. This was a new and rather odd experience. She had spent the day crying intermittently, something she was quite unused to doing, and now she was sharing a personal letter with someone she didn't know all that well.

"Poor man," said the person sitting next to her, who she was beginning to see as a friend she could trust with herself, someone with no expectations from this visit other than to help.

She stroked the chocolate wrapper Peter had enclosed with his letter, which must have been nearly sixty years old, though its pristine condition didn't give this away, and then passed it to Audrey.

"Quite a treasured possession," she said. "It reminds me of a serviette I've got from my first meal out with Kenneth. It's in the top drawer of my dressing table. He has no idea it's there. He'd think I was daft."

She thought of all the things she'd kept of her children's – tiny shoes; scarves; bibs even – and how just touching or smelling them could turn her into the person she was then, those old joys and fears experienced anew.

"He's very lonely," continued Audrey. "I can see that having a proper conversation with you was something of a novelty, not only because of the English, but he obviously doesn't get to have many chances for a chat. It's enough to drive you barmy. Can you imagine it?"

Had Audrey asked her that question a couple of weeks

ago, she would have had to say she couldn't imagine what it was like to live without sensible conversation while incessant demands were being made, but after seeing for herself and for such a short while, she could say it was as if a person's freedom had been completely taken away from them and that time to breathe was something lost.

"Then maybe you should go back and thank him for his letter," Audrey prompted. "I'll go with you."

Helen didn't respond.

"You need to get your things," her friend reminded her.

"God, Audrey, I've made such a mistake coming here."

"Don't be silly. For one thing, you've come all this way on your own. That's no mean achievement."

"I was just looking for Stephen. I thought, I don't know, I suppose I thought he'd…" She hesitated because she thought she was going to get upset. "I thought he'd be here. It's ridiculous."

"No, it's not." Audrey found herself struggling.

There were things in life that just didn't make sense, but what Helen was doing was no more stupid than when she put on Jean's scarf and lifted it to her nose so she could smell her sister on the garment. Sometimes, she could even make herself believe that Jean knew what she was doing. "Audrey, for God's sake, get on with your life," is what she would've said, but it didn't stop her wearing it.

"Maybe you did find him. You've certainly found out a lot about what he was doing here." To herself she thought that Helen had probably come here to cry and what had happened in the flat had certainly helped it along. It was funny, she thought, how some people needed distance, and for Helen, she seemed to need permission as well. "You know, I think we should go to Peter's," Audrey encouraged Helen.

Helen nodded. She knew Audrey was right, but she really didn't feel strong enough. She started to cry, then let out a big sigh in sheer exasperation at her inability to stop what felt like a disease that kept creeping up inside her.

Audrey reached for a hanky and passed it to her.

"I'm so sorry," Helen barely managed and she blew her nose.

"Don't be daft. Why do you think I'm here?" Audrey gently put her hand on Helen's wrist. "Look, why don't we go and collect your things, bring them back here, then go and get something to eat. You can just put a note under Peter's door. Sort the finances out later. He'll understand."

★

"What are you doing?" She could hear Stephen's voice in her head. He was angry. His briefcase had fallen off a chair and all his papers lay scattered on the floor. She was just trying to scoop them up.

26

"Is Karl coming today?" Elsa asked.

Peter smiled. "Not today, no," he replied.

"Did you get me a cup of coffee?"

"Yes, you drank it."

Elsa stared, confused, at the empty mug on the table in front of her.

"Can I have a biscuit?"

"You've already had two."

"Can I have a biscuit?"

Peter reached for the biscuit tin and offered it to Elsa.

"Is Karl coming today?"

"No."

"Can I have a cup of coffee?"

"You've already…" Peter picked up the mug and walked towards the kitchen.

The day the doctor told them Elsa had dementia was hot and sunny and such days since had often been scarred by that memory. Elsa held his hand so tightly he was worried he might have to release himself from her. Bulging tears collected in her eyes. He asked the doctor if she was sure. She said she was. Later, he thought it was a silly question. She wouldn't have said it if she wasn't sure, but he couldn't quite believe it and didn't want to have to digest it. Elsa had always had such a bright, enquiring mind. He must have asked other questions that probably equally had no sense, but he couldn't remember what they were and anyway, he had no idea what she answered.

On the way home, he tried to reassure his wife, speaking

earnestly and at a fast pace. Science was moving; there was medication; they'd get through this together; but really, he felt he was talking to himself. Elsa could only nod occasionally, her grasp of his arm like that of a frightened child. Conversation was sparse when they got home and they ended up watching a film on TV, she still holding him tightly, he too frightened to let her go. Halfway through the film she asked him never to leave her because she couldn't cope with this on her own. She was sane then and he told her that she shouldn't think such a thing. He would always be with her.

He put the second cup of coffee on the placemat in front of Elsa. She looked at it blankly.

"Did I tell you my grandfather was in Ypres in the First World War?"

"Yes."

"Did you know him?"

"No, no, I didn't."

"He learnt some French there, you know."

★

Her grandfather was in Ypres. He learnt some French there. He was in the First World War. He was in Ypres. He learnt French there. Her grandfather. He didn't know him. He'd never, ever, ever met him. Never. He had, however, met an English soldier, Freddy, in another war, the enemy, only he wasn't the enemy, he was a friend, someone with a different language, but a person nevertheless, who'd lifted him from the devastation of the war and from his mother's depression, and had allowed him to stop thinking, for one moment, about a father he didn't have anymore, the one who'd gone to the park with him and played football, who'd laughed and joked with him and ruffled the top of his head when they were walking home but hadn't been able to carry on doing all those things because one day he'd dared to talk honestly to someone he shouldn't have done about the despicable regime they were all having to live under. Two men had come to the house to speak to his father, they'd forced him into their car and Peter had never seen his father again. Freddy, though, had shown him that life was still possible. Amongst all the rubble and all the dirt, they'd managed to somehow find a little bit of conversation, which had encouraged Peter to learn more English, to study the old enemy's language, even when some had looked angrily at him. "What do you want to learn that for?" And so he'd ended up teaching it. He loved this; he loved sharing his knowledge, teaching the culture of another country, even if it was an old adversary. It was great when he watched an increasing enthusiasm amongst some of his pupils.

"Did you get me a cup of coffee?"

"Yes, it's there, in front of you."

"Is Karl coming today?"

"No."

"Can I have a cup of coffee?"

He'd fallen in love with Elsa and they'd married. Elsa, of the hysterical laugh, the passion for dogs, Sofie, Karl and anyone she could look after, the person who told him not to get so worked up about things, it would be all right. The woman who'd courageously turned her back on a Nazi father and said her life would be completely different. She had led a different life. She had enough optimism for both of them, which left resentment at what life threw at them in a corner somewhere, never to be found, so her inability to have children was not something she dwelt on and they both got on with a reasonable life, despite living in the East with all its restrictions and, not least of all, the Stasi.

It was an illness, then, that had brought everything to naught. He kept telling himself that. It wasn't them. They were still OK, they still loved one another, didn't they?

But it was like loving a child. This was probably what it was like, he told himself, but without the joy and the satisfaction the parental role held.

As reciprocity diminished in their relationship, he'd learnt not to ask the questions he'd been used to and what he'd always thought were part of a civilised way of caring for someone. For instance, he'd stopped asking her what she wanted to eat anymore because anything he suggested would always be met with a "no". It sometimes felt as if this was the only word she knew with its sense of rejection severe. Nor did he allow her the privacy of showering now because this invariably led to a lot of aggravation. Instead, he held the shower handle over her, watching her vacant expression as water cascaded down her body. He didn't think she would even know how to wash her hair. It was something that was probably impossible for her to contemplate. So they held one another prisoner, the one taking away the other's choices. Was this, then, any kind of love?

"Is Karl coming today?"

"No, Elsa, no, he isn't coming today."

She looked at him, confused. His tone had changed. He couldn't help it.

He was irritated. He was very irritated. This wasn't life. The life that Freddy had shown him. This was existence. And he hated his existence. There was nothing for him. There, he'd said it. For so long, he'd felt sorry for her; then he'd felt he should feel sorry for her; then he'd just felt sorry; then he hadn't felt quite so sorry; then he was wracked with guilt for feeling the latter emotions. Then, since he'd spoken with Helen and had seen what life had been like, he'd begun to accept he was sorry for himself; then he'd had the talk with Karl, got angry with him for daring to suggest that he couldn't look after Elsa anymore and had returned again to feeling more sorry for Elsa and had heard her pleas for him never to leave her; then he'd felt a little more sorry for himself again and had tried to contact Sofie but hadn't yet succeeded. Now, just at this moment, he felt very sorry for himself and his sympathy for Elsa had probably not been as low. He was worn out. Worn out. Shut up, Elsa. Please shut up.

"You are my beautiful little girl." Elsa was looking at the photo of the boy. "You are my beautiful little girl," she said to the photo and she started rubbing the glass of the frame with the sleeve of her cardigan. She stared at Peter. "This needs a clean," she said, asking him to solve the problem.

He stayed where he was, pretending he hadn't heard her, then shuffled some bits of paper lying on the corner table. He had his back to her, but he could still hear every word.

"This needs a clean," she pleaded again and again, her plaintiff, pathetic voice ringing in his ear like an annoying, tiny insect. "This needs a clean." She was getting cross and, in her sense of urgency, made the mistake of tapping him on the shoulder. "This needs a clean. It's dirty."

He walked away. He needed to keep walking. He went towards the front door. The insect was getting louder and louder. He wished he could spray the life out of it. Shut up, shut up. He reached the door and opened it. Elsa, perhaps in her terror as she wondered where he was going, became louder.

"This needs a clean," she shouted. "It's dirty."

"I'll tell you what's dirty," he turned and glared at his wife. "I'll tell you what's dirty," and he snatched the photo sharply from her hands and flung it on the floor, where the glass smashed into little pieces, the plain, white back of the photo discarded beneath it.

Elsa started sobbing. "My beautiful little girl," she said whenever she could and she got on her knees and scrabbled for the photo itself, cutting her hands in the process.

"Stop!" Peter got down beside her.

"You've broken my photo." She started punching him like an inconsolable child, while he tried to get her up and away from the broken glass.

"No, no," she shouted, trying to release herself from him. "You've broken my photo. I hate you."

"And I hate you," he shouted and slapped her across the face.

27

The air was thick that evening; it didn't seem to want to help anyone breathe. Even though the nights were drawing in now, the city was full of people outside, eating and drinking, waiting for a storm perhaps, but taking advantage of a temperature that would soon be lost until the following spring. It was an evening that made coming home from work so much more pleasurable because there was almost another day ahead.

The first thing Peter remembered was Helen's voice. She was kneeling on the floor next to the chair where he was sitting, her hand on his arm.

"Peter, what's happened?" she said calmly. "Your door was open, we just came in." He saw, then, that there was a woman he'd never met sitting on the edge of Elsa's chair, somehow instinctively knowing it wasn't hers to sit on.

He could see that she was looking very concerned.

He wasn't able to answer Helen's question. He didn't know what had happened. He wasn't sure where he was. The other woman stood up and said something about making a drink. He didn't have the words to tell her where anything was.

Helen waited patiently. She was in no hurry, but after only a few seconds a terrifying surge went through his body and he came alive. "Elsa! Elsa! Elsa! Where is she? Where's Elsa? Oh, God, where's Elsa?" His heart was pounding, he couldn't think properly. He ran out of the room, shot up the stairs and, when Elsa was nowhere to be found, ran out of the house. Helen must have run after him, but he wasn't aware of anything other than the need to find Elsa. He kept screaming her name. "Elsa! Elsa! Elsa!" If he shouted loud enough, surely she'd recognise his voice. *Please, God, Elsa, recognise my voice. It's Peter. I'm so sorry. I'm so sorry. What have I done?*

He didn't know how long he kept this up, how many streets he went down, how many shops and cafés he went into, how many people he asked. It was a blur that made no sense, had no reality, for the only reality would be him finding Elsa. Had they seen a woman in her seventies, about this tall, grey, curly hair? What was she wearing? He couldn't remember, oh yes, a blue blouse, white skirt. But no one had seen her. Sorry, no. Sorry, no. Sorry, no. Still, he ran. It was all his fault. By now, he could hear Helen's voice more clearly and as he began to slow down with exhaustion, she caught up with him. She had to shout at him to get him to stop; he didn't want to, but when he finally did, he just collapsed in a heap, sobbed and said it was all his fault. Everything. Everything.

She eventually persuaded him to go back to the house so they could ring the police and be there when they came. There was also a good chance that Elsa may be able to find her way back there, she said, and it was this that convinced him.

They walked back, he had no more energy to run, and as they did, he went into shops he hadn't before, desperately searching and asking the same questions: had they seen this woman? Were they sure they hadn't? He wanted to see her face. *Elsa, Elsa, come back to me. I'm so, so sorry. Please forgive me.*

When they got home, Elsa wasn't there, the promise dashed, just the woman standing and waiting for them. She made them drinks. He probably had something. He couldn't remember, only vaguely aware of Helen offering him a mug, which he took. He told her what had happened and how he'd hit his wife and how he couldn't believe himself capable of this because he would never do that. Did she know that?

It was only then that it struck him the broken glass was

no longer in the hallway and for a minute or so he wondered if he'd had a nightmare. He'd drifted off and for some reason the front door was open. He didn't think Elsa would open it herself, but she might wander out if it was already unlocked; maybe that was what had happened. He asked about the glass. It had been there. The woman had apparently brushed it all up. There was a photo, he said, but she replied she hadn't seen one.

"Elsa probably has it," he whispered and he felt he'd somehow been given a lifeline because, if she was clinging to it in her customary manner, it could be a way of the police and anyone remembering or identifying her.

The police came not long after they'd rung. Helen went to the door and ushered in a man and a woman. Both were young and had the concerned look of involved professionals. Helen signalled vacant chairs to them and they asked her if she was a relative, but she didn't understand, so he told them she wasn't and explained who she was. He said he thought the other woman was probably a friend.

"Mr Bayer has told us who you are," the female said in perfect English. "Is this your friend?" she continued, indicating Audrey. Helen said she was and gave Audrey's name.

She then looked at Peter. "Do you understand English?" she asked him. He said he did. She nodded and got a notebook from her coat pocket.

"When did you last see your wife?"

"Is anyone out there looking for her?"

"Two of my colleagues, who are aware of the situation and who are in a car, are looking, sir," she said in a voice that suggested procedure rather than urgency. "When did you last see your wife?" she asked again.

He found it difficult to answer because he'd lost all sense of time. He said he thought it was probably a couple of hours ago because he couldn't be sure, then gave the officer a description

THE WRITING ON THE WALL

of Elsa, although he thought they'd already done that when Helen called them. He said he didn't know where Elsa was likely to go.

"My wife has dementia, officer. She won't know where she is." He was cross at this examination and showed it, but she was used to anger and repeated they were doing all they could and she had to ensure she had all the relevant information.

"Can I ask what happened when you last saw her, sir?"

"The dementia, officer, it's so difficult, you understand." He put his head in his hands. "I'm not excusing—"

"He's not excusing his tiredness, officer." It was Helen's voice. "I'm sure you've met people with dementia. It's exhausting." The officer nodded. Peter put his arm out towards Helen as if to join the conversation while Helen looked at him and said, "You went to the toilet, didn't you?"

Peter started to speak, but again Helen intervened.

"You see the problem is, officer, you just can't take your eyes off someone with this illness. But sometimes, that just isn't possible."

"Is that what happened, sir?"

Peter nodded. In that moment he lacked both energy and courage. The truth could wait for another time. What he wanted more than anything was to find his wife.

The officer thanked them for their time and reassured them that they would do all they could to find Elsa. As they were leaving Peter remembered something.

"She may be holding a photo, officer. It's an old photo. Of a boy. It was her father when he was young. He always told her she was his beautiful little girl. She remembers that."

The policewoman made a note of this, thanked Peter and, with her colleague, made for the door. Helen showed them out. Peter then weakly acknowledged the woman who'd cleaned up the glass and walked towards the hallway to find a coat. He could hear the officer outside speaking on her phone.

"Elsa Bayer. Apparently she could be holding a photo."

The front door was open. He could see that Helen was still talking to the policewoman. He put on an old jacket. Outside, he could hear people in the street. Someone was laughing, joking about not being fit for work in the morning. It all seemed a long way away.

28

Elsa was sitting on a bench next to a stranger, a woman of roughly the same age but with a sense of dress that suggested she preferred to be associated with a younger generation than either of them. She said something about the lovely weather they were enjoying and then started talking about the summers when they were both children, though, of course, many were destroyed by the war and memories of the sun had disappeared somehow. At least that was how it was for her.

Elsa said, "My father and I used to go cycling. He taught me how to ride. I don't remember that exactly because I was very young, but he must have been a good teacher because I learnt quickly. We used to go out on a Sunday afternoon. Sometimes we took a picnic with us."

WAR WOUNDS

Yesterday, I saw a child's car. You know the ones, bright yellow and red plastic, with the look of an old-fashioned bubble car. They give hours of fun to tiny human beings who have no idea of the dangers of the road but who can pretend they're like the adults they know, driving from A to B in order to go about their business. "Watch out, here I come. Brrm. Brrm." My daughter used to drive one that was lying around the communal garden of her uncle's flat and she was very tickled by it.

I looked at this particular model sitting there with that view of the city behind it and felt greatly comforted, which was unexpected. It was a beautiful summer's evening, the city lights were just coming on, telling everyone the day was coming to a close. The owner of the car, who'd parked a little haphazardly, was probably fast asleep. Tired, after their long day at the wheel. The only sign of life in the house was a light from the television and, a few feet away, a pair of adult hands moving their fingers across a piece of technology. It was all I could see of the person because this was a house that required walking a few steps down to it, so what was on view was almost an aerial picture. Out of step with the rest of the city, it was still in darkness, unwilling to accept, perhaps, that the evening had come. The car was parked at the top of the back garden. I'd caught sight of it as the house was an end terrace, its painted white wall separated from the next wall by several feet, with the gap between its side and the side of the next house offering a glimpse of something beyond.

My grandfather lived in this house. He was a man who was

frightened of fear. It was something he couldn't bear to think of in himself and something that bothered him when he saw it in others, particularly in his family. "You're not frightened of that, are you?" and even at a young age, I picked up that the answer was "no". I think part of him couldn't understand the fears of everyday life and was confused when they touched him.

He was a slight man, not that tall, bald on top, with white hair around the edges, rimless round specs, who usually wore a collarless shirt and a cardigan. I remember being told that he'd been given a medal, though to this day I'm not sure what type of medal it was. My mother told me he had been in the trenches, when I didn't know what a trench was, and that he'd been in the cavalry and when I asked what that meant, she explained he was with the horses, "Poor things."

My grandparents then built their lives in this house that now had a plastic car as a friend. It sits high on a hill in Brighton and is very near the racecourse. I know it. I went there once with my husband and daughter. It was a similarly hot day and we enjoyed the galloping horses as we looked outwards towards the sea. I remember the sight of cold buckets of water being poured on their hot and steamy bodies after a race and my husband, though temporarily vexed he hadn't taken our then teenager's advice on an outsider, whereby we would have left with several hundreds of pounds in our pocket, soon reassured himself that a loss was a positive step.

My grandmother enjoyed a flutter and I amused myself reading the names of the different horses in the local newspaper. It lay casually on her favourite chair with biro marks on the ones she favoured or the ones recommended by a television pundit. My grandfather hated her doing this and frowned upon it, as he might a frightened relative. He adored horses and hated them being used for gambling. It was probably all a bit frivolous for him.

A few years ago I discovered why he'd received his medal. It was because of his love of horses. I picture my grandfather in a trench with a horse for companion. He strokes and reassures it and asks "What the hell are we doing here?" He thinks of London, his place of birth, and his beloved Tottenham Hotspur. Suddenly, there's fresh gunfire. His horse rears up, terrified. He's terrified as well, of course, but at that moment more for his horse than himself. It's as if it were his child. The horse goes over the top. My grandfather does likewise. It's instinctive. The two of them work together. Bullets are fired. Two hit his back. The horse is saved.

The bullets hung around. Like malevolent time travellers, they were greedy for the souls of others, so they settled into my grandfather and watched over his life, ensuring that peace of mind never truly returned, wreaking havoc and disturbing sleep. They made sure he was always anxious, mithering about this, worrying about that, "What if this happens? How will that work out? The bullet wounds are still on my back, does anyone want to see?"

He married and had three children. My father was one of them. Not content with a single generation, the bullets seemed to take a liking to him as well. A man of great kindness, he was also a very worried one. I sometimes think of my grandfather, anxious as he asked, enquiring whether my father was frightened and his son obliging him by replying that he wasn't. Instead, my father developed nervous tics that my grandfather probably didn't notice because he didn't want to see. No one near him could be frightened because then we'd all be lost.

My father's most discernible tic involved his mouth twitching slightly while his tongue disappeared into one corner of his mouth. The bullet rolled around his mouth like a piece of chewing gum he could never spit out. This occurred when he was worried about money, which was often, work or having to say something he knew was going to be unpopular, and there were many occasions for all of these, like the time he suggested gingerly that perhaps we shouldn't have another dog when my heart broke in pieces after our West Highland terrier, Bernie, died, and I blamed my parents wholeheartedly for putting him in a kennel while we were on holiday, which was where he lost his life. Apparently, his heart had broken too. My father's mouth twitched a lot then.

It twitched when my grandfather was dying. I remember I watched him putting his tie back in the wardrobe – there was a wooden bar on the inside of the door especially for ties – his mouth moving at a fast rate. I don't think he realised I was looking at him, but my mother saw what I was doing. He had just returned from visiting my grandfather who was dying in this house from stomach cancer. My grandfather was in so much pain that my grandmother had told my father to go – there was no point in staying any longer; she didn't want her child to see his father so distressed – so my father walked out, knowing he would probably never see his own father again. Apparently, he could hear cries of pain in the street.

I looked at where he must have walked. It's a steep descent from the house to the main street and winds round to the left as it disappears from view. I try to imagine what he was thinking and with the benefit of years behind me can understand more clearly now the initial shock of realising something is lost forever. I didn't appreciate that then. I just picked up a sadness and, with it, a fear.

My father died of cancer too. He vomited into any bucket that was available and lost an inordinate amount of weight. I was frightened of this, of course, as anyone might be, but I was fearful long before. Perhaps the bullets have me, too, and hamper me from trying this or saying that. Some days, I think they're a damned nuisance. On others, I'm angrier and can think only of their destructiveness.

My eyes drifted up the hill and cast their glance back at

the house. I could still see the car, though with the creeping darkness it had lost all colour and was now a mere silhouette. I had put off coming back here for a long time. It was something I had wanted to do for many years, but going back to anything brings with it a fear of its own.

It promises to be a good day again tomorrow. The owner of the car will probably run down to the garden, start up their car and drive it around and around, until one or the other runs out of steam.

I turned round and looked at my husband, who had encouraged me to visit my childhood, and as we walked back to the car, I smiled to myself because it occurred to me that with all the courage my daughter shows, the bullets are beginning to lose their power. As I took one last look at the house, I noticed that someone had put a light on.

MRS BLACKBIRD

When Mrs Blackbird told Florence to stop hassling her, Florence knew it was time to think about a holiday. She would mention this to Alan, but Alan wouldn't be very keen. Alan was never very keen. His enthusiasm came to fruition during the second week of planning. Usually day ten or day eleven.

So she waited a little to see if Mrs Blackbird would pick up that worm. Poor Mrs Blackbird. The ground had been very dry recently. She would really be better trying to find some berries in the bushes. But she caught the worm and when she had, she flew into the tree at the bottom of their garden. She wanted no more to do with Florence and Florence, for her part, went into the house to begin thinking about her ideas. She wasn't sure what she had in mind but sitting on a beach somewhere far off or swimming in a pool were definitely not on the agenda. She honestly couldn't remember them ever doing either of these things, even when the children were little.

She went upstairs to the room they now called an office, though she'd probably always think of it as Mark's bedroom. Putting her research for Nora's book to one side to make space for an empty notepad, she turned on the computer. Things were going to get quite tricky when Alan retired. She could imagine all sorts of dilemmas if they both wanted to use this room simultaneously. Alan's radio club seemed to take up a lot of internet time as it was, so goodness only knew what was going to happen after next March. Sometimes she quite dreaded the thought of it.

She tapped in "holidays with a difference" and went downstairs to make a cup of tea while it sorted itself out. As she got the milk out of the fridge she had the thought that it might be good to go and see Mildred that afternoon just to see how she was getting on. She was slightly concerned that she hadn't heard from Arthur for a few days and a bit worried something not very nice might have happened.

She sipped what she considered to be a very fine tea. She must change to that brand permanently. Celia was right. It did have a lot more flavour than most. She must tell Joan about this particular brew, though she'd have to get her on a better day than yesterday. She'd been in the middle of telling her a bit about the history of the yew tree, the *Taxus baccata*, talking about its extraordinary longevity and how, after five centuries, it's actually in its prime, when Joan had suddenly seemed quite irritated, had looked at her watch and said, "Good Lord, is that the time? Florence, you've made me late with your yew tree! I've got a dental appointment." Poor Joan. She'd always tended to be a bit scatty about these kinds of things. Once, when they were making lunch for the old people's club, she'd turned up at the church hall at 10.30, having forgotten to go to the butcher's for the mincemeat first, with the result that everything was put back nearly an hour. The club members were not happy bunnies that day. Luckily, Mildred had saved the day a little bit by producing some soup from her freezer, which they'd warmed up nicely and which had kept everyone going. Yes, she must go and see Mildred and Arthur this afternoon.

When she was back by the computer she looked at the options the internet had given her. Ah, yes. She thought the paranormal would raise its head, something she was quite interested in but, unfortunately, not Alan. He'd complained of an acute irritable bowel after they'd been part of a group who'd stayed up all night in the same church hall where Mildred had produced her soup, waiting for Thomas the Roundhead.

She'd thought he was being a mite silly and had told him his condition was far more likely to be the result of the draughty conditions that they'd had to endure than the prospect of the unlikely appearance of Thomas and his severed head, poor thing, whose lot had been up, so to speak, when he'd misjudged the whereabouts of a cavalier who was lurking in what was then a stable, they believed. Still, Mrs Cumberland's flask of hot chocolate making an untimely tumble probably hadn't helped.

She didn't fancy a disused arsenic mine and though she was enjoying her later years, she didn't wish to be reminded of it by a holiday company of the same name. But, just a minute, this looked interesting.

★

They were waiting for Lucy, their conductor, when a fellow soprano sitting next to her, who Florence hadn't met before, said she was glad they were singing something joyful for the music festival. She was, she had to admit, getting pretty fed up with choirs insisting on requiems most of the time. Florence agreed it did sound jolly, but did she know that, in actual fact, the piece was written to reflect the fear Austrians were feeling about Napoleon's conquesting armies?

"Ah, here's Lucy," her companion said and the two-hour rehearsal began.

Lucy was a very enthusiastic conductor and probably more passionate about music than any of her predecessors, but Florence thought that she sometimes lost sight of the fact that they were all here because singing was a hobby and not a lifelong vocation. Her irritability with Maureen was therefore quite unfortunately pronounced when, for the third rehearsal in a row, her choir member was scrabbling away in her bag for something she thought she'd lost.

"Please, Maureen, could you put your bag down!" she shouted, causing them all to sit up a bit in a way that was uncomfortably reminiscent of an atmosphere at school prior to someone being given a detention. Florence was concerned about Maureen, who had seemed to get mithered a lot recently and had almost got lost when Ruth had let her out of her sight for just a few minutes on the last WI outing. Whatever Lucy's talents as a conductor, Florence was of the opinion that Maureen could well do without her curt remarks. She was glad, though, that the WI had come to mind for she must remember to collect the last two or three people's money for the Mystery Trip next month, though she dearly hoped no one else would pose the question, "Where are we going?"

★

"A lighthouse!" Alan smiled and his eyes lit up in a surprising way. This was going to be easier than Florence thought. "Yes, I could go along with that," he continued, then proceeded to re-immerse himself in *The Collector's Guide to Radios*. Habits die hard, Florence concluded to herself. *In about ten days' time he'll wake up, as if from a dream, and ask where the lighthouse is. Then he's in for a nice surprise.* She had to admit, she was really quite excited about this one. They would have to travel to the south coast, which would probably be roughly a four-and-a-half-hour's drive. Or perhaps five, with Alan's needs, which these days were politely referred to as comfort breaks. But the information promised the sighting of numerous ships across the Channel and, when Florence looked it up, the average daily total ran to over five hundred. There was, she knew, a mandatory two-way system, with ships travelling east to west on our side and vice versa on the French. She was particularly amused by the French law forbidding non-standard vessels from landing and had given herself the task of finding out what these non-standard vessels might be but had never got round to finding out.

★

Mildred's health was, as she'd suspected, failing, and Arthur was having a bit of a job, both practically and emotionally, keeping up with this. Last week, she'd made some chicken broth especially, but Mildred had taken only a few sips and Arthur didn't seem particularly interested in her telling of its nutritional content. It was a standard broth she'd cooked when the children had been poorly. She'd always known when they were getting just a little better because they'd say "yes" to a bit of broth. But, sadly, it didn't work its wonders on Mildred and Florence didn't think Arthur would have to cope with the care of her for much longer.

★

"The lighthouse. So where is it?" The long-awaited question came at 3.30 one Saturday afternoon as they were drinking tea and enjoying some of her homemade scones. Thank goodness they'd remembered to buy some butter. Alan articulated as much when he took his first bite of the freshly baked goodie. These things wouldn't be half as delightful with that healthy grease – now there's two funny words put together, they agreed – we have most of the time. "At least this comes out of a cow," he said, which, if she was being honest, slightly put her off her first bite, but she relished the enthusiasm with which Alan spread the butter and jam, his concentration like that of an artist adorning his canvas. She told him it looked out onto the English Channel, that the accommodation looked perfectly cosy and that there was an available week just before Christmas.

"Bit of an odd time to go," had been his response.

Well, yes, she agreed, but it was very expensive during the summer months and, given his propensity for sunburn and his general dislike of the heat, it was an extremely exposed place on a hot afternoon. He mulled it over for a few minutes.

"Well, you seem to be set on it," he said, glancing at the mass of information she'd produced to help him make up his mind.

"Have a look at all that," she replied. "Never mind about me, you have to like the idea as well. I'm just going to ring Mark and ask how little Oliver's teething problems are getting along."

She hadn't left him for long when, reading one of the bits of information she'd given him, he just said out loud, "Ah," and was, in that moment, very taken with the idea of this holiday indeed.

Florence rang her son who told her that poor Olly still needed gel rubbed into his gums, but they were getting a bit more sleep than they had been getting, which was obviously a great relief. She was very pleased about that and asked him to give their love to Melanie and to let her know she could always pop down on the train and do a spot of babysitting.

"Thanks, Mum, I'll tell her."

"I need to see you all soon because I've bought a book for Olly, which I hope he'll enjoy. It's all about birds and when you open the pages different types of birdsong come out, though I'm not sure they've got the thrush quite right. It doesn't sound flutelike enough to me. Still, I think it'll make him smile."

"I'm sure it will. Let me talk to Melanie and we'll set a date. You can leave Dad for a couple of days and let him get on with his radio stuff."

"Well, little Oliver seems to be perking up a bit," she said when she got back to Alan and the lighthouse information. "Apparently he's almost managing to get through the night."

Alan agreed firstly that that was a huge step forwards and secondly concurred that the lighthouse was a splendid idea, even in December.

"Right then, I'll go ahead and book it," his wife replied.

★

When she explained to Matthew, the vicar, that she wouldn't be able to make the Christmas Fayre this year because she and Alan would be on holiday, he seemed perfectly fine about it and received the news better than she'd anticipated. He said he had quite a few volunteers this year, he wasn't sure exactly where they'd sprung from, but thanked her for letting him know and he hoped both she and Alan had a good break.

"Oh, I can fill you in on that, Matthew," she'd replied, and she told him that the new wave of volunteers had come from the village art fayre in October when Mrs Thompson had, for some reason best known to herself, got it into her head that he needed more people for the Christmas Fayre as the cake stall in particular, she had told everyone, had been a bit of a fiasco, though Florence said she didn't feel she could support that view and had thought it had all gone rather well. The consequence of this had been that Mrs Thompson had managed to gather quite a few names for volunteering.

She then went on to ask him what he thought about this Winter Festival idea, which a lot of people were beginning to say would include more of those who didn't celebrate Christmas. "Of course, originally it was a Winter Festival and considered to be the most popular in many cultures, funnily enough, because agriculturally less work needed to be done during the winter."

He told her he didn't see anything wrong at all with other celebrations complementing Christmas but that it was his prime responsibility to keep the spirit of the birth of Jesus alive and well, but he had to go and address the parish council about the costings of three new windows in the church hall. He said he thought her holiday sounded excellent.

Oh dear, she thought as she watched him walk away. She'd obviously slightly offended him with all that Winter Festival stuff and she sincerely wished now she hadn't opened up the topic. It was just that she'd heard this interesting discussion on the radio the other day. Never mind. She'd apologise when she next saw him. She was quite sure she wasn't the first member of the congregation to discuss something controversial with him.

★

When the third week in November came, Florence began to think about packing and what exactly they were going to need.

"The lighthouse." Alan always began his thoughts on their holiday, she realised, with this pronouncement. "I forgot to ask when we booked, it's not working, is it?"

They were eating a vegetable casserole, which really would have benefited from a little more time in the oven as the carrots were a bit crunchy. She was surprised at the tardiness of Alan's question. It was quite a crucial one and unlike Alan not to have thought of this when he initially agreed to go.

"No, it's not," she replied. "It ended its working life in 1988. Don't worry, we won't have to cope with foghorns and glaring lights. That would not have been an attractive proposition."

Still with her mind on packing, she asked him if he needed any jumpers washing. There may not be foghorns, but it was going to be jolly cold. He said he thought he was all right.

"What about the grey one?" she asked, slightly irritated by his complacency. Oh yes, come to think of it, it did need a bit of a wash, he conceded. She thought so. It was his favourite jumper and one he wore at any given opportunity. Tom and Melanie had bought it for him three Christmases ago. She'd seen the one in the store they were talking about and she'd agreed he'd like it very much. And they'd all been right. If anything, he was rather too attached to it. Now, what was she going to take?

★

They stopped at the agreed service station for a comfort break, food and a newspaper. There had always been a slight disagreement about the holiday newspaper. Alan liked to know what was going on no matter where they were and they'd often had a spot of bother trying to find an English paper when they'd ventured abroad, while Florence had always firmly held the view that a holiday was exactly that, a holiday from everything, and in particular one from the dismal and often grisly happenings of the world. She was of the firm opinion that if he wanted to read anything, he should pay more attention to where he was, but Alan had been content to leave that kind of research to her.

"Well, it looks as if that minister's going to resign after all," he said over his egg mayonnaise granary sandwich in the café, which was far too clinical and noisy for Florence. She hardly heard what Alan had said for the woman on the next table was screaming at her child to be quiet. She must have looked confused because he said it again.

"Don't tell me, Alan," she replied, putting her hands to her ears. "I don't want to know. I'm on holiday," and she got the AA route planner instructions out of her rucksack so she could be as familiar as possible with her navigation when they were in the car again.

It was four in the afternoon when they reached the nearest village to the lighthouse, but it might as well have been midnight. They called in at the mini-market to get provisions and were met by a very buoyant and, Florence thought, glamorous owner whose enthusiasm for the lighthouse was, to say the least, most encouraging and just what they needed to hear, as the cold and dark had left them a little dampened in spirit.

"You'll love it," their enthusiastic mentor said as she bundled bread, cheese, milk, bacon and half a dozen eggs into a bright blue plastic carrier bag (which Florence was slightly dismayed about, but what with all the chatter she'd forgotten to produce the cotton bag from her rucksack). "Everyone does."

"Yes, we're very much looking forward to it," said Florence. "Did you know it was the first lighthouse to use an electric light?"

The owner didn't and didn't seem to appreciate being told anything about the lighthouse she wasn't already aware of. She stopped smiling and asked Florence for £8.75. Florence handed over a £10 note and while waiting for her change asked, "Am I right in saying it's right at the bottom of the road, then left at the very end of that road?"

"Yes, you are," said the owner, in a flat voice that reminded Florence a little bit of the way some girls used to speak to her at school. It was odd and she'd never altogether understood it. She picked up her change, which had been left for her on the glass counter immediately above the bars of fruit and nut chocolate.

Though she was loath to admit such a thing to Alan, it all became unnerving as they drove away from the village and Florence suddenly felt glad of her ghost-hunting experience. The terrain was certainly very dubious, causing the car to slightly rock from side to side and Alan to express fears about the tyres. He assured her they were going the right way several times, while Florence's mind was never far from thinking about cliff edges, something certainly not helped by a triangular danger road sign they'd come across depicting a man falling down a cliff into the sea. Surrounded as they were by only black, a cliff edge was no more distinguishable than anything else.

She asked Alan to stop for one moment so she could read the letter from the holiday company again. Despite Alan's assurances, she felt they'd driven too far and should've reached the gate they were looking for by now. Her suspicions were right, so they were forced to reverse back quite a few yards before taking a left turning they'd missed, an action that made the darkness only more dubious and the ground beneath their tyres more precarious.

But it did nothing to question Florence's faith in her decision to come to the lighthouse, the imminent appearance of which excited her even more, and when it was finally before her, a dark, tall but well-built shadow that rather resembled one of Dr Who's daleks, she thought, though she was never a fan of that particular programme, she tapped in the number to open the key box with great relish. She had to admit, she didn't particularly like this arrangement. There was something far more reassuring about collecting keys from a person. The box opened and she collected the keys and as she walked back to the car she found herself caught up in a momentary feeling that the lighthouse could well have been following her. As they drove nearer, this feeling changed to one of almost being enveloped, but it was as exciting as anything she could remember and Florence found herself wanting, as children do on Christmas morning, to hurry things along and open the car door before the car had stopped. Getting their bags into the lighthouse was no mean feat as they battled against the wind, but their reward was most satisfying as the warmth inside enabled their muscles to relax a little and they took a good look around. The kitchen had obviously been renovated only recently and its pale blue and pine were a lovely bright contrast to the darkness outside. This was going to be very nice to cook in, she concluded. All mod cons. The sitting room was more old-fashioned with floral covering to the sofa and chairs that reminded Florence of her childhood, especially the chair near the window, which might as well have been the one favoured by her father, it was so close in shape, so that she could almost catch a glimpse of him sitting there with a newspaper and a cup of tea perched precariously by his left foot. That chair, that newspaper and that cup of tea were probably his best friends who kept him away from his family for many an hour while her mother, instead, made sure his surroundings were clean and his tummy was fed. She thought her mother was probably bored a lot of the time and that her mind was quite empty of anything that might possibly stimulate it.

So Florence made it her business to keep finding things out for her mother to think about when jobs that hardly required any thought at all took up so much of her life. She supposed it had helped create some particular connection between them, though at the time Florence just thought that all children were born partly to entertain parents who had the hard task of bringing them up. But the facts in themselves did little to encourage the idea in either of her parents' heads that maybe she needed this brain of hers to be more formally led and challenged, mainly because her father was never part of these conversations and took only a minimal interest in her schooling; so when, at the age of fifteen, she had watched him come into the house with news that a secretarial school was opening only a mile or two away, her professional life before marriage was well and truly set. The facts, though, never went away and even when her mother became so ill and up until a week before her death, Florence was still making her smile with the knowledge she'd discovered that the hazel dormouse loves residing in honeysuckle, which was probably why there was an odd lump of its bark strips all clustered together at one end of their plant. Unfortunately, she hadn't yet seen the animal himself. Her mother had died six days later and though she may not have known it at the time as she was preoccupied with a whole series of funny tummies and horrible headaches, her heart had broken a little because of the underlying knowledge that this was one less person in her life who'd appreciated and known her really well.

"I'm going to put some soup on," she told Alan. "I think we need a little warming up," and she marched into the kitchen to try the new appliances and find out exactly how she was going to get on with them. The wind was whipping itself up into quite a frenzy now. Her only understanding of how far off the sea lay belonged to her mind's eye and the pictures in the brochure that had originally caught her attention, for there was no hint of it in the pure darkness that existed outside the window and she closed herself and the kitchen in by pulling the curtains to. She'd seen enough darkness for one day and basked in what felt like the beauty of bright lights, reminding herself that this lighthouse was indeed the first to use electricity.

She opened the carton of winter vegetable soup and wondered exactly how wintry runner beans were. Nevertheless, it would do them both good.

She liked the royal blue tableware very much. It had always been a colour she'd fancied, but, for some reason, Alan had never been keen, preferring instead a conservative white with only the tiniest hint of pattern. Maybe he thought it a bit too modern for them, but she'd often thought there was an energy about this blue she found pleasing. The soup was ready and, if the hob was anything to go by, she was going to get on very well indeed with this oven.

★

Sometimes, when they got up in the mornings, and this was particularly the case on holidays when there was no Mildred to visit or no choir practice to think about, Florence found she missed the children and their enthusiasm for the day ahead. And when she saw, for the very first time, the amazing vista before her from the kitchen window the following morning, she couldn't help that desire for them to be there and for all of them to share it.

"Come and have a look, Alan," she shouted enthusiastically towards the bedroom from where she could hear her husband emerging. "I can see France," and a memory flittered across her mind.

"Do you realise where we're standing?" Alan asked as he entered the kitchen, articulating something that sheer exhaustion had prevented him from doing the evening before.

Yes, she did. It was where Guglielmo Marconi had stood in 1898. She looked across to Alan. It was good to see him looking more relaxed. He'd been looking a bit tired of late. But this morning he had a colour back in his cheeks she hadn't seen in a while.

"Let's have a walk after breakfast," she ventured. "It's beautiful out there and it most likely won't be fine all week. We'll have to wrap up, though. It was mighty cold when I just went out to the bins."

They were still both admiring the view, something that could quite easily take up a whole day.

"Do you remember that day we went to Calais?" Florence queried.

"Gosh, yes, that was a rough day."

"Yes, I don't think Tom enjoyed that very much," and they both smiled a little, not in any unkindness, but because of a shared history and a time lapse that allows the odd smirk at things that haven't gone quite to plan. "I'm not sure if he's ever been on a boat since," she continued and Alan didn't reply, so he obviously couldn't think of an example of such an event either.

He couldn't think of a time when Tom had talked about being on water. Poor thing. He'd been pretty poorly.

"Now, today's the sort of day we should've gone."

Yes, it certainly is, she thought. When they'd landed at Calais the rain had been relentless and they'd parked themselves in a small, family restaurant for shelter, though they'd been worried how Tom was going to cope where there was food. But it had been all right. It was the sort of sickness that disappeared after they were on dry land.

In her mind she saw vividly the restaurant with its faded net curtains hung from halfway down the window so that it was just possible to see the tops of heads considering the menu, deciding whether or not it was appetising enough for them to use it to shelter from the rain. Most did. It wasn't difficult to attract customers on such a grisly day.

Alan looked at the tranquillity before him and envied the sea its calm. It had been five days since the doctor had told him it was cancer. The fact that it hadn't surprised him had done nothing to stem the shock of realising that his life really was limited, a fact he'd rarely embraced in any meaningful way when health had been on his side.

He didn't know when he was going to tell Florence. Percentages had been told him systematically by a doctor who didn't seem to appreciate how similar his delivery was to that of an insurance salesman. The odds weren't completely dismal and if he had an operation in the next month, there was room for optimism. He loved Florence, a fact that had been part of his life for nearly forty years now. He loved the way she'd always been satisfied with things, the way she'd embraced life and simply got on with it. So many people seemed discontent these days. It was an age of spoken hurt and complaint and her stoicism was something that he saw to be increasingly rare. It was as if girl guides had given her a manual for life that she'd continued to refer to. But her mind, something that interested him enormously, and her inquisitiveness, which always made the most stimulating of conversations, could also be quite claustrophobic, something he'd realised only in the last five days and with considerable consternation. There was no escaping Florence's desire to get to the bottom of everything and though he'd always enjoyed her interests and shared in them, he had no wish for her to pursue his illness in this way. He smiled to himself because it wasn't an unkindness in Florence. Far from it. And not even an insensitivity, for in her telling to friends about the dysfunction of the cells in their bodies, she genuinely thought she was being helpful. It was the sort of thing she would want to know, so why wouldn't they? He'd watched as they tried to change the subject but had never had the courage to interfere because telling Florence not to find out facts would be like telling her not to be alive. But, at the moment, he didn't feel he could bear the inevitable array of facts and figures that would follow his revelation. He would tell her after the holiday and the holiday would be the reason why he'd left it so long.

He took a deep breath and began to quietly sing. Slightly startled, because Alan wasn't given to doing this very often, Florence gave a quizzical glance. Alan held up his right forefinger, asking her to wait as the sense of it might become clear. She listened carefully to the words, which told of ships trying to find the English Channel in fog, helped in their quest by this particular lighthouse.

"I can see you've been doing your research as well," she said, pleased at her husband's enthusiasm, which came as an unexpected surprise. "I think what we need to do is find the English Channel for ourselves."

★

Over the next few days they did a lot of walking and Florence did quite a bit of talking. She told Alan about the house at the bottom of the cliff that once belonged to Noel Coward and they chuckled about some of his sillier songs while Florence remembered her mother and the way she would softly hum some of the more reflective ones, their notes lingering in her head a little while longer than she wanted them and reminding her of when she would follow these notes around the house, half hoping her mother would soon finish them and talk to her instead.

Alan congratulated himself on his ability to conceal his horrible fear, which he was determined would not interfere with Florence's obvious enjoyment, even though the fear surged inside him so powerfully at times that he could almost feel himself wanting to vomit it up. At night-time, when he was confident Florence was asleep, he got up from their bed and, with hardly a sound, took himself off into the living room, opened the curtains slightly and looked out onto the vast darkness, which could be broken only by speckles of light coming from the ships as they crossed to and fro. His stomach rose; then it fell. He had his own tidal wave rising and falling alongside them.

When he left the room, Florence opened her eyes and could just make out the shape of the dressing table opposite her. This was the third night Alan had got up. It wasn't like him. He was usually such a sound sleeper. If anyone had had a broken night's sleep during their marriage, she had been the one tip-toeing downstairs to make herself a cup of tea. He seemed a bit distracted at the moment. And he didn't seem to be the slightest bit interested that Marconi had carried out important research in this lighthouse.

She must've dozed off a little for she was suddenly startled by dazzling light shooting through the curtains and onto her face. The gravel outside their bedroom crackled, almost like rice krispies, she thought, then stopped. But the lights continued to illuminate her face and she sat up for there was no chance of any sleep. It was disconcerting because there was no one in the other flat. As a slight fear started to creep up on her, she rationalised the presence of others by saying to herself that maybe a family had arrived from a long distance, maybe they'd just got off one of the overnight ferries. As her body gradually woke up, she could hear the sound of a car engine gently purring, but there were no voices and no sound of car doors. She got up. Neither the lights nor the engine seemed to have any intention of switching off. The night storage heaters were throwing out a lot of heat, which was very welcome. Even so, Florence wrapped her dressing gown around her and made for the living room.

Alan was startled as she came in. He was lost somewhere between his illness and the life he'd already enjoyed, so when Florence entered he was thinking something about a day they'd had out in Wales and how he couldn't remember the name of the pub they'd gone to. He did remember a delicious cottage pie.

He apologised for having woken her, but she assured him he wasn't the cause of her wanderings. She told him about the car that didn't seem to care how much petrol and battery power it used and confessed to finding it a little worrying.

"I was wondering if anyone was in trouble," she offered, not entirely clear in her mind whether it would be safe to go outside.

"Can I see?" her husband asked, so she took him back to their bedroom so he could see and hear for himself what she was talking about. The car lights were still on and the engine still running.

"I really think someone needs help." But Florence was nervous.

They put cagoules over their dressing gowns and wellies

on their feet and unlocked the main door. The biting wind flew in and nearly took their breath with it. Florence reached for the large torch they'd brought with them, took it off the shelf by the door and switched it on, making it possible for them to see the small eating out area with its table and chairs thrown all over the place by weather showing little pity. They stepped over them, hardly hearing their feet crunching against the stones below. Opening the outer gate, they were greeted by even stronger winds, so they held one another's hand, both for the practical reason of ensuring they remained standing and to comfort the other's trepidation.

When they got to the car, they could see a man in the driving seat. As they drew nearer they saw his face was contorted.

"Quick." Florence opened the driver's door.

The man was holding his left elbow with his right hand, unable to speak because of the pain he was in. He let out a shriek when Florence moved a bit towards him but managed to point to where the pain was when she asked him.

"I think he may've injured his collarbone," she shouted at Alan, for the wind made it virtually impossible to communicate. "It would be best if we could get him indoors."

She asked the man if he could walk. He nodded and began to ease himself out of his seat. Both Florence and Alan bent towards him, but there was little they could do without fearing they may hurt him further.

After a few minutes he stood up. The wind competed with his cries of pain and almost lost as the three of them walked back to the lighthouse, with Florence and Alan propping up the man as best they could.

Once successfully indoors, Florence took the man into the kitchen and asked Alan to phone for an ambulance. The man said he'd be all right. It was the first time they'd heard his voice, which was cockney and urgent. His face was prematurely lined, Florence suspected, and his clothes hadn't received much attention recently. She insisted a professional see him and though he looked as if he wanted to argue, his pain and a general fatigue prevented him. She opened the cupboard above the cutlery drawer where she knew the first aid box was and lifted it out.

"I'm going to take it that we have a collarbone injury here," she told the man.

He thought she seemed to know what she was doing, so he didn't argue. What the hell was this old couple doing here anyway? Did they live here?

She asked him to put his left fingertips on the collarbone that was OK and then she took his right hand and placed it under his left elbow.

"There, that's what we want," she said, satisfied that everything was as it should be. She took a clean hand towel from one of the drawers and placed it against his chest, then took the cellophane off a wrapped bandage, opened it up and started making some sort of shape with it.

"Have you had a prang?" she asked him.

He looked at her.

"Have you had an accident?"

"Yeah," he answered and she started saying something about how he got his injury, but he was in too much pain to listen.

"The ambulance people said they'd be here as soon as they can," reported Alan, "but warned us they might be delayed because apparently it's started snowing down there."

"You told them what we suspected it might be?"

Alan nodded. "They said to ring again if things get worse. They'll give us advice over the phone."

"Oh, I'm sure they will," said Florence, who noted the look of alarm in the man's face at the prospect of any delay.

She looked at his poor, troubled expression, which seemed to have to do with more than a collarbone, and felt there probably wasn't anyone unduly concerned about his whereabouts. There wasn't much she could do about that, but she could help out with a painkiller and, having taken the precaution of checking this was all right with the ambulance team, she gave him the soluble sort, holding the glass and getting him to slowly sip the powdery water. She could smell the cold coming off his face. He was in a sorry state and she almost thought he wasn't going to make it as his chapped lips quivered against the rim of the glass. As the drops of water fell into his throat and his Adam's apple rhythmically moved to take it down, her mother's poorly face came to mind and she remembered the story of the dormouse. She smiled to herself. She never had seen him.

"Good," she said as he finished the medicinal drink. "That should help a bit," and she gently patted powdery remnants off the sides of his mouth. "Do you know where we are?" she asked him.

"The lighthouse." He grimaced and looked slightly annoyed at the question.

She confirmed his reply and then wondered if he knew its history. His blank look proved to be no match for her determination and Florence continued, undeterred and encouraged to see that his expression had improved to a state of vacancy rather than pain.

So she began her story about Guglielmo Marconi. If he could try to listen, it might help him take his mind off things.

"Who?" he asked and she smiled broadly. It had been a long time since anyone had asked her a question.

She told him about who Marconi was, his work with radio and how he'd worked in this very kitchen to bring about the first ship-to-shore message between where they were sitting and a ship called the *East Goodwin* in the English Channel and she looked at the closed curtains as if to indicate where the Channel was. She told him how important this had been.

How, for instance, so many more people would have drowned after the *Titanic* had sunk if there hadn't been the use of radio between ships. He knew about the *Titanic*? He nodded.

Her witterings bored him at first and he wanted to say, "Just shut up, you silly old bat, I'm in agony here," but the painkillers she'd given him, though not really doing much of a job, seemed to have, at any rate, stopped him shouting out, and he found himself listening to bits of what she was telling him. Something about an old geezer who'd found a way of ships talking to people on land. She was obviously very into what she was going on about. And when he winced she'd tell him to hold on and said the ambulance wouldn't be long. But she'd said that a few times now and though he hadn't wanted them to call one, he wanted it to get here as quick as it could now.

She had quite a nice face but not the sort of face he could tell stuff to. How he'd got into this bloody mess. That bloody ex-wife of his. God, the pain. Still, it was worth it. Ramming into the back of lover boy's BMW. Well worth it. And nobody could trace it back to him. So he'd run into a tree. Accidentally. He'd thought he could push his old banger off the cliff. But that hadn't worked out.

She was telling him about this radio bloke doing his work here. Where they were. He was in agony, but it was quite interesting, so he asked her about who he was exactly. Some guy called Marconi. Italian. Sounded like one of those blokes in that old film his uncle used to watch. His uncle. Yeah, yeah. Whatever you say, Mum. Anyway, she was talking about this guy and radios and how it had started all this communication. Had helped the *Titanic*, apparently. That film. God, how Shelley used to go on about it, even though she'd first seen it when she was just a little girl.

"You wouldn't stick our arms out on the edge of a boat."

No, he bloody wouldn't. What kind of a prat does that?

"You're not romantic, you." How many times had he heard that one? How many times? And he always hated how she said "you" at the end of it as if there was no greater crime on the planet than not being romantic. Never mind that he'd said "yes" to two kids and done his best with them. Still, his best was obviously not good enough for our Shelley and that bloody mother of hers. What they meant was, he didn't earn enough. Well, they knew what they could go and do. This old soul probably didn't even know the word, but she did seem to know a lot about this Italian bloke. So he found himself asking questions, like when did this all happen? Eighteen something or other. Christmas Eve. Felt like Christmas now, what with all this snow coming down. What happened after that? The first international transmission to France, apparently. What happened to him then? The Italian government wasn't interested in his ideas of wireless communication. Ha, losers. So he came here.

The phone rang. Alan picked it up. They could hear his monosyllables. Then he walked back into the kitchen.

"The ambulance said it's trying as hard as it can, but the weather means it probably won't get here for another half-hour or so. They asked if we were OK and I said we should be all right for half an hour," and he looked at the man, who gave a small smile.

"Yes, that should be all right," agreed Florence. "I think we all could do with a cup of tea and I'll carry on with my story," and she grinned as broadly as she could remember at the stranger.

He had to laugh. In absolute agony and here he was, about to have a cuppa. But there was no getting away from it. What she was saying was interesting. He might even go and look up this guy.

TRIFLE IN THE TOPIARY

Figs? What on earth was Roger talking about now? She must have had a little doze and was coming out of a dream in which her dear friend was claiming to grow figs in Wiltshire. Or had she just missed a bit and the reference was actually to his Tuscan garden? Really, she was quite cross with herself if she'd disappeared into the land of nod. Mind you, at least she'd heard a bit, probably woken by Cecily making quite a clanking noise piling up the plates ready to put back into the hamper. Bless her, she'd provided a delightful supper for them all. How many years had they been coming? And she'd never missed a trick.

Did that mean figs were going to feature in the dessert? Or perhaps with the coffee? We shall have to wait and see. She certainly didn't remember them appearing in the Waldorf salad. Oh dear, and it was such a lovely evening. She sat up a little to savour the view.

Cecily asked her if she'd like a cushion to sit on, but she declined. She was quite all right. She feared making herself too comfortable. Otherwise, Mr Sleep would reach for her again and Roger would, in all probability, be the proud owner of a camel. Either that or her dream would consist of Roger being asked by the BBC to take them round his Italian villa. But she remembered now. That had happened and Roger had politely declined, saying it was only an excuse for a group of voyeurs to have a holiday on public money. And he hadn't wanted to run the risk of resultant tourist interest, especially after what had happened to his friend Oscar, safely ensconced in a very nice little pad, a few kilometres up the road, but who now faced the dreadful prospect of the second and fourth Sundays of every summer having British holidaymakers plodding around the estate. And that was only after some gardener TV bloke on a curious channel nobody had ever heard of decided to spend a week eating poor old Oscar's grub and generally using his facilities for a show that lasted only forty-five minutes. Poor old Oscar. He never could resist a bit of pressure. Far too nice a bloke for words.

Yes, she'd thought at the time, far too nice a bloke, as Roger always insisted on referring to Oscar, who was now pocketing quite a bit of money. Poor old Roger, he often thought he was making a strong stand when actually he didn't always think things through properly.

The air was expectant and quietly jovial and there was a general bustle and laughter, punctuated by conversation where sentences such as "Oh no, Bengal would be far preferable" and "The rocket's from our Sussex garden" could be heard, understated utterances that didn't in any way suggest the peacock was parading its feathers. Just normal talk.

She looked out at the slightly sodden view. How wonderful rain was, for despite the slight inconvenience of it not having achieved the accolade of a beautiful summer's evening, this was beauty of a different kind altogether and the rain, like Brasso on silver, had brought back nature's finest colours. It was truly magnificent and she pondered over how many different shades of green she could see in any one view. In reality, probably about half a dozen, but in such an enthusiastic moment, and this is what music always did to her, it felt like hundreds of varying hues. She absolutely adored how far out she could see, how many miles beyond where she was sitting. The possibility of so much more.

Though captivated by what was before her, she could still hear Roger. He was telling everyone how damned hard he worked. She recognised his voice, of course, but she also knew the words. They were, after all, his mantra. She would never try to deny it for she was sure the words were absolutely true, but the thing Roger couldn't quite get hold of was that so did everybody else. She was very sure, for instance, that Roger and Diana's daily worked very hard indeed. Carol wouldn't be allowed a penny if she didn't. But she was far too old to make this remark to her beloved nephew, not because the energy to do so was sapped out of her but because Roger would consider the remark of someone so much his senior as unworthy of much cogitation. Not that Roger ever cogitated much, being pretty much the opposite of reflective and dwelling almost entirely in the present.

Her attention was taken by a young man sitting on the grass near a summerhouse where a small group of people were enjoying a crisp white tablecloth, candles and a small vase of roses she'd noticed them setting up about an hour before. The man was rummaging in a plastic supermarket carrier bag. Out came a piece of chicken, followed by a roll and what looked like a tomato. Using his bag as a plate he tucked into the food with enthusiasm and hunger, his cutlery his fingers. Not a champagne glass anywhere near him and no crockery in sight. Cecily probably wouldn't approve, but secretly, she thought the food was almost certainly tastier. Like fish and chips out of newspaper.

"Figs, Hester?"

She was just admiring the cypress and slightly resented the figs appearing again but turned her attention from the beautiful tree to the others, if only to resolve the mystery. Diana beamed at her. She had a lovely smile. Quite lovely. Roger should remember that when he was counting the coffers.

"Hester," Diana began and proceeded to give her news that the others had decided they were too full for dessert at the moment and thought they'd settle for coffee. Was that all right with her and did she want a fig with her coffee? So coffee and figs was the idea. She replied that she'd like figs very much. Diana apologised for not remembering whether she took sugar. Diana was forever apologising. No, she didn't take sugar.

She thanked Diana when both arrived and remarked on what a treat figs were. She couldn't remember when she'd last eaten them. And Diana smiled in good part but nevertheless wearily, saying how Roger wasn't going to let her forget his prize produce. Adrian, their gardener, had persuaded them to grow figs and much research had gone into the project. But she begged Hester not to say anything, even if she thought them the most delicious things ever.

She'd sometimes thought in the past that Roger and Diana were a pretty odd coupling. He was so loud, so grandiose in his demeanour; everything the large gesture, the theatrical stroke. And Diana was so contained she often wondered how her nephew's wife had never, as far as she could tell, exploded with sheer exasperation. But to this day, she'd supported him throughout all his business ventures, even the slightly misguided ones. When was it he'd come up with "aprons for the twenty-first-century woman" with their mobile phone pocket? Maybe sometimes he should check his ideas with his dear old aunt and she smiled, closed her eyes and listened.

If the saxophone, playing to the right of her, was a little softer, it would be within a whisker's distance of taking her into a hotter clime, heavier and almost putrid with its smoky, sweaty aromas and she would be tipsier than she should be and laughing coarsely in a way no one on these shores had ever heard. Her society in England had taught her long ago that nothing good ever came of a lady's belch or belly-laugh. She hadn't minded. Belching was unattractive and nothing had greatly amused her.

But that summer she'd come to understand the extent of

her previous deprivation when Nathaniel had piled far more on her plate than seemed polite and had regaled her with stories and insights that had reached for her stomach and pulled out a laughter that was a complete stranger to her. And she watched him make slight mockery of her sense of the order of things when he'd officially introduced her to the members of his band, but he was so kind there was nothing offensive about it. She was so unaccustomed to everything she was encountering that novelty far outweighed overstepping the mark. "Nathaniel, Nathaniel, wherefore art thou?" she supposed she should've asked and taken herself back to the hotel, full of luxury and her family, but her body was shaking with joy and she didn't know Nathaniels existed, so she surprised herself by falling into the arms of this man with whom she seemed to share little, different in everything from experience to skin colour, at a time when those things mattered to people who knew nothing. For two weeks they'd fallen in love and when she'd returned home letters, not kisses, had passed between them. She'd collected them at the post office. Nobody ever knew. She smiled. Good thing those letters had been written. Good thing she'd taken heed of Nathaniel and set up this jazz festival. How inspirational he was. How wonderful no one had found out it had been her. Something that had begun in that damp church hall and was now housed by a family's garden. They adored the music and said it deserved better. And the trust had agreed.

She tapped to the music with fingers that had what she liked to think of as an arthritic elegance all of their own, taking knuckles and nails off in unusual directions. What would Nathaniel have made of them? "Hester," he'd have probably said, "these fingers show me just how tedious youthful beauty can be," because she'd heard him say it once to a woman probably four times older than they were then.

"The figs are delicious, Roger, you've quite surpassed

yourself this time." Dear oh dear, she thought, Diana wasn't going to thank Cecily at all.

She turned her head back into the cloister where the musicians were thoroughly enjoying themselves and the growing evening was allowing beautiful lighting between each archway to show itself off. It was such a small space she could have touched the singer. Leaves cascaded down from the columns and there was definitely a smell of sweet peas in the air. The musicians took a short break and one perched his bass against the small font that sat in the middle. This wasn't England, she thought to herself again and was amused at how she surprised herself with this thought each year she came. So continental, she could almost hear Italian plainsong.

There was music elsewhere, Cecily informed her when those musicians had finished and they all trundled off to the area where the topiary was, with Diana and Roger carrying the fold-up chairs. Safely settled in these, they could see another band, louder and brasher than the other, and Cecily winced a bit. But she loved it and she loved the couple who'd taken it upon themselves to dance a salsa in front of the pianist, so sensual in their movements it almost felt voyeuristic. But nobody cared.

Diana persuaded everyone it was at last time for dessert and produced individual trifles, rich and creamy with fresh raspberries at the bottom that were also, no doubt, from their garden. *Let's hope they're as good as the figs*, she thought. They were, but in deference to Diana she didn't say anything. She scooped out a spoonful of cream, custard and fruit – there was alcohol in this – and thought of a time when she and Nathaniel had danced, weaving around one another with steps that were challenged by almost constant giggling. And not a fig in sight.

ROLL YOUR OWN

These days it always seems to come back to age because the girl on the opposite seat reminded me of Audrey Hepburn and though the girl – young woman, I suppose I should say, but being a similar age to my daughter she felt like a girl – though she probably knew Ms Hepburn by posters, it was pretty likely she didn't know her work, as is said these days. She probably didn't even appreciate her as an icon. Yet look like her she did, even though it was Audrey in thick, rectangular-rimmed glasses, purple baggy vest T-shirt and long, green and silver beads more reminiscent of hippy San Francisco than chic New York. An Audrey less constrained, you might say. An Audrey making, what seemed to be, a small factory's worth of cigarettes. Ironic, really, as cancer had deprived the star of old age.

The train was travelling through the French countryside. Audrey had got on at Lyon and I was immediately struck by this one-woman business unfolding before my very eyes. Such industrious behaviour in what was, for me, a journey of leisure seemed even more incongruous than someone on their phone or computer. Maybe it was just that I wasn't used to witnessing the making of cigarettes on such a large scale.

She wasn't really interested in anyone nearby. As soon as she sat down, on a seat where the other three around her were empty, she began to pull things out of her rucksack, again something I didn't imagine the real Audrey possessing, at least not on set, and I smiled, if only because it looked like Mary Poppins with her bag of surprises. Were all my references of the celluloid variety? So out came what looked like a large black and orange stapler, a yellow, round box of Camel tobacco with the vacuum foil still half attached to its top and a silvery grey box, which I thought might hold tools of some sort but which carried, what turned out to be, cigarette papers. Audrey momentarily glanced out of the window and caught a glimpse of the sunny day and a countryside deprived of people, then quickly returned to the matter in hand. She pushed back a tiny thread of hair from her face and tucked it behind her ear. Her hair, piled high as if Tiffany's beckoned, though more dishevelled, gave the impression she was more concerned about a cat lost forever than a piece of jewellery.

I thought how confident she seemed. How years of feminism had gifted her with this. Though as her fingers delicately twirled the cigarette paper to a point where it could satisfactorily fit into the stapler machine, she most likely didn't see it that way. She chewed gum; she intermittently answered text messages, with barely a break in the factory process. The machine was loaded and the tobacco deftly dropped at, I would have estimated, a height of about an inch. Yes, well, we're back to the age thing. Don't get me wrong. I love European. But when it comes to measurement, I'll always think feet and inches. Old habits and all that and from the end of Audrey's manicured and varnished fingertips, there was definitely about an inch. She pushed the machine up and down three times for each cigarette, ensuring it released any unwanted tobacco and forming as it did so, a perfect shape. The process was faultless and would've made a factory owner proud, but this worker had her own autonomy, her absorption something to behold. And after each cigarette was born, its life was confirmed with a personal inscription written carefully on and with seemingly great satisfaction.

I went back to my book. I didn't want to appear too nosey. She was probably already wondering what on earth she was doing that so fascinated the middle-aged woman opposite. Her phone rang and unlike other calls that had obviously not interested her enough to deter her from her task, in fact one had caused transparent disdain, she picked this one up. Yes, she said, the train was on time. She'd be in Marseille by six. A small bundle of tobacco was picked up from the tin and gathered into an appropriate amount, the phone between her ear and shoulder. A series of *pourquoi*'s followed. Why? Why? Why? Then she said no quite sharply, and abruptly finished the conversation. A deep sigh followed and another cigarette completed. It was given her signature. Another box, which had started its journey empty, was filling up with the signed articles.

"Hello, it's Francine." Her voice was quite deep and assured, the kind that tells you your room is ready and breakfast will be served between seven and nine. "How are you? OK, I think. Not great. But I know I've made the right decision… Yeah… No, I'm on the train now… Yeah, no, I know you're right. It just feels a bit odd. But you're so right 'cause he just rang. I couldn't believe it. He was still going on about how he could improve my writing! Like he thought that was going to bring me rushing back! I said, 'You're not my professor now!' Anyway, good to talk. I'll give you a ring when I've got my stuff sorted a bit. Yeah. Cool. Bye."

She started tapping her phone, then checked the box with the finished cigarettes, as if she was doing some sort of calculation.

I got my purse out of my bag. All this concentration on another's life was making me thirsty, so I ventured down the hairy pathway of several coaches towards the buffet, holding tightly the tops of seats to avoid falling into someone's lap. I was one generation behind such speed. My stomach and brain hadn't quite caught up, being at the tail end of small carriages for six with sliding doors with their very definite click when pulled shut and most pleasing, individual soft lighting that meant you could still glimpse the world outside at night-time. This journey would've taken forever but would've been kinder to my body.

"Hello, madame."

Audrey, or Francine I suppose I should say, was speaking again and I was sitting very comfortably and relieved my coffee had survived the return journey, with a book I wasn't reading. Was this what it was like to be a spy?

"Yes, thanks for getting back. I knocked on your door last night, but you must've been out... Right. Yeah, it is sad... That's kind, madame. You know I don't want to hurt anyone. I'm upset about Gilles. He was very kind, but then he works with your son, so it was all a bit complicated really... Well, thanks. I'm going back to the flower shop in Marseille... Well, I hope so. My friend, the owner, and I are great mates and she's talking about me going into business with her and the pair of us doing event organising or something like that... Yeah. Well, I should have a pretty good idea, shouldn't I, after all those uni dos... Well, that's really nice you saying that... Yeah, I have to say I was pretty upset about him taking my ideas and presenting them as his own to the publisher, but hey ho... Yeah, I think so too and he's got it on his conscience... Um well, I'm glad you said that, madame! Yeah, that would be nice. You too. Bye."

She stopped the cigarette making for a while and concentrated on the scenery once more, which was beginning to look hotter. There was still no one to be seen. Just the odd church or a red-roofed house. She put on an olive green cardigan that had been languishing next to her bag and shuddered slightly as she did so. Her phone rang again.

"Hello, Papa." She sounded bored. "Oh, Papa, you've been drinking again. I can hear it in your voice! I tried to talk to you! ... Well, that's not my fault, is it? ... What? I can't

hear you properly. I don't know why you're going on like this.
Well, maybe I do. But you didn't even want me to go to uni...
university. You didn't want me to go. You said it was just full
of a lot of hoity-toitys who turned their noses up, and I quote,
'at the likes of us'... Hah! I was right. I thought money was
at the bottom of it. Well, stuff you... No, I won't and I'd say
something stronger if I wasn't on a train. There's someone
near me and I'm sure she doesn't want to hear all this...
Marseille. I'm going to work in the shop again. I don't care
what you think. It's enough for me to get by on and that's all
that worries me at the moment... Well, that's not my prob...
Problem. Your debts aren't my problem. Bye."

"Tickets, please. Tickets, please."

She rustled in her bag, I in mine.

"Thank you, madame. Thank you, madame. Ooh, it's
running a little late, madame, so about ten past at the moment,
but we could make up the time."

"Thank you, monsieur."

"Hello, it's Francine. I need to talk. I've just had my dad
on the phone. God. It's such hard work... Oh, have you been
talking to Nicole? ... No, it's not a secret. People are going to
find out soon enough I'm back in Marseille... No, I'm not
going to put it on Facebook... Well, I'll put that I'm back in
Marseille. Obviously. But I'm not going to say why. Tempting
though it is to out that sleaze ball for the plagiarist he is. God,
when I think of the hours and hours of work he made me
do. Do you know, he once had me up all night in his office?
... God, no. Gross. He's at least twice my age. No, we were
working on that speech for the Paris conference. You know,
the one in April. Anyway, it wasn't like that 'cause we had old
Professor Lefevre in there with us. Have to say, he's quite a
nice old thing, really. He was annoyed about the plagiarism,
anyway. But I think he's a bit torn 'cause they've been mates
for so long. God, all those rewrites and him checking every

tiny little bit of punctuation. I was like, oh my god, it's just a comma. The man was obsessed. Anyway, how are you?"

The train stopped. Avignon. *Sur le pont.* Only about another forty minutes to Marseille. We had made up the time. I watched people get off, tired and stretching limbs that had been stuck in the same positions for hours. Those waiting for them wore only T-shirts. It must be hotter than Lille, but in this air-conditioned environment it was difficult to tell.

The cigarettes had a lid put on them, the foil on the Camel tin was gently folded over and the stapler returned to the bottom of the bag.

"Hello. Word gets around! ... Yeah. Yeah. I know, I could be making a big mistake, but I really don't think I am... No, well, that's good to hear... Yeah. I do feel better. I've just had his mum on the phone... No, it was actually OK 'cause she was the first person who really pointed out his arrogance. She thinks he's a bit of a misogynist. She came into his office while I was there once and he'd gone out to grudgingly make her a drink – at her insistence, he didn't really want to, 'cause his secretary was on leave, he hated that – and she asked me how he was treating me. I was a bit shocked, but, at that time, said he was fine and I remember she raised her eyebrows, even then. Anyway, must go. I'm getting into Marseille soon... Yeah, I'll text you or something. OK. Bye for now."

I reached for my jacket, which I'd shoved onto the rack above my head what seemed like yesterday, though it was only a few hours ago. The book I hadn't read was put into my bag, ready for another day and I made sure there was nothing of mine on nearby seats. There were only a few of us left.

Francine gave an exasperated sigh and answered her phone. She looked at me and begged my pardon, as if she knew I might not like what I was about to hear.

"Why are you ringing me? I've told you, I'm not coming back... No. No. No. Oh god, how many times do I have to say this? The plagiarism, the conference. The Paris conference or have you forgotten? You know, when I delivered the talk, just as we agreed, how everyone applauded, was interested, asked questions, and then you went off with the professor for a meal and didn't even ask me to join you... Oh god, I can't do this anymore. Goodbye."

There was another sigh and another apology. I smiled and said it was fine. She said, yes, it was and picked up her phone.

"Hello. It's me. I'll be there in about fifteen minutes... Yes, can't wait to see you either... For my flat? That's kind... Oh, roses, please."

CAN YOU KEEP A SECRET?

1980

I was asked if I could keep a secret. I answered that I didn't really know as I had never tried. The nearest I'd got, I suppose, was when our father told my sister, Joyce, and I that we were all going to make our mother a birthday cake. It was all very exciting and we were in the kitchen stirring and mixing ingredients and generally getting extremely messy when she came back earlier than expected from a grocery shop. Our father signalled to us that we move ourselves and everything from the table to the pantry, which was silly, really, because there wasn't time to clean up properly. Well, she came into the kitchen, carrying a huge, heavy bag – we could just see her through the pantry door keyhole – and was obviously not in the mood for any surprises or shenanigans, as she probably saw it, and said quite loudly as she plonked the bag on the floury table surface, "Oh, Arthur, I know you're in there with the girls."

And funnily enough, because this does sound rather odd, I had never got into the secrets sort of thing at school. Dolly, my best friend and I used to talk about lots of things, but I don't ever remember her saying, "Oh and by the way, don't tell so-and-so." At least, I hope she didn't. And I really don't recall saying any such thing to Dolly. Come to think of it, no one asked us to keep their secret. Maybe they didn't trust us. I don't know.

So it was a bit strange, looking back, and seeing how my daughters and their friends were always keeping secrets and getting into little huddles, shush, whisper, whisper, "Mummy's coming!" It's peculiar to think I had somehow managed to get to the great age of twenty-one and not kept anyone's secret.

Everyone knew I wanted to go to university. Absolutely everyone. I remember I was twelve and a half when I decided that was what I wanted to do. I was in my bedroom and I could hear a conversation taking place between my father and a colleague of his who he'd brought home for an early evening drink after work. My father was saying how he hadn't gone to university, even though his parents had had the desire and the money for him to do so, and how, looking back, he regretted very much that he hadn't gone along with their wishes. He confessed he had, instead, followed his youthful urgency for employment and a wage. His colleague, quite a nice man from what I could hear, tried his best to reassure my father that his decision had been for the best, but when pressed by my father, who never took reassurance easily, admitted that, though the work had been hard, he had had a fine old time and it had been good to escape the shackles of family life before having to support one oneself. He talked about theatre clubs, debating societies, language societies (now, that was the one that got me hooked) and lots of parties, which, he laughed, included a lot of roaming around streets singing and only the odd bit of complaining from locals or, indeed, the local police. He said one got away with a great deal.

Yes, I was very taken with what I'd overheard, though I knew, even at that age, it was going to be a pretty hard wall to climb as a girl.

But it's funny how a whisper, or a moment, can change absolutely everything. How a man I never saw, whose words I wasn't really supposed to hear, changed me from a potential housewife or secretary into an undergraduate.

And that was where they found me. At Westfield College in London. I was in my second year, reading German with

French. We were at war and at that time the universities, in their supposed wisdom, said if women were not intending to teach after their degree, then they would have to leave. Well, as much as I wanted to go to university, I knew equally well I had absolutely no intention of entering the teaching profession. I'm afraid it offered nothing to entice me.

I think I must have started talking to people about how I was interested in war work, I can't remember who exactly, but word must have got round and suddenly, one day, I had an application form from the FO, the Foreign Office, sent to me in the post. I later learned that colleges were being asked about likely students, so my name must have been put forward. I know one of my professors, a lovely man, had a real thing about us women doing more with ourselves than teaching, so it may have been him. He had a mischievous twinkle in his eye and was a very good sort. When I look back I feel a tad guilty about how horrified I was when he asked me once if I wanted to teach. I mean, it was a bit rude of me to be like that with my professor.

It was my language skills they were after. Particularly, obviously, my German, which I was reasonably confident about. It was all very hush hush.

I suppose it was quite strange that I just looked at this form without asking how it had come to me, without questioning anything. But after one read through I just thought, *Well, why not?* You didn't question your elders in those days and I definitely thought it was an elder who had put my name forward. I can't imagine my daughters doing the same for one moment.

I was fortunate, living in London, because the interviews, well, many of them at least, were held there and I got up that morning feeling excited because I wasn't sure what it was all about. I felt a bit like a child when an adult gradually unveils something; it was all very tantalising and the anticipation made me tingle a little. But I remember, as I walked to the bus stop, it was far too optimistic a day that didn't belong to wartime, sunshine and a slight breeze, and I suddenly felt an overwhelming desire to retreat into teaching. On such a day, as a teacher I could almost forget there was a war. I think my college had made me feel safe, really, and that morning I realised, with the whiff of the breeze across my face, that things were very uncertain indeed.

So, as I say, they asked me if I could keep a secret and I don't think they were particularly impressed with my reply, so after a second or two of the old pin-dropping silence I added, "But I'm sure I could."

One gentleman, who was top flight army and who looked extremely stern, told me that discretion was of the utmost importance and though he didn't want to imply that I was lying or that he couldn't trust my reassurance he would, nevertheless, have to ask for the names and addresses of three people outside of my family who they could put this self-same question to. The exact nature of the work I would be doing wouldn't be revealed, he said. I thought for a couple of minutes, then offered the names of three professors, including the one I just spoke about. It seemed a bit silly because I had never shared a secret with any one of them, so how they would be able to give a reliable verdict on the matter, goodness only knows. But my interviewers seemed satisfied with the information I'd given them and that was that. I didn't see those professors much after the interview as term was ending and when I did, they observed the social grace that demands tight lips over anything potentially tricky, so my future employment was never the subject of discussion.

The most difficult thing for me was not being able to talk about the interview with my family, which I was bursting to do, but it was made clear in no uncertain terms that this was forbidden. Yes, that was difficult.

Anyway, I passed my interview and was told I was going to be somewhere called Bletchley, a place I hadn't heard of before then. They told me it wasn't too far from London, about fifty miles, but I would have to reside there and that they would find me somewhere to live. They were pleased with my level of German, thanked me for my time and wished me luck, at which point, I must admit, I started feeling a little worried. Well, if I'm being totally honest, I panicked a bit and began to wonder if this place Bletchley was actually a code name for Berlin. My imagination started playing havoc with me and I was extremely restless until I received the long-awaited envelope from the FO. *At last*, I thought, when the letter dropped on the mat, but my relief was very short-lived because, when I opened it, I had instructions that quite definitely had something of the Agatha Christie about them as I was to go to Bletchley railway station, find a telephone kiosk there and then I was to ring this number – they provided a telephone number with the letter – and await further instructions. *My goodness*, I thought, *I really am going to be parachuted into Europe*, which, looking back, was ridiculous because I'd been given no training whatsoever for such a task.

My parents and sister had to be kept in the dark. This, as you might imagine, worried them quite considerably, exacerbated, of course, by the fact we were at war, but Joyce, my sister, apparently gathered some cachet amongst friends for having such a secretive sister. But it was really very odd for us as a family because, as I said, we weren't the secretive sorts. My father took the view that teaching wasn't a bad price to pay for getting a degree, and my mother said that if I was determined to leave university, there were some very fine prospects in the John Lewis Partnership. Celia's daughter, Patricia, was doing nicely there and enjoying every minute.

Obviously, I could understand their grievances. They'd put an awful lot into my education and I had wittered on about going to university for an awfully long time, but I suppose I justified it to myself because we were in the middle of a very extraordinary time. I remember one Sunday afternoon when the arguments about me being a teacher reared their ugly head once again and I felt myself getting pretty cross with both my mother and father. I got up from the dinner table and said, quite sharply it has to be said, but they had tried my patience, "Well, I hope you'll be jolly pleased with yourselves when I'm having to teach you German, because that's what will happen if I don't join the war effort!"

Gosh, to think I imagined I could win the war single-handedly! It's quite funny, looking back. I remember running up to my bedroom, shaking, and not quite believing I'd dared to talk to my parents in that way. But it's fair to say, they must have realised how passionate I was about not teaching because the subject was never brought up again.

So there I was at Bletchley railway station. I have to say I didn't like it very much. It was a dull old place. My heart sank and I found myself thinking, *Gosh, is this what I've given up university for?* And I had a secret hope that maybe this wasn't the journey's end. You know that feeling when you go on holiday and you get to some God awful village and you're fervently praying for another ten miles to somewhere a lot nicer.

Anyway, I found my way to the telephone kiosk and duly rang the number they'd given me. Someone on the other end asked me one or two questions about myself and then, when they were satisfied they were talking to the right person, told me to go to the main road and gave me further instructions – I can't remember what these were now – until I came to some iron gates, where there would be three sentries. I was to present my letter to them and they would then give me instructions as to where I should proceed.

It was quite a lot to take in and I was particularly worried because they said could I repeat the instructions back to them as they didn't want me asking the locals. I then put the telephone down and kept repeating what I'd just said over and over in my head. Fortunately, I didn't lose my way and when I got to the sentries they directed me to a captain to whom I had to show my letter again. The captain nodded approval at my letter, gave me a brief smile, which meant a lot, I can tell you, and then from what seemed absolutely nowhere, two women appeared, not much older than me, who were asked by the captain to escort me to the house. It all felt very mysterious and I started to quite foolishly get it into my head that I was going to be asked to be a lady-in-waiting or some such thing because I wondered if members of the royal family were holed up here or something. And my head was whirling with their German connection, of course.

None of us spoke. The women didn't seem to have an ounce of curiosity about me and, being the newcomer, it didn't seem right for me to question them. We arrived at the house, which, on first sight, was impressive yet rather odd. It was a strange amalgamation of styles that didn't seem to fit into any particular period, but I was quickly distracted from thoughts of architecture because of the countless number of people milling around. I don't know what I'd been expecting, quite, but a small town hadn't crossed my mind and I remember the first hour or so being a little overwhelmed.

They gave me a meal of some lumpy soup and a jam sponge, which I ate with what appeared to be hundreds of others in a large, oak-panelled hall. I was so grateful for something to eat, I think I was less critical of the food than if it had been of the university's fare and I gobbled it all up very quickly.

It all felt tremendously odd and had I not been to university I think I would have felt quite homesick. But even with my experience, I suddenly yearned for a meal with just the four of us at home. A cosy intimacy was lost to me and I suppose I wanted it because it wasn't mine anymore.

Shortly after I'd finished my last mouthful, I was escorted, along with a few others, who I presumed were also new, by another two women into an office, which had a great long table. I remember it was covered with what seemed like an old blanket. Three army officers sat bang in the middle and I had this horrid feeling I was about to be scolded. It felt a bit similar to being called into the headmistress's office and I started to feel quite nervous and desperately wished I hadn't had pudding. But it turned out they were perfectly nice, though extraordinarily serious. The whole thing felt very funereal.

Then the officer in the middle began by welcoming us. He ended this, I remember, with a little smile and I thought he seemed quite a decent sort of chap. But this bonhomie was short-lived and his tone transformed as he told us why we were at Bletchley, what would be the nature of our work and its huge importance to the war effort. I think I must have gone into a bit of a state of shock because I remember feeling very light headed and was terrified I was going to faint or something awful. I don't know what I thought I was doing there exactly, but suddenly the gravity and expectation of the work took hold of me, and excitement and terror just sort of intermingled, making me feel pretty wobbly, I can tell you. Would I be up to the task in hand? It all felt very responsible.

Then the chap to the right of him read the Official Secrets Act to all of us, again not something to steady the nerves, and told us, in no uncertain terms, that we weren't to breathe a word of what we were doing at Bletchley to a soul. They made us sign a promise to that effect and we were told there would be dire consequences, such as imprisonment, if we did. It all felt very peculiar. I suppose I didn't feel important enough to be signing such papers. Was this a Tudor court? Certainly the word "traitor" was used. I think we all wanted to steal a glance at one another but were too intimidated. We left the room very quietly and then the women took us to one side individually and informed us about our sleeping arrangements. The woman who spoke to me – very trim, I remember, with tiny eyes and a mouth I couldn't imagine smiling – told me I was to sleep at Bletchley that night, for which I was most grateful as I felt too weary to travel elsewhere, but the next day I was to be billeted out to Fenny Stratford, which, she explained, wasn't far off and I would be taken there by a member of staff on one of the buses. This would then be my mode of transport for getting into and out of Bletchley. I was to be living with a family by the name of Johnson. She wasn't someone to whom one responded or asked questions, so I just nodded and thanked her, then began to go over and over again in my mind what this family might be like. I think, looking back, I was quite shocked about being thrown into the lives of a family I didn't know. How on earth were we going to rub along? I found it quite difficult to sleep, which wasn't helped by the hard, most uncomfortable bed. I could only look forward to something better with the Johnsons.

"No mention whatsoever may be made either in conversation or correspondence regarding the nature of your work." That's what I thought as I got up the next morning and prepared for my first day at work. I hadn't felt quite as nervous since my university interview, but this time I think I was, if anything, more tentative because it felt as if there was a very real sense of responsibility towards others. My thought was that I didn't want to let anyone down and for the first time I remember I started to doubt my linguistic abilities. What passed for all right at university might be downright inadequate here and mistakes would be catastrophic. So, when I even think about it, I get the chills. It was awfully nerve-wracking.

After I dressed, I walked into the corridor outside and was soon met by yet another woman, about ten years older than me, who told me we were to breakfast together. She had a warm smile and I felt for the first time that working at Bletchley could turn out to be perfectly OK. Someone resembling a human being, at last, I thought. You know that way some people have of letting you know you're the sort who's going to fit in. I ate two pieces of hot buttered toast, munching it with a total relish, as Sylvia explained I was to be working somewhere called Hut 6. I began to ask exactly what I'd be doing, but she said firmly, without giving me the notion that I was being reprimanded in any way, that we would talk about that when we were in the hut. Where I was going to be was all she could say and she continued, instead, to ask me about university. Had I had a jolly time there and what was London like as a place to live? She'd always been enthralled by the idea of it but admitted to not being plucky enough to actually live there. Cambridge had suited her very well, which was stated as something merely factual.

We walked across to Hut 6. It was a bitter day and there was little, if any, relief when we got inside. It was extremely cold and most people were donning scarves, thick coats, and one or two chaps hadn't removed their balaclavas.

When people say to me today that they're chilled to the bone because they've escaped central heating for more than five minutes I think to myself, *Well, you should jolly well have tried a Bletchley hut.* I still have the mittens I wore whenever work would allow. I remember my mother popped them in my suitcase at the last moment. They were a particularly old pair and I said, "Mummy, I'm never going to use those!" I was quite cross with her for mollycoddling me, but how wrong I was and how thankful she'd had the common sense to pop them in. But I never let her know this, being far too young and too proud. The electric heaters barely did anything in terms of warming up the room. It was like asking a car heater to deliver in a mansion. Often, in the winter months, you found it troublesome trying to concentrate properly when all you could think of was whether or not your toes were still in place.

Anyway, I sat at a desk with Sylvia and quite a handsome man, Mr McIntyre, quiet-sounding and a little too tall for me, I thought, which was a bit cheeky, really, because I'm sure he wasn't the slightest bit interested in me. This is all a bit difficult. Would you really like me to talk about my work? Excuse me a minute, I think I need a drop of water.

Mr McIntyre chewed on a pipe and throughout most of the conversation bore furrowed brows, leaving me feeling he was slightly puzzled as to the reason for my being in the same room. Not long into the conversation he started speaking in German, asking me all sorts of questions from family matters to what I thought about the progression of the war. He seemed particularly interested in talking to me about naval matters and, though I was slightly thrown when this questioning began, by the time he returned to English again, I thought I'd fared pretty well, even though much of what I said assumed a low level of knowledge of the navy. He must have thought I'd done all right too because he smiled, held out his hand and told me it was good to have me on board.

At four o'clock I was told to go to the main house, pick up my things and report to the main entrance by half-past. At precisely that time the woman who had spoken to me the day before about the family I was to stay with said, "Hello again, shall we?" and placed her right hand efficiently in front of her. Both she and I walked out of the front door and onto a bus where a driver greeted us in an over stern manner, almost as if he was acting a part in a play, the drama of Bletchley, as it were. He scowled a little, which felt perfectly in tune with the disposition of my escort, who had very little in the way of humour at her disposal. I remember hoping that I'd be able to get along a bit better with the family I'd be living with. We were in the middle of a ghastly war, but surely we didn't have to be quite so dour with one another. Hopefully, my family would at least attempt the odd dance with frivolity.

I needn't have worried. The Johnsons gave me a hearty welcome. Much had obviously been explained to them because Fred, Mr Johnson, began by saying he knew they weren't supposed to know anything about me and they wouldn't be asking any questions. Just as long as I was in by eleven, what I did was nothing to do with them. My escort, quite unnecessarily, I thought, told them I certainly wouldn't be telling them why I was in Fenny Stratford, leaving an awkward waft in the air.

I introduced myself and thanked them for their hospitality. I said I would be in by eleven, if not quite a bit before and I would try as hard as possible not to be noisy or cause them any bother. Fred answered that he was sure I wouldn't bother them and they were very happy to have me. We were then left by my escort, who said she had to go and she would leave to give us time to get to know one another. I think we were all heartily relieved when we'd said our goodbyes to her. I really can't remember her name; I'm not sure she ever told me.

Then Fred said, "Look, I don't know how much you know about these arrangements, but I want to make it clear that we're getting quite enough from His Majesty's government, so to speak, to have you here. We could charge you for things like hot water and whatnot, but Beryl and I have talked it over and we're quite satisfied with what we're getting, so you're to use our home like it's your own. Like family."

It was a very sweet speech and I thanked him a great deal for his, and his wife's, kindness. I didn't know then how truly fortunate I was because I learnt only later that plenty of girls were getting stung for the slightest amenities. Some of them could barely walk upstairs to their bedrooms without incurring a fee. And stringency was another thing. One poor woman I spoke with once told me how her landlady was very mean with light bulbs and the poor woman spent a whole two weeks without any light in her bedroom. She said she didn't mind the dressing and undressing so much, but it was the fact that she couldn't read at bedtime that really got under her skin. You may think in a war this is all very trivial, Mr Donovan, but it was the only kind of chitchat that was at her disposal. As I said, work was never a subject of discussion.

I was very sensitive to the fact that my being in the Johnsons' household was an extraordinary invasion of their privacy and I'm not sure my own family could have done the same. My mother, for instance, was so partial to her daily routines that I think the slightest change would have sent her quite loopy. I knew, absolutely in the first instant, they were a lovely family and I remember I felt terrible about the way Fred kept alluding to my family and my former life. "Bet this is smaller than what you're used to," he would say. And I thought, *Well, yes, it is an awful lot smaller*, but of course I would never have said that. Often I didn't reply, but once I answered, "But it's not half as warm, Fred," and he said he did seem to have a particularly good coal fire.

Beryl seemed a bit wary of me at first. She just used to answer my questions monosyllabically and a few weeks went by without me knowing much about her at all. It was Fred who did all the talking, though his son, Ken, asked a lot of questions of his father at mealtimes (I must say, some of them were quite near the bone and not ones that Joyce and I would ever have been allowed to ask, let alone get answers to; for instance, he once asked his father why he was out so late the evening before), until he had the confidence to turn his line of enquiry on me, to which Fred gently told him off with something like, "Now what did I tell you? No questions."

I finally got to know Beryl a little more one evening when, for some reason, I think as a result of her having saved up a few rations, she was making an apple pie and I asked her if I could help. She was a tad reluctant at first and I thought, *Oh, golly, I've probably ruined this woman's enjoyment of what she's doing by sticking my nose in it*, but because I knew absolutely nothing about the making of apple pies – that was always my mother's arena – she had to give me instructions and after a little while she started telling me how relieved she was that Ken was too young to join up. She knew what other women in Fenny were going through. She then told me to roll out the pastry and I said I'd never done this before. "Go on, give it a go," she replied, so I pitched in and Beryl said she didn't think I'd made half a bad job of it.

Their daughter, Susan, was a precocious little thing and, at half her brother's age, seemed to know twice as much. Beryl said it was a wonder to her where Susan got all her knowledge from because they didn't have any money for books and even her teachers couldn't believe what she told them a lot of the time. I remember she said that if she were honest, she was a bit jealous of Susan as she'd always been so shy.

Am I digressing? They were such a lovely family. I didn't see them as much as I'd have liked. Time off was rare and even when I did have an evening meal with them I'd make excuses to retire to my room as I genuinely had no energy to talk. They would be very polite and bid me goodnight.

The work was hard. The level of concentration required was so arduous. And the fear of making a terrible mistake. Not to mention the rules and regulations. They quite buzzed in one's head. I can remember them as if it were yesterday:

Do not talk at meals.

Do not talk to the transport.

Do not talk travelling.

Do not talk in the billet.

Do not – and this was perhaps the hardest – do not talk by your own fireside, meaning to one's family. Yes, that was difficult. But one got used to it, Mr Donovan.

But it did sort of get in the way of things. You can see that, can't you?

It wasn't all doom and gloom, though, by any means. Sylvia, for instance, was very pally with a chap who was billeted in a pub, so that gave us all a good excuse to go there and have a jolly time every so often. The landlord was very amicably disposed towards us all and it wasn't long before his darts and billiards room became a bit of a BP Social Club. We rarely said Bletchley Park. It was always BP. There was a rhyme going round amongst the Wrens at the time, something about, what was it? Oh yes, "I joined the Wrens to see the sea and what did I see? I saw BP."

Anyway, the point was, we always had a good evening there. It was just the tops to be able to let one's hair down. Quite literally, as it happened, in Sylvia's case who, it has to be said, always looked pretty shabby by the end of an evening. Looking back, I think the landlord, Don, I believe his name was, probably quietly ensured that we use this room, rather than the main part of the pub as there could be something of a stony silence when we walked in. There was an enormous suspicion of us amongst the locals, particularly those, I suppose, who weren't hosting any of us in their houses so weren't benefiting in any financial way from our arrival.

One friend, a gentleman, I stepped out with on a couple of occasions, dated I suppose you might say, was booed several times. I was flummoxed the first time it happened and had to have Nigel point out that it was because he was in civilian clothes and there was an erroneous assumption he was a conscientious objector. It was hard to disentangle that one, Mr Donovan, because once inside the Park you felt so completely and utterly part of the war and these people had no knowledge of the fact that Nigel had, in his own way, been responsible for the death of many Germans.

On very warm days groups of us would have our lunch by

the side of the lake. It had that kind of tranquillity that can take you quite away from everything, a little like a favourite piece of music, I suppose.

I think those were the times I felt as right as rain because it felt as far as anything from the war. The boffins, who were doing all the deciphering, all the really clever stuff, used to get in and have a swim. Quite a few of them were homosexuals. It sounds awful nowadays, but there were whispers and giggles. I suppose we didn't really understand. I think people thought they were a bit idiosyncratic. I remember we were watching them one lunchtime, having fun and generally letting off steam and one of the girls remarked on what a shame it was that none of them were interested in us because one or two had absolutely gorgeous bodies.

Quite a lot of cycling went on as well. Some of the intellectuals, being billeted out like myself, used to cycle in. It was obviously good exercise, but I think it kept their minds trim as well. Helped them think. I used to see one of them from the bus or on the odd time I walked in. He always looked very anxious. You could almost see the cogs twirling around. Looking back, I feel very privileged to have been so near such brilliance.

For my sins, I became a member of the BP Drama Group. One year, we put on a production of Shakespeare's *Much Ado about Nothing*, which was great fun. I've always loved the bickering between Beatrice and Benedict.

Anyway, I was one of the props people for the production and I had a huge crush on a young man who was in Dogberry's group of fools. I won't say his name because I've no idea where he is or what he's up to now, but he was so handsome. It was a thought, needless to say, that many of us girls shared and on the odd occasion he spoke to me, usually about something to do with the blinking props, I felt myself go completely scarlet and I could never produce a coherent answer to what he was asking of me. Very embarrassing. In my defence I was very young.

What really galled me and what was quite disheartening was that many of the mathematical boffins were superb at acting as well. It didn't seem fair that so much talent rested in one individual. Though I say it myself, the productions were very good. Some people, of course, went on to become famous actors. Susan, my comrade in properties, and I used to spend a lot of time scouring both Bletchley and the local area, via shops in particular, for worn-out bits of blackout material and we seemed to spend a lot of time dyeing bandages. It wasn't completely self-indulgent of us, you know, prancing on the stage and everything. Many said afterwards how much it had helped them cope with the tensions they were under. I believe the proceeds went to the services charities as well, which was a very good thing. You know, for their families.

The work? Well, I do find it very difficult to talk about. It's odd, really, I suppose it's always been something I thought I'd take to the grave with me. Bletchley was just so very, very secretive. I can't emphasise that enough. All those hundreds of people milling around and all we could ever talk about were matters that had nothing to do with the work we were doing. So, in that sense, no one ever knew one another. It was just, "Oh, I'm in Hut 3. Where are you? Hut 6." It was most extraordinary. And it made quite an impression on me, of course, because it was my first real job.

I do remember there was a sort of edginess, you might call it, between us civilians and the forces, though I did become quite friendly with a couple of Wrens and the three of us decided to put all that nonsense to one side and get on together. We were a bit like musketeers and adopted an "all for one" approach to things. We were, after all, working towards the same end. But it could be difficult. For instance, the drama group and the other things belonging to what was called the Recreational

Club were mainly for the forces. Susan and I were lucky to have got in on it. I think it was probably largely due to Lillian and Marjorie, my Wren friends. We all used to take ourselves off to the cinema, which was a great relief because you could truly forget about the work and lose yourself in a story. *The Man in Grey* was a particular favourite.

The thing I found most difficult, Mr Donovan, no, I'd really rather not call you John if you don't mind, was not being able to talk about anything to my parents and sister.

Yes, that really was very hard. And, being young and a bit naive, I suppose, I initially felt pretty insulted that anyone would think they would be indiscreet. I mean, we talked a lot with one another, but we all had very definite boundaries, if you like, and my mother was certainly not the sort of woman who discussed things with neighbours. I can't imagine her discussing much with friends, come to think of it. So I felt a little peeved, I must admit. But then someone, a little older and wiser, shall we say, pointed out that actually it was as much for their protection as anything and when I thought about the "do not" list again, the bit where it says, should there be an invasion, it's best that family know nothing due to Nazi brutality, well, I obviously wouldn't, for one moment, have wished to expose them to something so terrible. Nevertheless, it was hard. I had to invent a life for myself. And remember, of course, what I'd said on my last visit. It was like those Russian dolls, you see. You know, the ones you open up and there's a smaller one inside. I felt as though I was in a world of secrets within secrets. It all got extremely complicated at times and I wondered if I'd ever return to the life I once had with them. I began to find myself being thankful that, because of the amount of work we were expected to do, leave to go home was very infrequent and short-lived. Homesickness was replaced by a relief that ultimately cleverly disguised homesickness. But I got used to it. I suppose.

They all thought I'd landed a secretarial job that gave me quite a good salary. One of the consolations for my father was that, in the light of things, German wasn't a language one would want to be studying anyway and he was taken by the idea that I was doing administrative work for the navy, which was my story. He said he thought it was crucial war work and was very proud. "They're very lucky to have you," he said, which was very sweet. I think he eventually came round to the idea his daughter was doing her bit. My mother, bless her, was completely at sea when it came to understanding me in any shape or form. The thing the war did was to move women forwards in a way that was quite alien to her. And my sister just thought the whole thing was tops and spent a lot of time and energy trying to extract information from me. She was the one I had to be careful of. You know, nosey sisters and all that. But it has to be said, I began to enjoy not telling her anything.

I decided it was best if I told them I had a pokey little flat just outside London (I said I was outside so they didn't worry unnecessarily about the bombings) and because I was working for the navy, they could write to me through a box number (which they really were going to have to do) and that I was sharing the flat with a girl I knew through work. I suppose I didn't have to go into quite such an elaborate plot, but I thought, *Oh well, I'm not allowed to tell them about my work, so I might as well invent a private life for myself.* That way, I'd have something definite to talk about and have less chance of letting things slip. I gave Sylvia another name, I thought that would help me separate things out a little; my "flatmate" was Mary and we got on rather well, which was, of course, the absolute truth. We did get on well. One time I was talking about Mary and me enjoying ourselves in a pub and Joyce said she did like the sound of Mary but didn't think she seemed quite as nice as Hilary, who'd been my best friend at school. I said, but you haven't met Mary, you're making a judgement on a completely unfair premise, to which she declared she was completely bored with my life and waltzed off into the kitchen.

Then, for some reason, I think I must have been tired and not thinking very clearly, I suddenly told my parents that Beryl was very kind and she often made me a hot drink before I went up to bed. My mother, who was darning some socks and who I didn't think was listening properly, looked up from what she was doing and enquired, "Why do you go up to bed? I thought you lived in a flat!" Stop smiling, Mr Donovan.

Anyway, I wriggled out of it quite successfully and said I must have been thinking of this house. But I was jolly glad Joyce hadn't been listening. And it made me realise how careful I had to be. As I say, if I'm being honest, I came round to quite liking the challenge.

We did have a lovely evening that once in the pub. It was summer, July, I believe, and Sylvia and I managed to encourage a few others who were going to be off-duty to come along with us. We were all under a great deal of pressure, as you can imagine, Mr Donovan, working very long hours and having hardly any time off whatsoever. It was the evening I first met Malcolm properly. We weren't in the same hut and I'd only seen him walking by the lake once or twice.

We all met, I think there were probably about eight of us altogether, outside the main house, and got one of the buses into Stony Stratford. A charming place, Mr Donovan. Have you ever been there? You should. I think it's just your sort of place. We decided to go to the Cock and Bull there, which, given our clandestine lives and the tales we were telling, seemed rather appropriate. I thought Malcolm was quite a poppet. He was pretty lively for a mathematician. Many of them seemed very withdrawn and were quite difficult to get to know. A bit dour, if you like. Of course, none of us talked about our work, so we mainly discussed our lives before the war, our families, our interests, that sort of thing. Malcolm told us he'd always loved fishing because it helped him think. I remember he kept that up. He always said how good the fishing was after he'd returned from holiday and it invariably determined where he went.

So, as everyone began to warm up a bit, the evening became quite enjoyable. Aside from the looks we got from the local people who, as I've said, didn't like us very much. Well, Malcolm was explaining a bit about his fishing when we were ordering our drinks at the bar and one of the locals, an oldish man, looked him straight in the eye. He said it was a pity his son couldn't fish. Malcolm looked as if he was going to answer with some light-hearted remark but was stopped by the man. "Trouble is," said the man, "he's six foot under. He was doing his bit." And I remember very vividly, he put all his emphasis on "he". *He* was doing his bit. We all told Malcolm he was obviously grief-stricken and not to take it to heart. But I think he did. He certainly was quiet for the rest of the evening and was probably still mulling on the remark long after we'd all put it out of our minds.

Of course, I kept to the time I'd agreed with Fred and Beryl to return back to their house, although I put the key in the door much later than usual. About a quarter to eleven, I think it was. Malcolm had kindly walked me from the Park, which was quite a stretch, but he didn't live far from me. It wasn't completely an act of chivalry, Mr Donovan, though I was very glad of his company. No, he wasn't interested in me, so you can put that thought out of your mind.

Fred was still up when I got in, which was out of character. I had to go through the kitchen, where he used to sit, to go to the outside toilet and he was just sitting there reading his newspaper. He said he couldn't sleep and the war was preying on his mind, but I think he was waiting up for me, which was very touching, so I apologised for being so late. He waved it to one side and said he was glad I'd enjoyed myself. "I think we have to wherever we can. Otherwise we'd go mad, wouldn't we?" I said that certainly office typing could send you that way and he smiled.

I didn't see Malcolm for a little while after that evening. As I say, he was in a different hut. I can't impress on you enough the hundreds of people that were working there and once we were in our respective huts we were locked in almost like criminals, the only difference being that the lock was on our side. Sometimes, I ached to fling open the door and shout, "Hello from Hut 6," just for the hell of it. The one thing I can say is we did have decent lunch breaks and I would sit by the lake and use them to write home.

I still have one of my letters, in actual fact. I retrieved it from my mother's drawer after she died. It was all about Betty, the family cat, who'd apparently succumbed to fleas, and telling Joyce to crack on with her mathematics homework, a subject she hated. It was very light, mainly written to tell them I was all right.

Even after all this time, I still imagine them reading it. Me banging on about how tedious typing was, but it was war work, so I had to get on with it. Daddy would have read it out loud and have been extremely positive about everything. "Sounds like the old girl's enjoying herself," that sort of thing; my sister would feign boredom but would have been quite intrigued secretly, imagining what she was going to do with her life; and Mummy would have just listened very quietly. They were reading a lie, of course, Mr Donovan.

Things got a bit sticky once because Joyce wrote to me to ask if she could come and see me. It was a particularly hectic time at BP, getting time off was practically impossible and the asking for it very much frowned upon. So I had to put her off, which I felt terrible about, especially when she wrote back to me saying she couldn't possibly imagine what I was doing at weekends that was so important I didn't have a moment to see my sister. She said she was quite put off by her family at the present time, what with me wanting to have nothing to do with her and Mummy and Daddy making a complete mountain out of a molehill and not wanting her to travel in the first place. She did tend towards the dramatic, Mr Donovan, a fact that offered me a crumb of comfort, but I do think my work at BP affected our relationship quite badly, really. It did spoil things, I suppose. But we were all pretty much in the same boat at BP. When I was reading this sour response of Joyce's, I was sitting in the mess room of the mansion, eating one of their sponge puddings. I quite often took things to the mess to read. Malcolm came up and asked if he could sit next to me. I must have looked quite upset because he asked me if I was all right. I got a little teary and explained that my sister had sent me a rather upsetting letter. He was lovely and said how tricky he found all the secrecy as well. He reminded me of the good our work was doing and reiterated its importance. He was very kind that day, Mr Donovan, very kind indeed. And I tried to return the favour another time when something he was working on failed, but unfortunately, his mistake was irreversible.

★

When the war was over, I thought, what now? As wonderful as it was that we were now living in a peaceful time, I couldn't help but feel I had been given an extraordinary sense of purpose that would be very difficult to find elsewhere. Daddy tried to come to my rescue, bless him, and said he was quite happy for me to finish my university degree, but I felt I'd grown up too much and it would have been a rather retrograde step. It was years later that I did eventually decide to return to university, after Robert and I had moved to Birmingham.

I suppose, at that point, I was keen to go back to London

and actually spend time leading the life I would have had had there not been a war. You know, have a flat, do a job, even though it might be a boring one. But at least I'd have my own money and independence in a time of peace.

It was towards the end of the summer of 1945 when I finally left Bletchley. I packed my bags at Fred and Beryl's and we bade each other farewell, with an unspoken assumption we would probably never meet again. Fred said it had been a real pleasure having me there and Beryl just gave me a big hug, which was quite something as she wasn't a demonstrative sort of person. I felt very sad leaving them. They were, it has to be said, two of the kindest people I've ever met. I walked away from Bletchley with a letter from the Foreign Office tucked in my handbag. It told anybody who wished to employ me that I had been working for them but that my services were no longer required. It said I'd performed my duties satisfactorily but that the Official Secrets Act precluded them from being able to give any information as to what my duties had been. I remember thinking that I would never possess any such letter again.

I love coming to Dublin, Mr Donovan. It's such an old city. I love the Georgian architecture, the beautiful doorways with their shell-shaped windows and Robert says if you see the Ha'penny Bridge on a fine day and catch a perfect reflection, an eye watches over you. We've come here three times. We fell in love with it. I think what I like is its size. It's not as endless as other cities. Sometimes I feel paralysed by places where leaving seems almost an impossibility. I believe cities should exude a sense of freedom, don't you?

You asked about my friendship with Malcolm. Well, after Bletchley, it was a long time before I saw him again. If I'm being honest, I found it very difficult to adjust to life outside the Park. Living, as I had, amongst such intense secrecy, I found it tricky to just get along with people, I suppose you could say. Sylvia and I kept in touch, which was a lifeline really because, for quite a while, it was only Sylvia with whom I felt truly comfortable. Comrades in arms, I suppose you could say. I wrote to Susan, but I didn't get a reply and neither Sylvia nor I had an address for Malcolm. So I don't know what happened to him immediately after the war, Mr Donovan. It was quite a surprise to discover his family came from Dublin. I don't remember him ever talking about that. But not talking about things was part of our *raison d'être* and though some people did share their family lives, Malcolm never did. At least, not to my knowledge. And even when we met up again later on, he didn't talk to me about his personal life. Just fishing. It was always fishing. He was someone who concentrated on his work.

Shall we order some more drinks? I don't know about you, but I'm rather parched.

I'm sixty next year, you know, Mr Donovan. Thank you, that's most kind of you, but most of it is due to make-up and hair dye.

I do remember one remark of Malcolm's at Bletchley. He didn't say it openly so much as muttered it and I'm not sure he wanted anyone to hear. He'd had a couple of drinks, so the reliability of his words was perhaps questionable. They certainly struck me as quite odd. We were in the main house and it was late in the evening. Sylvia was saying something about how awful it would be if the Germans did win and we did have to live under their rule, like France and pretty much everywhere else. She made some quip about how I would have to teach them all the language and everybody laughed because they knew I'd come to Bletchley in order to avoid teaching anyone anything and they started pretending to be naughty children. Malcolm, though, was quite quiet. He picked up his glass and I caught him almost whisper as the beer reached for his mouth, "It's not the Germans we should be worried about." Nobody else heard because I'm sure if they had, they would have asked what he meant and I heard only because I turned to him in an attempt to try to get away from their teasing. As I said, it struck me as terribly odd, but I put it down to him being slightly worse for wear. He didn't know I'd heard. I'm certain of that because, at that moment, he didn't seem to be aware of anyone. There was an intensity about him sometimes that left him oblivious of his surroundings. I often thought teaching was quite a strange choice for him. And that, Mr Donovan, was how we met up again. The irony has never been lost on me, I can assure you.

I met Robert two years after the war ended and we married a year later. He was a lecturer in mathematics – I think Bletchley must have left me with a fascination for mathematicians – at Reading. When we married we bought a house there because Robert didn't want to commute. I was sad to leave London, prematurely as I saw it, but we've always been quite happy, so it was obviously the right decision. The only thing that niggles Robert just ever so slightly about me is my unwillingness to talk about my jobs. I suppose I should celebrate having a husband who's interested – let's face it, most husbands aren't – but I was so highly trained at Bletchley not to discuss anything, it's a very difficult habit to break. Robert likes talking about his students, his department, that sort of thing, but, I don't know, I just like to keep things separate and, if that's his only complaint, it's hardly one to worry about, is it? But there is quite a lot I don't tell him, I suppose. I overheard Karen, one of our daughters, saying to a friend once, "Mummy's a teacher. But you can't ask her about her job. You can't ask her what she did in the war, either. I don't think even Daddy knows." She's quite right, of course. Robert doesn't know. Do you find that strange? You can consider yourself very honoured, Mr Donovan.

We moved to Birmingham in 1961. Robert was offered a

professorship at the university. He was excited about it because Birmingham had a very good reputation and I was excited for him. The girls, Karen and Anne, were still at primary school, so, fortunately, hadn't yet reached that awkward age when they might have put up a lot of opposition to moving because of friends, so it wasn't bad timing. At that time I was still more or less a full-time mother, though I did do the odd bit of translating here and there, so I didn't have any reason not to move.

We moved to a house near the university and I found I settled better than I'd anticipated. This was not entirely unrelated to the fact that I knew we were able to afford a house we couldn't possibly have afforded in Reading. It certainly softened the blow of uprooting. Sylvia was sad at the time because I'd often gone up to see her in London. Well, we both were. But, as I said, we've managed to keep in touch. And Robert took to the university like a duck to water. I have to say, though, he talks in superlatives about Trinity and if he were that much younger, I'm sure he would be most interested in taking up a place here. Would they take to an English professor, do you think?

Are you married, Mr Donovan? Do you think your wife would tell you about things that had disturbed her at work?

I trained to be a teacher when Karen and Anne were teenagers. It's funny how life teases you, isn't it, and scratches at what you feel to be your most heartfelt beliefs? The person I'd been twenty-five years beforehand would have thrown up her hands in despair. "Teaching!" she would have exclaimed. I decided to use my German, it seemed a waste not to, and train for secondary-school education. I'd had my fill of messy play and small children with whom you can have only limited conversation.

After my training I had a horrible two years working in a diabolical school where learning seemed to be the last thing on anyone's mind, including the teachers, who were really just disciplinarians. But then I managed to get a highly coveted post at King Edward's High School for Girls. You probably haven't heard of it, but it's a very prestigious school and I was chuffed to bits to get the post. I sometimes think my time at Bletchley helped prepare me for what was quite a rigorous interview. And what was pleasurable about it was that it meant I was near the university, so Robert and I met up when our timetables would allow.

You may very well smile, Mr Donovan, because I'm getting to the part of my story that really interests you. For a detective, you seem a patient man or have I got police work all wrong? I suppose it's not always in your interests to rush things, is it? Did you say you were going to Australia because of all of this? I hope you like it. I've never been. I think the heat would be too much for me.

It was quite a shock to see Malcolm walking down the corridor of King Edward's that July afternoon. If I'm being honest, he hadn't aged well. More lines than I would have thought and hair that had receded more than I'd have expected. But then, over thirty years had passed since we'd last met and, in a way, the shock was recognising in Malcolm my own ageing. He said my name and stopped walking. I was pleased he'd recognised me. He said the usual, "Fancy meeting you here," and said he was being interviewed for a maths post. I knew the post, of course. A rather nasty woman, something of a bully, was leaving to move to Suffolk and my first thought was that Malcolm would be a very welcome change if he succeeded in getting it. So I was secretly quite tickled when I heard that Malcolm was joining us. *Another Bletchleyite*, I thought and it was as if thirty years had come to nought.

But it wasn't long before the penny dropped that getting to know Malcolm again wasn't going to be half as easy as I'd imagined it would be. He seemed, in many ways, quite changed. But when one is young one perhaps misses the nuances, wouldn't you say?

He had the reputation of being very good at his job and, from what I could gather, the headmistress seemed delighted she'd chosen him. I can't say he was well liked by the girls, he was a bit too quiet for them, but he certainly got results and, in their own way, I think the pupils respected him.

Sometimes, we would sit next to one another in the staff room and once he whispered that this wasn't Bletchley, was it, to which I just smiled but actually disagreed because in the classrooms, in the canteen and in the grounds, I felt there was much to remind me. But our conversations were fairly limited and pretty superficial and if I'd wanted a connection with my past, it was not to be found in Malcolm. All I knew really was that he had married but only for a short while. He didn't have children. He said that he and his wife had disagreed on many fundamental things. He never told me her name.

Other teachers, who saw us talking, sometimes asked me about him because they found him difficult to get to know, but I didn't tell them anything. How could I?

They asked me how I managed to get him to talk for as long as I did. Did I know him from somewhere else? Were we related? But, of course, I couldn't say anything. I've never spoken about Bletchley.

It's difficult for me to remember much immediately before the pub bombings, Mr Donovan. That night stole memories of previous ones and I've tried, as you suggested, to think about Malcolm's behaviour around that time, but it was six years ago now, Mr Donovan, and all that really comes to mind was my complete relief that Karen and Anne were no longer living in Birmingham because they may well have been in the city centre that night had they been so. Then I remember the trauma of the girls at school the following morning. Lessons were more or less cancelled as teachers spoke of girls not concentrating and wanting only to talk, quite understandably, about the horrific events of the night before. Three sixth formers were in the city centre that night, not far from the Tavern, and spoke of limbs lying on the pavements. And all the blood. They were out of sorts for some while afterwards. I remember it was the first time I'd ever truly appreciated my parents' agitation about Joyce and I living in London during the war.

I don't really know much about Ireland, Mr Donovan. Just Oliver Cromwell and the Potato Famine. It's always felt very complicated, something that to understand fully requires a great deal of time and enthusiasm and I can't profess to have either, I'm afraid, though I do love this city. It's very lovely. I told Malcolm once I didn't have the time to learn about the Troubles – I can't remember how the subject came up – and was met with an uncharacteristically frosty response.

"Well, you should," he said quite sternly. "You really should." I felt a little cross with this reprimand and wondered on what basis he felt he could be so high-minded. But, as I say, I didn't talk about him with anyone, so I couldn't discuss possible answers and he seemed too distracted for me to ask him. No, I didn't talk to anyone about him. He was still my Bletchley friend and I always felt close to him, in a funny sort of way.

When I thought about it and with the benefit of a certain detachment six years brings, I do remember he seemed to have quite a lot of sick leave that autumn term. And he did say something strange at our staff Christmas meal that year, a subdued affair, coming as it did, only a couple of weeks or so after the bombings. It was a little like Bletchley when we let our hair down. He'd drunk quite a bit and I offered him a lift home. I think he was embarrassed about me seeing where he lived because he said "no" very emphatically, it was a long way and he'd be absolutely fine, but I insisted he let me take him home and that he should come for his car the following morning. He became cross, as many people do when they've drunk too much, and told me, in a not very polite way, to mind my own business.

I'm so glad to be in Dublin again. It was Malcolm who suggested it to me one day when I said once that Robert and I didn't know where to go on holiday.

"You should try Dublin," he said, "and make sure you go to Christchurch Cathedral," which surprised me because I'd never thought of him as being religious in any way. But he was right. It is very impressive. The interior is exquisite and the link bridge, very unusual. When the foxgloves are out, it's particularly beautiful.

When Mrs Thompson, the headmistress, asked me to come into her room because a Chief Inspector from the Irish Police wanted to talk to me on the phone I was extremely taken aback and couldn't imagine what any policeman would want with me. It's fortuitous, isn't it, that when you rang Robert and I were soon due to visit Dublin? I find face-to-face conversations so much more satisfactory, don't you?

That night? Yes, well, I was undeterred by his behaviour, which reminded me of a boy in one of my classes, except that Malcolm had liquor inside him. I kept saying he wasn't safe to get himself home in any way, shape or form and eventually he agreed but wanted to come back to our house. I thought, well, if this was the compromise needed to ensure his safety, then so be it, though I was unclear as to why this should be the case and also concerned that, in his state, he might be indiscreet about Bletchley. As I said, never to that day and never, indeed, to this have I told my family about my time there and I was as determined as was earthly possible for that to remain unchanged. But nor did I want the fact that something horrible had happened to Malcolm on my conscience. On the way home I started talking about Bletchley, the main house, the huts, the pub at Stony Stratford. I thought if we got it out of our systems on the journey home, the subject would be done and dusted by the time we got to the house. He said he'd personally had a very successful time there and was proud of what he'd done, which was true to a large degree and I didn't think it fair to remind him in the state he was in that one or two things hadn't quite gone to plan under his watchful eye.

When we got home I set up the sofa in the living room. Both of our girls were home that weekend, you see, and the guestroom was full of Robert's research for a book he was working on. He kept thanking me over and over again. You know the way people are when they've had too much to drink, overly sorry, overly grateful. I said it was quite all right, told him where everything was and that I was very tired so I really must go to bed.

As I walked away, his hand grasped my wrist, which would have shaken me a great deal more had he not been drunk. Malcolm was not a tactile person.

"Please sit down, Isabel," he said quite insistently. We sat on the sofa.

"We were both in the huts?"

I nodded, thinking he was far drunker than I'd thought. He put his finger to his lips.

"So we don't talk?"

Again I nodded but was obviously wondering what this was all about. To be honest, I felt a little frightened. I'm not sure he even knew I was there. I didn't feel he was really talking to me.

"The bombings," he almost whispered. "Those six guys. It wasn't them. They're innocent. Completely."

I answered, and when I look back it was perhaps foolish to try to argue, that there was divided opinion about the six of them, but maybe this wasn't the time to get into it, but he wasn't listening and he just kept repeating their innocence. I couldn't stop him. It was almost like a mantra.

Are you saying you think he's in Australia, Mr Donovan? The last I saw of him was the end of the summer term the following year. No, I didn't think it was important to tell the police the confused rantings of a drunken man, Mr Donovan. What exactly had he told me? Just that he thought these people were innocent. So did a lot of people. I would have been wasting police time if I'd gone to them with this story. Surely you can see that and in answer to your question, no, I don't believe Malcolm has anything to do with the Irish Republican Army, Mr Donovan.

Have I told you everything? Absolutely, Mr Donovan. Absolutely.

A TOAST

1

Thank you everyone. It's wonderful to be here today in these beautiful surroundings with their truly splendid gardens, which were originally designed by that well-known eighteenth-century landscape artist... *(LOOK THAT UP)* I have never eaten such a delicious meal in such affluent surroundings and if my earnings remain at their current level, I doubt very much if I'll ever eat this way again. *(PAUSE, HOPEFULLY A LITTLE RIPPLE)* Thank you, Sally and Ian, for such generosity. *(PAUSE)*

I'm very honoured that Emily asked me to speak at her wedding. I've always thought of that "unaccustomed as I am" nonsense as being the domain of the other sex, even though I'm only thirty and live in a world where women do pretty much anything. I guess weddings in my mind still belong to that bastion of conservative thinking in which men and women have very clearly defined roles. *(PAUSE)*

I have known Emily for twenty years. We were at the same girls' school here in Hampshire – I won't say which one in case any of you are thinking of sending your daughters there and are completely put off doing so by our behaviour today. *(RIPPLE, FINGERS CROSSED)* The first time I saw her, Em was standing in a corridor looking lost. It was the third day of our first term there and that year she was in a different class to me, so I hadn't spoken to her before. I asked her if she was lost to which she said thank you, but she wasn't. She seemed as if she didn't particularly want to move and I remember walking away from her thinking what a strange girl she was. But I was intrigued nevertheless. *(SMILE AT EM)*

The next time we saw each other was in Miss Herbert's after-school choir – do you remember, Em? – and I was told off for talking to the other girls too much. I had wound up poor old Miss H quite a lot and thought the detention she gave me was fair in the circumstances, but she did shout very loudly and I remember I spotted you in the soprano section and noticed you were crying. I felt a lot worse about you, I can tell you, than I ever did about winding up Miss Herbert. Anyway, the good thing was I had the great common sense to go and apologise to you, we became firm friends and the rest, as they say, is history. *(PAUSE)*

It's customary on these occasions to come up with an anecdote, so I will do nothing to change that tradition.

Em, as some of you may know, is a very keen horse rider and Tim, as you also may realise, is as keen a walker. Put the two together, it seems, and disaster strikes *(RAISE EYEBROW, PAUSE)* for they met by virtually colliding into one another. I say virtually because a certain horse called Amelia was an important part of the equation. Tim tells the sad story of a man on foot, lost and thirsty, who sees a woman on a horse coming towards him. He asks her the way to the village he's trying to get to and as she tries to tell him, Amelia refuses to play ball – this is an intruder after all – and proceeds to keep circling round so Em's incapable of pointing in the right direction. Not content with that, Amelia misjudges one of her turns and, let's just say, her rear end and Tim's face are quite well known to one another. Of course, Em always professes Amelia's innocence. She does manage to tell Tim the way eventually and, during a few pleasantries, makes the fatal mistake of telling him she lives in the village he's just come from next to the church. A week or so later, an invitation to a party comes to Amelia from Tim. Immediate attraction is a very misguided thing, ladies and gentlemen, and can lead you to date a horse. *(PAUSE)*

Joking aside, I'm so glad Em and Tim did meet one another because I couldn't wish for a nicer bloke for my best friend than Tim, whose kindness and consideration for others seem to know no bounds. *(PAUSE)* I'm sure Em would join me in acknowledging that many of her recent successes are due in no small part to the self-confidence Tim has helped her find. *(PAUSE)*

Because, as those of you who knew the younger Em will realise – the toddler; the schoolgirl; even the university student – her current, smiley, outgoing personality is a relatively new phenomenon.

As I said, I felt far guiltier about her crying at our choir practice than I did about any upset I caused our teacher. Miss Herbert was a pretty resilient woman who could withstand quite a lot. Not so, our Em. *(PAUSE)*

I remember my mother's view of Em was that she was a timid little thing who was always very polite and she probably wondered why someone as robust as me would want to be your friend. But it took her a while to see, and she did see it, Em, that you were so much more than either of those things. She saw what I saw. Someone with a wicked sense of humour whose take on the world was both quirky and interesting. But, unfortunately, to those who knew you less well, who merely saw you from a distance, you seemed aloof and disdainful of those around you. Some girls told me they were a bit frightened of you; you had a sharp tongue, they said. I suppose I could see what they meant. Isn't it funny how we seem to adopt the very traits that have caused us so much pain? *(PAUSE)*

I suppose it's only in the last few years that I've started to get a glimpse into the life of Em's childhood. Don't get me wrong, ladies and gentlemen, I was part of it and spent many hours at the Frobrishers', but I never really saw Em's childhood, if that makes sense. *(PAUSE?)* Families are very good at tricking us, aren't they, and there's no reason on earth why the Frobrishers should be any different in this than the rest of us. And they are very good, ladies and gentlemen. At tricking us. And themselves. They are not exempt.

I looked forward to going round to Em's after school. Everybody seemed to get on so well; the food was delicious; a house full of homemade cakes and biscuits; a beautiful garden to play in, one that I can now appreciate equals anything we can see here today. The herbaceous border was always perfect. What, as they say, was not to like? A family that was at peace with itself, one that could even laugh at its own idiosyncrasies.

(AVOID LOOKING AT JAMES) It was Em's brother, James, who pointed out that, as a family, they had a habit of adopting cosy names for things: biscuits; clothing; home helps. It was something they usually did for visitors, he said, to convey an image to the onlooker of a fairytale from long ago. Did I remember? I said I did. We were sitting in a hospital corridor. It's a tradition also, on an occasion such as today, to give everyone a version of our family that we want them to see. How full of bonhomie we all are. How close. How loving. "What a lovely family" is a phrase we want to bask in, and we delight in the accepted view that things are going very well for us. Tired but fulfilled, we go to bed congratulating ourselves on what a wonderful day that was.

When James was in that hospital corridor, ladies and gentlemen, he couldn't possibly have thought he belonged to a lovely family. We were sitting on uncomfortable chairs drinking coffee. He said there were all sorts of different days, when the same kind of thing happened. Thinking about it, he recalled, there were probably hundreds. One afternoon he particularly remembered and when he thought of it, he felt sick, as he did when he thought of much of his childhood, because it was full of all the usual sneering between his parents and culminated in the all-too-familiar shouting. It started, as it often did, in the car. There was usually some recrimination about the road taken, followed by either a defensive remark about there being roadworks on the other road or passing the blame back by saying this was the chosen route because she always said how much she hated the other road, how depressing it was, all those high-rise flats, how she'd then go on about how she would never understand why councils built those monstrosities, but people had to be put somewhere, but that she hated them almost as much as she hated men. There would, he added, be copious amounts of swearing and he smiled as he said, "Of course I was a man, albeit only nine years old."

He said that some years ago, he'd tried to recall this specific afternoon with Em, but she didn't remember it that way. Instead, she said she quite liked the trips out on a Sunday afternoon. It was to look at houses, wasn't it, and she thought it was quite enjoyable looking inside other people's kitchens and living rooms. Anyway, she'd always read a good book in the back of the car. He said that was the trouble. Reading in a car always made him feel sick.

There were many visits to that hospital, ladies and gentlemen, and James talked, often in a corridor and often accompanied by a cup of coffee, about life at the Frobrishers, where there was an unwritten rule that his parents were the only ones who were allowed to express anything, whether it was anger, negativity about their children, or how their lives would be so much better had they not had James and Emily. But their children were not allowed to express anything. They shouldn't make a fuss. They certainly couldn't have any of the vast amount of alcohol that was drunk. Their job was to achieve, so at occasions such as these and in their daily contact with friends they could be seen to be producing something successful. They could, in effect, report a very good turnover. *(PAUSE)*

We were in a psychiatric hospital, ladies and gentlemen, and the person we were visiting was Em. I expect there are very few of you here who knew that. Families, ladies and gentlemen, and what they tell us. *(PAUSE)*

As you can see, though, Em has made a wonderful recovery. She has to be congratulated on overcoming such a tremendous struggle and all the things she had to try to come to terms with. Something, I know, she is still doing. Well done, Em. She is my best friend and along with Tim, James and everyone here, I would like to wish both Em and Tim a long and happy life together. Please could we all stand and raise our glasses. *(PAUSE)* To Em and Tim.

2

Thank you everyone. It's wonderful to be here today in these beautiful surroundings with their truly splendid gardens, which were originally designed by that well-known eighteenth-century landscape artist... *(LOOK THAT UP)* I have never eaten such a delicious meal in such affluent surroundings and if my earnings remain at their current level, I doubt very much if I'll ever eat this way again. *(PAUSE, HOPEFULLY A LITTLE RIPPLE)* Thank you, Sally and Ian, for such generosity. *(PAUSE)*

I'm very honoured that Emily asked me to speak at her wedding. I've always thought of that "unaccustomed as I am" nonsense as being the domain of the other sex, even though I'm only thirty and live in a world where women do pretty much anything. I guess weddings in my mind still belong to that bastion of conservative thinking in which men and women have clearly defined roles.

I have known Emily for twenty years. We were at the same girls' school here in Hampshire – I won't say which one in case any of you are thinking of sending your daughters there and are completely put off doing so by our behaviour today. *(RIPPLE, FINGERS CROSSED)* The first time I saw her, Emily was standing in a corridor looking lost. It was the third day of our first term there and that year she was in a different class to me, so I hadn't spoken to her before. I asked her if she was lost to which she said thank you, but she wasn't. She seemed as if she didn't particularly want to move and I remember walking away from her thinking what a strange girl she was. But I was intrigued nevertheless. *(SMILE AT EM)*

The next time we saw each other was in Miss Herbert's after-school choir – do you remember, Emily? – and I was told off for talking to the other girls too much. I had wound up poor old Miss H quite a lot and thought the detention she gave me was fair in the circumstances, but I saw that you were giving all this your full attention, so afterwards, I came up to you and said hello and we became firm friends. The rest, as they say, is history.

It's customary on these occasions to come up with an anecdote, so I will do nothing to change that tradition.

Emily, as some of you may know, is a very keen horse rider and Tim, as you also may realise, is as keen a walker. Put the two together, it seems, and disaster strikes *(RAISE EYEBROW, PAUSE)* for they met by virtually colliding into one another. I say virtually because a certain horse called Amelia was an important part of the equation. Tim tells the sad story of a man on foot, lost and thirsty, who sees a woman on a horse coming towards him. He asks her the way to the village he's trying to get to and as she tries to tell him, Amelia refuses to play ball – this is an intruder after all – and proceeds to keep circling round so Emily's incapable of pointing in the right direction. Not content with that, Amelia misjudges one of her turns and, let's just say, her rear end and Tim's face are quite well known to one another. Of course, Emily always professes Amelia's innocence. She does manage to tell Tim the way eventually and, during a few pleasantries, makes the fatal mistake of telling him she lives in the village he's just come from next to the church. A week or so later, an invitation to a party comes to Amelia from Tim. Immediate attraction is a very misguided thing, ladies and gentlemen, and can lead you to date a horse. *(PAUSE)*

Joking aside, I'm so glad Emily and Tim did meet one

another because I couldn't wish for a nicer bloke for my best friend than Tim, whose kindness and consideration for others seem to know no bounds. I'm sure Emily would join me in acknowledging that many of her recent successes are due in no small part to the self-confidence Tim has helped her find.

Indeed, Emily has come a long way since those days in the choir. They certainly didn't seem to put her off because, as most, if not all of us know, Emily has pursued a very successful career in music as a superb and extraordinarily talented violinist, whose rise has been quite phenomenal, given that she started playing again in earnest only about seven years ago. And now a member of the London Symphony Orchestra. *(PAUSE)*

Sally and Ian, you must be extremely proud of your little girl. I remember when she first expressed an interest in wanting to play the violin in our first year and I thought how little I envied her family. A beautiful instrument in the hands of an accomplished musician... *(PAUSE)* You must have had a lot of patience, all of you. I only heard Emily once she'd been playing for a while. We were all sitting around your living room *(LOOK AT SALLY AND IAN)* after one of Sally's scrumptious meals and Emily played a duet, with you on the piano, Ian. It was quite beautiful.

Her progression continued from school to university concerts and we all thought then that a promising career was only just round the corner, but, of course, Emily decided to travel for a couple of years and so her musical career lay in wait. It was at that time that I got to know her brother, James. I obviously can't cope without a Frobrisher in my life, ladies and gentlemen. *(GIVE EM AND JAMES A REASSURING LOOK)*

But after she'd finished travelling, Emily resumed her musical career, and she's been travelling with various orchestras ever since, so please feel free to test her geography.

Obviously, much of this has been helped, as Emily often says, by the support of others. She wanted me to thank her parents, so of course I will. Sally and Ian, I remember your home: the food was delicious; a house full of homemade cakes and biscuits; a garden to play in, one that I can now see equals anything we see here today. The herbaceous border was always perfect. And Emily says she always remembers the family outings on Sunday afternoons, in search of an even better house, if one could be found. Somewhere, there was an even more perfect herbaceous border, perhaps.

She would also like me to thank her brother, James, who I am more than happy to acknowledge, for Emily owes so much to him. Thank you, James. I know I wouldn't have the friend I have today were it not for the fact that she has such a loving and dedicated brother.

And, of course, there's Emily's husband. *(EMPHASISE AND WAIT FOR APPLAUSE)* When Tim first saw Emily on her horse, she had recently returned from her travels. Thank goodness he did, for he soon saw that Emily's passion lay in music and he gave her all the encouragement she needed to pick up the violin again.

In turn, Emily is terrific for Tim. He always says she has given him so much support in his career as an architect; he knows he can talk to her about anything and everything and that she is the kindest, most understanding person he has ever met. He loves watching her play in the orchestra and just wants to burst with pride. He is, he says, the luckiest man alive. *(PAUSE)* He also said he felt guilty about this and didn't want to cast her in a traditional role, but she is an absolutely fabulous cook. Everyone round to their house on their return from honeymoon. *(PAUSE)*

Ladies and gentlemen, I would like to wish Emily and Tim a long and happy life together. Please could we all stand and raise our glasses. *(PAUSE)* To Emily and Tim.

9.58 SECONDS

"When was that operation?" Hilda asked.

It wasn't really a question to him because she was looking into space with that expression she had that showed little awareness of anyone else, but Reg answered it anyway, probably because this had generally been his role, to plant words into a social void, whenever it was required. She'd never bothered much about awkward silences, which, he had to admit, he found unusual in a woman.

So he tried, "It was just before your mum died, wasn't it? When was that, then?"

The glance into space and an accompanying question had not been unfruitful.

"It was 1989," she said, completely ignoring the help she'd received, so it was touch and go as to whether she'd actually heard the words of her husband that had floated into the cloying air of the living room. "Of course, it was 1989," she repeated, pleased that her hard work had paid off. "Our Carol had just had Joshy. How could I have forgotten that?"

"Oh yeah, that's right. You were blubbing on the ward that you couldn't see your grandson." Reg turned to Amanda. "She was blubbing on the ward that she couldn't see her grandson. 'Joshua Jenkins,' you kept saying and you burst out crying every time you said his name. 'I want to see him, not be in this poxy hospital.'"

"I doubt if it was 'poxy' I said," she corrected and they both burst out laughing.

"Yeah, well, we've got company. We don't want to shock her, do we?"

"Nothing she hasn't heard before, is it, love?" and they all decided that laughter was the best response.

He continued. "I said, 'Stop saying his name, it's upsetting you.' She told me to bugger off, didn't you? Said, as I didn't understand, I might as well go home. I was more of a hindrance than a help, you said. Yes, it was 1989," he said and nodded, as if to say, "Write it down, it's correct and we might forget again in a minute."

He quite liked the look of this support worker – he thought that was what she called herself; these titles were all the same to him – they just needed some help. She seemed to know her way around a form. He hated the damned things. They always seemed to be trying to trip you up, asking similar things repeatedly, like they were checking you knew your story. He had visions of people sitting in offices, triumphant they'd got someone on question twelve, subsection four a. Not only that, his writing wasn't at all good. Over the years, he hadn't had it put to the test, except at school, where he'd been told he was a disaster and would never get a proper handle on it. Consequently, forms just mithered him. They had that effect on both of them. Hilda felt just the same, probably because she hadn't ever written much either, apart from birthday cards and shopping lists. He'd once asked her, "Is that how you spell cauliflower?" and they'd both had a good laugh as it had flummoxed both of them.

Anyway, this woman seemed to know what she was doing. She'd barely sat down before she'd written the first page of this form, though that was partly due to Hilda knowing her National Insurance number off by heart. He was proud of her for remembering.

"How do you know that?"

"I just do. It's the one with the letter at the end of it."

"Blimey, I don't know mine." He didn't even know about the letter. It got him thinking. How long would any of us have one of these numbers? Their son, Barry, had said only the other week when he came over, "Dad, twenty years' time, there won't even be an NHS." Mind you, our Barry could be a bit of a prophet of doom. He'd told them years ago their roof would collapse in the next twelve months, but it was OK. Admittedly, a tile had fallen off after a bad storm and landed on Sherlock, their last poodle, which had subsequently incurred a huge vet's bill, but that was all. Still.

"Oh, and there was that time when I was in for my knee." Hilda looked at him, so he came out of his reverie and cast aside thoughts of Sherlock not being much of a detective.

"Now that was 2006," he weighed in. "It was during the World Cup," and he laughed.

"He's laughing because he kept missing matches so he could come and see me in hospital." She looked at him with a mocking sternness. "You weren't laughing then," she chided.

"I was worried about you," and they both chuckled.

"So worried you kept going out. To the loo." She raised her eyebrows and twinkled at the woman, whose name they'd found out was Amanda. "He was ringing Barry, our son, to find out what the score was."

He smiled. She loved having the last word. But she was right. He had been heartbroken about the World Cup. *All this for a disabled parking badge*, he thought. *No wonder a lot of people give up.* Like George down the road. Couldn't make head nor tail of it, he'd said.

Hilda shuffled in her seat. "All right, love?" he checked because he could see she was in pain. Their lives revolved around discomfort. He said as much. He wanted Amanda to put this on the form. He wanted her to write, "We need a bloody badge because my wife's in bloody agony if she has to walk ten steps, tears streaming down her face and everything."

Or words to that effect. Surely that should be enough. He'd take Hilda up to that swanky council building and get the lot of them to watch her. "All right? Can we have our badge now, please?"

"Reg, where's my repeat prescription? Amanda wants my prescription. Where did we put it?"

He looked at that lovely face he'd adored all these years.

"Reg!" Hilda came running towards him, squealing with delight the whole time. He gave her a great big hug and lifted her little figure off the road. "You won't be able to lift me like that for very long," she laughed.

"Your prescription. Now where did that go?" He walked towards the dining table, where he shuffled a pile of papers that was strewn across a barely visible, tired and grey tablecloth. "It's not there. Now, where is it?"

It took him a good few minutes to locate the green and white slip of paper, which had somehow found its way to the top of their fridge – maybe it was when he'd put it down with the crossed-off shopping list the other day – and all the while he could hear Hilda filling what would otherwise have been an embarrassing silence with a story of one of their travels.

"We went to Hong Kong, you know. Have you ever been? No? Well, it's a fascinating place and I'm glad we did it, but oh my goodness, the sweat. It was so humid. Reg used to have a shower in the mornings, and then he'd go out and get a paper. He'd only be all of half an hour and he'd have to have another one when he got back. Sweat dripping all over him. But the views. We were very lucky. We had a room in the hotel that was very high up, so we could look down on all the buildings and the harbour. Amazing place, really, but if you don't like the heat…"

"Here it is," and he waved it in the air with a triumphant smile. "Two blummin' pages of it. Excuse my French."

He handed the prescription to Amanda.

"Take that, Mr or Mrs Council Worker," he announced defiantly. "You rattle with the stuff, don't you?"

Hilda nodded and wondered if Reg remembered he'd once found her sexy. The thought passed and she entered into the joke.

"Barry said we'd need a suitcase just for all of this," and she tapped the prescription. "The last time he said that, I told him he needn't worry. Fat chance of any travel." She laughed and Reg asked her what was funny.

"I was just thinking about what Beryl told us," and they both chuckled. "A friend of ours," she explained to Amanda, "pinged as she went through airport security. It was her replacement hip. She said it was the most excitement she'd ever got from a replacement anything. Even better than the replacement telly her children had got her that Christmas. 'Me, a criminal,' she said."

Amanda began writing down the list of medication on the form. She recognised the tablets for Hilda's heart condition and presumed the others were for her arthritic arms and legs, and the vertigo she'd described so vividly. How once it had resulted in a bleeding forehead outside the post office – what a commotion that had been – and then the time when she'd fallen here, in this lounge, and nearly done for the coffee table. She'd been on the floor for almost an hour when Reg came in from doing the shopping. "What you doing down there?" he'd said.

"Do this a lot, do you?" Hilda asked Amanda and when the reply came that she did, Hilda had got what she wanted. It wasn't just her, then.

"Have you lived here long?" The question was Amanda's, who was aware that another awkward silence was developing as she wrote the never-ending long words across the paper.

"Thirty-two years," they both said in unison, as if this was a question they were frequently asked. It was a natural question, but sometimes Reg felt he was like an exhibit in a museum.

"We bought the house just after they'd finished building it," he offered. "We were one of the first people in the street."

"Yes," joined in Hilda. "It was us, the Whites and the Robertsons and Joan. I think she was even here before us."

"Oh yes, she had a beautiful garden at the front by the time we moved in."

"We're the only ones left standing from the old brigade, though, aren't we?"

"Yep, the Robertsons moved about seven or eight years ago. That was when their daughter had a baby. Moved all the way to Manchester, didn't they? Then Bill and Joyce left because of Bill's job, and poor old Joan just recently."

As Amanda wrote on the form the long, depressing list of her everyday medication, Hilda wondered if there was anything else she did but take the stuff, wait to take it and recover from taking it. She looked closely at Reg, who she'd come to rely on for almost everything and though there was no doubt in her mind that she loved him still, there was something about their more recently established relationship with all of its inequalities that got under her skin. Her never-ending need, requirement almost, to be always grateful made her just the teensiest bit resentful. For instance, she could hardly point out that these days she preferred plain digestives as she found the milk ones too sweet or that she didn't really like the smell of lemons in her shower gel. It would have seemed churlish, spiteful even, when the poor bloke had bust a gut fighting wind and rain to get to the supermarket and then trundled around pushing a heavy trolley.

She turned her head because he was becoming aware she was staring at him and she didn't want him to ask her why. Instead, she looked out of the window at number thirty-five. Empty now because Joan, her friend of thirty years or more, had taken her last breath there. They'd carried her out two weeks last Tuesday at 2.45. Poor Joan. She'd missed her afternoon cuppa.

She watched Amanda, who was quietly reading out a question about how far she could walk, and thought, *God, has it come to this?* Yes, it did take her a quarter of an hour nearly to walk a hundred metres and all the while she was in bloody agony.

She thought about the athlete on those adverts. It had taken him 9.58 seconds to run the same distance. Crikey, it took her longer than that to get out of her chair.

Amanda went back to the question about the tablets and read them out just to check there was nothing she'd missed.

"No more medicine you take every day?"

"No, love. I'm not sure my body could take any more. Do you?"

There was a small smile from her inquisitor and probably an inner relief that she was in her own shoes and, when needed, could jump out of the chair she was sitting in quick as you like. All the questions were beginning to depress Hilda and she was beginning to seriously regret Reg and her children suggesting one of these badges for the car. If they hadn't, at least she'd be watching a bit of telly now, lost in a murder mystery she'd seen umpteen times before but only concentrating on the tablets the murderer had used.

"What's the name of your GP?"

"Dr Jones," she replied and she could see in her mind's eye the neatness of her doctor, a well-fitted dress hanging beautifully off her slim figure and hair pulled back into a bun so harshly it almost made Hilda want to wince. Everything about her was so taut it was barely possible to imagine her smile and there seemed to be an air of constant irritation about her. The effect this had on Hilda was to always, even though she promised herself the next time would be different, play down the pain or discomfort, which invariably led to a follow-up visit when the current medication wasn't working, coupled with a look of exasperation on her doctor's face that seemed to worsen each time. Sometimes, she felt she would be given a detention.

"Mr Southfield," she said, as she went through the names of hospital consultants she'd seen. *Funny how they become Mr again*, she thought. "He had a lovely way about him, didn't he?" She was looking at Reg, who saw no argument with that statement. "It was as if he had all the time in the world," she explained. "He obviously didn't, but he made you feel like he did." *Quite the opposite of sour face*, she mused. "Yes, a charming man. He almost apologised for taking up our time, didn't he? I wish they were all like that."

"Anyone else?" Amanda asked.

"There was that surgeon at the General, wasn't there? But I can't remember his name."

Reg was stumped as well. He couldn't even begin to think what that bloke's name was. It seemed such a long time ago. And they'd thrown away all the paperwork. Didn't think they'd ever need it again.

Hilda tried to think of a time without doctors and what her life was like when it seemed years since she'd last seen one. It was probably when the children had left home. She'd quite often had to go with one of them, but once they'd left, there was quite a bit of doctor-free time. That seemed an odd idea now and she smiled at the thought that months, if not years, had passed with no need to ring the surgery.

"How do I walk?" she repeated the question. "How long have you got?"

"You don't really, do you?" Reg joined in.

"Well, that's a bit of an exaggeration, but it's not a pretty sight," and she laughed because it was the better of two options.

"She needs me with her all the time, don't you?" He smiled at his wife, but it lacked an enthusiasm that would have been there had her dependency on him been less than it had become.

"I do have to have Reg with me, but I've also got my

walking frame." It was as if she were simultaneously confessing a crime and arguing extenuating circumstances. "And I have my wheelchair if we go out for the day anywhere."

"Yeah, I don't know where you'd be without them. Not that we go out much."

He said, "There's a pub over there. We could stop for a snifter."

"Don't be daft," she snorted. "We've only been walking an hour. What's the matter with you? We've got to earn it."

He looked disheartened and she overtook him, marching almost, not traipsing as he was, and well set up for at least the same distance again.

"Come on," she urged, looking back and beckoning him with her left hand. "Get a move on."

"Don't know what you're made of," he muttered as they made their way through the village and out into the countryside.

She laughed. "Oh, stop your moaning. I know for a fact there's another pub on the other side of that hill. We'll be there before closing."

"Over that hill?" he asked incredulously. The sun was beating down, with only the occasional cloud to shield them.

"We'll make it in no time," she said. "There before two."

The questions kept coming. Maybe Reg could see she was getting tired because he'd started to answer for her.

"No, you can't walk upstairs, can you? We've got a stairlift. I help her in, don't I?" His head moved quickly from side to side, as if he felt preyed upon and was keeping watch. "Then you just sit there and it does the job, doesn't it? 'Going up, Home Furnishings, Cooking and Dining,' I say, don't I?" Yes, he did. Sometimes, it was Electricals, particularly if the lift was making a funny noise that day; other times it was Sport and Leisure, something she thought was a bit insensitive in the circumstances.

Do people really read this? she thought. *And if they do, what do they think? Silly old woman? Is she making this up? Or God how awful, who'd live like that?*

"There was that time in the shopping centre." Reg was still doing the work, but she knew what he was talking about. She had lost her balance. All of a sudden, she'd come over dizzy and had lost her temper with him because she was so frightened. He was fussing and she hated that. She hated him asking her lots of questions when she was in trouble. She was like a little animal and wanted to be on her own, so that day she'd told him that she'd had an altercation with a kid's fizzy drink. He hadn't believed her and he knew she knew that, but their charade was better than facing the fact that something was wrong, especially as, up to then, they'd had a lovely time looking for Joshua's birthday present. What had they bought him?

"The next questions are about your arms," Amanda said, turning the page of the form over and then turning to Hilda with pen poised to write.

It was all something to do with reaching to put money in a parking meter. Fed up with saying she couldn't do things, Hilda just showed both of them how painful it was to move her arms more than a couple of inches above her lap. Her face creased up and Reg leaned over and carefully put her arms safely back where they'd been. Amanda wrote what Hilda supposed was the vision she saw before her.

"I do get breathless, yes," she answered, relieved that she'd been told they were nearly done. "After only about seven or eight steps." It sometimes felt as though she'd drunk in the worries of the world and couldn't cope with them, and she'd have to stop and let her body catch up. She remembered Joan telling her off a number of years ago. "The trouble with you, Hilda, is that you take in everyone else's woes. 'Breathe out,' she'd say. 'Blow them away. Let them all get on with it.'" Her body seemed to be finally rebelling, probably because she'd never been one for taking advice. "Told you so," it was now saying and each time she had to stop, it gave out a self-satisfied laugh.

They'd walked at least a couple of miles, sometimes breaking into a run. It wasn't Agnes's nature to take things slowly. She enjoyed speeding through life quite literally and hardly ever saw what she was passing. It was crucial to her that her legs moved as fast as they could and Hilda never saw her as happy as when she was on the move. They both loved it and on a sunny day would spend most of it racing against one another, though the competition was always fun and never unfriendly. That afternoon, they were going to do what they often did on a Sunday, which was to take as many apples as they could from Mr Grey's garden. It was a favourite occupation, the element of danger modified somewhat by Mr Grey's inability to run very fast, even if he did see them, which he usually didn't. They wore dresses with big pockets and, between them, managed to escape with around twenty fine Cox's. That particular afternoon, a beautiful late summer's day, filled with that slightly melancholy air suggesting things were coming to an end, they hadn't bargained for Mr Grey's son, Alfred. As they finished bundling the last apples away, an unfamiliar voice roared from Mr Grey's dilapidated shed. They were already on the move to "What do you think you're doing?" and with the loss of one or two of the fruit and no enthusiasm for the sprint ahead, Hilda ran as fast as she'd ever done before, convinced she could never reach the gate before the voice would take hold of her and give her a good hiding.

The questions ended. She finally took Joan's advice and let out a deep sigh. The only thing that remained was for her to give permission for any of these officials to talk to Reg, if necessary. Who else would they talk to? Of course that was OK.

She took the pen off Amanda, who was passing it over to her, and as she signed her name, she suddenly felt as though some things had disappeared forever.

THE £10 NOTE

She never really knew her dad. So often, she'd make him up in her mind's eye. And usually, within that often, he'd look like one of those American movie stars she'd heard her mum and Auntie Betty talking about. All tall, dark, handsome and Brylcreemed. She'd seen the odd photo, of course, and the man her mum showed her looked nothing like that. Every part of the man in these photos seemed to be round: round face; round belly; even round, podgy fingers, which she particularly noticed in the photo where he had her on his lap. The chubby digits were holding one another, forming a human safety belt for her own rotund eight-month belly. Nothing about him suggested a movie star hero. She couldn't help feeling a bit disappointed. And though he had the appearance of one of the kindest, warmest human beings she'd ever seen captured in black and white, these weren't qualities an eleven year old was looking for in a father. She wanted a bit of glamour so she could show him off.

"This is my dad," she would've told Madge and Ada, her best friends at school, and watch their eyes widen in amazement that anyone as plain as she was could've been fathered by something as handsome as Arthur Gladstone. But, unfortunately, the man in the photo available to her suited the job perfectly. By the time she reached the grand old age of eleven he'd have been even rounder and his shiny skin lined with the odd ageing river trickling down his face. A plain, eleven year old standing next to a plump, pretty non-descript-looking bloke would've looked smashing together, suitable as bubble and squeak, and everyone who saw this photo would've observed that father and daughter was the obvious relationship.

But in her fantasy world, there he was. Long, lean, posh, complete with trilby hat and winning smile. She absolutely adored her fantasy world. It was so much more enjoyable than her real one.

And when she thought of that, of course, she felt guilty for ever having the temerity to wish her father was anything other than he had been. Because it wasn't a film star she wanted. It was a father.

"Killed?" If she'd heard a stupid classmate say that once, she'd heard it a hundred times, though only a few had taken it any further, daring her to be nice to them when her expression defied the odds. Eric, the cheeky chappie – she could see that now, but at the time she hadn't liked him one bit – said, "What's that?" He wasn't very bright, Eric, and when she saw him years later, milk bottles in hand, delivering to grumpy Mrs Hartley, she could see that eight or nine more years of education hadn't really changed things because Mrs H was saying she never had milk on a Tuesday.

For years she hadn't cared for cars. Not the noise of them, the smell of them; the damned petrol always made her feel sick, and she couldn't for the life of her understand why so many men seemed to like the look of them more than they did a beautiful woman. Ah, beauty. Well, there's the rub. Give her a bouquet of flowers any day. Now there's a thing of beauty. So it wasn't as if she hated everything to do with her dad dying. Because every year on 17th March, which apparently was her dad's birthday, their mum took them to his grave to put down a bunch of flowers, usually daffodils as they were all she could afford, though once or twice she did remember her mum buying a few roses. And yet she still loved flowers, even though they were brought into the house as a grim reminder of everything she and her brother lacked in life. One year, this solemn family occasion coincided with Easter and she was old enough to remember the vicar, whose name she forgot, saying something about her father being blessed having his family visit at such an important time in the holy calendar and she couldn't help thinking he was one of the most idiotic adults she'd ever come across. He did her a favour, though, because when she later became a nurse she was always most careful what she said to any family member who knew that neither medication nor doctors and nurses were going to be any aid to their relative's predicament.

Did she ever feel angry at the cards they'd been dealt? She didn't think so. It wasn't like nowadays where everyone's either angry or crying. Crikey, she got right fed up with people bursting into tears whenever they were on telly these days. No, it wasn't like that then. And it wasn't as if she really knew her dad. She'd never spoken a word to him because he died before she could talk. She was eleven and a half months when he stepped off the pavement and that bloody bloke – it was a bloke, probably one of those who loved the look of his car – went bang into him and her dad could no longer talk to her.

Their mum used to go on a bit about the good old days when they were of an age to appreciate what she was saying. Not just good in that a lovely man had been taken from them, though that went without saying, because the one thing she knew about her mum was that she loved her dad and she couldn't ever imagine her mum loving anyone who wasn't worthy of that love. No, the good old days were also spoken about in relation to the material comfort they'd all enjoyed under the umbrella of dad's good wage. How they could have tinned salmon for the odd sandwich and not always have to rely on paste, though of course she never benefited from this, not having much in the way of teeth before he died, or they could look forward to the odd day out and, occasionally, a little holiday. Sometimes, she slightly disliked her brother for having basked in the glory of the good old days more than she had. Being eight years older, he would sometimes chime in with their mum and agree that that picnic they'd had by the river had, indeed, been very nice.

About nine £10 notes had arrived and been used over nine Christmases before she started to ask questions about them. So she and her brother had had nine treats because of each note. The first few, of course, she wouldn't have a clue about. Her memory couldn't possibly stretch back that far. But she did remember the Christmas when she was about six and a glorious doll Santa had given her who she called Lucy. She told Lucy lots. Lucy knew practically everything about her. And she knew her secret thoughts as well. Things that she wouldn't have ever told anyone else because it would've seemed, well, disloyal really. Like how she wished she had a happier mum. And one that didn't have to go out and clean everybody else's house as well as theirs. Other mums seemed to giggle quite a bit. Hilda's mum never seemed to do anything else, though she did think sometimes Hilda got a bit embarrassed by it. But her mum never seemed to smile much, or hum, or do anything that might have indicated to her and her brother that things were OK. Her mum didn't seem to ever want flowers in the house. She didn't really understand that, because she and Lucy agreed that flowers were pretty and they made you smile.

So there was Lucy. Then there was the skipping rope, which gave her hours of fun. It made her smile thinking of the first time she'd got to fifty skips without her ankles and the rope intermingling. And the first time she got to twenty on the fast skips. It must have driven her mum bonkers when it was raining and she'd be skipping in the house. There'd be the sullen or exasperated look and sometimes her mum said, "Please, Vera," and touch her forehead, but she never got cross.

Then, when she was twelve, she got her first bicycle and, by that time, she just about cottoned on to the fact that it wasn't Santa who'd given it to her. So she felt a bit confused because if her mum had communicated anything it was that there wasn't much in the way of money to go around. "No, we can't afford that", "Clean your plate because there's nothing else when that's gone", "I'm sorry, Vera, but we can't go to the cinema, do you know how much that would be for all of us?" were sentences she was familiar with and she'd got used to them as much as she'd got used to getting a cold; they were never welcome, but they were a fact of life.

She was so very excited, but she couldn't help herself. "How?" she tentatively asked.

"Never you mind," had been her mum's initial response, but when this hadn't worked because she knew her daughter was cleverer than that, "You can save quite a bit when you set your mind to it, you know." But she knew her mum was lying. And she was pretty sure it wasn't her brother, who by this time was bringing in money from the colliery but who gave her his own present. Anyway, he couldn't have kept a secret to save his life. She'd have soon known that he'd chipped in to buy her a bicycle.

So she just accepted the way things were and got on with it. She loved her bicycle because it meant she could get away from both her mum and brother if the fancy took her and ride off into a world where no one could interrupt her or expect anything from her. She could take a deep breath. The bicycle, it turned out, was a bit of a lifeline. And luckily, her mum didn't seem to worry about her in the way other mums seemed to, so she was free to go off, providing she'd done her schoolwork, as often as she liked and she liked to do it a lot. She became, unusually, quite the envy of girls like Hilda, who could barely move from the front door without her giggling mum wanting to know exactly where she was going and when she'd be back.

One day, when she'd been out on her bicycle for over a couple of hours taking in the lovely fresh air rather than the words of others and, as a result, had in her a confidence that the constraints of the rules of the house didn't allow, she took off her clips and, pretending she didn't care, asked her brother where he thought their mum's money came from when it came to Christmas.

He looked up from his paper. He loved the local rag.

"We don't know for sure," he answered.

It always riled her when he said "we", as if he and their mum were in some kind of secret society together, gradually letting out information to her when they deemed fit. At least the air had given her the guts to stare him out.

"But we think" – now he was doing it deliberately – "that it might be the bloke."

He didn't have to say any more. They all knew "the bloke" was the… well, the b—, the bloke who'd shattered their lives.

She wasn't sure if she was curious or furious. She was very shocked, but it didn't stop her asking questions. How did they know? How did their mum get the money? How did he know where they lived? Her brother said he was tired and he didn't want to talk about it and when, in her confusion, she said, "Do you mean he's come to the house?" because he had said something about this envelope with the £10 note in never having any writing on it, he told her to shut up and go away. He'd never spoken to her like that before and he never did again, though equally he never apologised for his outburst.

She felt a bit sick. And, to her dismay, she suddenly felt differently about her beloved bicycle. And, for that matter, Lucy and the skipping rope. It all felt mighty unfair and she was cross with herself for asking the questions because, if she hadn't, she could've cycled blissfully on for years to come and never been any the wiser. Maybe her brother and her mum knew her better than she knew herself.

But curiosity was always going to be her downfall. Like on the ward rounds when she had this habit she couldn't seem to break of asking one question beyond what was expected of the doctor and was told by the very worst sort that hers was to do, not to ask, by the medium sort the answer but with great irritability, and by the best the answer as if he, and it was generally, if not always, a "he" in her day, was enthralled that she was so interested and even a smile sometimes came her way.

She remembered the first time she got told off by one of the very worst sort of doctors for apparently misunderstanding his instructions from the day before, though to this day she was sure the error was on his side; she took refuge in the staff kitchen as soon as she could. It was night-time, probably about two in the morning, and all the patients' flowers from the ward were still lying in a bucket, looking for all the world as if nobody cared about them. She reached high up and opened the pale yellow cupboard door where they kept the vases. It was very quiet apart from the odd snore or the occasional cough, and the moon cast its light on the table. She arranged the roses for Mrs Thomas – she had a lovely husband; the pink carnations for Miss Ford, whose mum and dad had been so worried about her, but she was going to be all right; and the freesias, how grand they smelt, for Mrs Harris, whose niece had said how much she loved them. She thought they might be her favourite flowers too.

She didn't ride her bike for quite a few months after that conversation with her brother, though in the long run she got so fed up hanging endlessly around the house that she took up with it again. So much for principles. Lucy and the skipping rope had already been put in a box marked "charity shop", though no one had ever taken them to one.

At a time when she was trying to find boyfriends who didn't seem to be trying very hard to find her, she found herself looking out of her bedroom window one evening, wishing, as she often did, that someone could've taken her out, like boys had Madge and Ada and Hilda, and given her a kiss under some mistletoe. It was 21st December, dry, crisp, everything you wanted from a Christmassy night. Even the moon was doing its bit. It was chilly in her bedroom, so she put another sweater on.

Her mum called out, "Vera, do you want a hot milk?"

Oh well, if it had to be hot milk, it had to be hot milk. "Yes, thanks, I'll be down in a minute."

A bloke got out of a very shiny big car. She could tell it was shiny because the moonlight showed its sparkle, but the night didn't give away its colour. But it looked new. Not one of those second-hand ones one of her friends' dads had, though they thought they were mighty lucky to have that. No, this one had a look about it that hadn't seen many journeys; you could almost smell its newness.

He was very smartly dressed, a darkish suit, again she couldn't tell exactly what colour, and a trilby hat. She thought him extremely suave, though he was someone her mum would've called a smarmy kind of bloke. It was true, there was something about him you probably shouldn't trust. Nevertheless.

But she then started to feel herself go very hot. The man was walking towards their house. She could see that he had an envelope in his hand.

"Your milk's ready," her mum called, but she wasn't about to miss this. She had to see this. Sure enough, the man, no, the bloke, the Bloke, came up to their door and hastily, very hastily, pushed the envelope through the flap. She could hear it drop onto the mat, though her mum probably couldn't hear a thing because she had her music playing quite loud. Some classical concert on the radio.

"Vera!"

"I'm just coming," she said, barely thinking about the hot milk and almost solely concentrating on the bloke who was quickly getting into his car. He'd taken off his hat and she could just about see through the window his shiny, Brylcreemed hair.

She felt really panicky. She wanted to run down and shout at him. But she didn't. She was rooted to the spot.

Her mum was quite cross when she finally appeared as the milk was now reduced to lukewarm. She'd passed the mat on the way and she gave the envelope to her mum who just took it from her without a word.

She took her milk upstairs and when she looked out of her window, the bloke was still there. He was gazing at their house, as if its appearance mesmerised him in some way.

She stared at him, gripped by a similar force, until they just caught sight of one another and he immediately started up his shiny car and was away before she knew it.

She got herself a hot milk. Seventy-five years later and she still loved one at night. She sat down and looked at Dad's Ted, scruffy as anything, witness to a war and a house that got bombed over the road, to her marriage to Stanley, to their lively children, Joyce, Bob and Alan, who he'd barely survived, and to her increasing old age. Well, he couldn't talk. He was as old as she was. She knew this because her mum told her that her dad had given it to her when she was six months old.

A BROKEN HEART IN
TWO LANGUAGES

Her heartbreak could often be seen on the painted faces of her friends. Or in her photos. For instance, the small street where she lived, a perfect image for the tourist guide, with its warmly lit melancholic antiquity, held many of her tears. If she'd kept every one of them, they would have definitely filled a bucket and she could have added paints, then frozen and sculpted them. Perhaps into one gigantic teardrop. Instead, words that could be spoken to a counsellor or a sympathetic ear were brush strokes on the faces of willing friends. Sometimes, a wintry scene full of icicles and crisp branches or an animal, maybe a tiger, who would walk her back towards her childhood, and she would be standing excitedly, at some level knowing everything was in front of her, in that purple and pink woollen dress, her face a painted cat. If only she could be that little girl again, making the cat smile so her mum could take a photo to look back on when she was as old as she was now. She wanted to revisit a time when she didn't know what heartbreak was; she just bawled her eyes out if someone upset her or didn't let her do what she wanted. She didn't know then what grief was, even though crying and crying and crying was her response to being told she would never see her favourite wellies again because some arse had stolen their car and the two little protectors of her feet were sitting, minding their own business, on the back shelf. She couldn't understand why she wouldn't see them anymore and sobbing was the only thing she knew.

Today, she'd woken up, as she usually did, crying, but twenty years on from the wellies, she knew this was heartbreak. She understood this was grief because, as with the wellies, she knew she would never see her boyfriend again. Someone had stolen him. She, too, was on the back shelf and could be put in the bin. So here she was every morning and for much of every day, with a whirling stomach, metaphorical vomit in her throat and a feeling she was freefalling without a parachute. It was as if there was no one else on the planet or her freefall had taken her somewhere else, where the beings that were walking about had no idea of what she was feeling because they were laughing and talking. She thought she must be mad. Certainly, too barmy for the work required to get from five minutes to ten minutes past the hour. Nobody could offer any comfort and it would be quite a while before she truly appreciated how much they listened. One day, though, she had found something of an intermission in her crying and panic. She picked up a brush that lay on what was laughingly called her work table. She hadn't been to college for a while. The incessant crying had put paid to that. She put some black paint on it and passed the brush up and down a scrap of paper, then left and right. She did this a few more times and found she was mildly pleased with what she saw. Her heartbreak, no matter what else it had done, had been singularly unsuccessful in depriving her of artistic ability.

She couldn't return to England. She'd come to realise that as she carefully painted, each stroke just gently slowing down her heartbeat a little every time. He'd ended the relationship while they were miles apart, but it had been a cold and unceremonious dumping of her that relied on a phone and a text message and, as such, had, if anything, encouraged her determination to stay where she was, even as she sobbed. While her brushes changed people's faces, something she particularly liked doing, her mind whirled around mistakes she'd made. It was true she could have texted replies when her instinct had told her responses weren't needed, but, even though her time away was short, the distance was too much for him. He wasn't someone who was used to distances when they involved people close to him. So probably she should have seen that with her in France and him in England the relationship was destined to fail. She would have to go back to her course soon or she would fail that as well. She just wanted to be quiet, so painting pictures and faces was just the job.

In the English café things were different. In the English café people talked, though this being an English café conversation was discreet. It was a bookshop too, so many just read and as comfy chairs were provided, some could be there for quite a while, the hours ticking by without them realising. There were days when she found the peace comforting; in her broken state she found the undemanding company of others reassuring, but at other times this quiet disconnection allowed her to bathe in broken-hearted thought and she'd conclude that a voice demanding her attention or a busy road would have proved to be a useful distraction. She sat at the small round table on an equally round chair, waiting for the person she was going to meet and glad that this time it was Madame Maes, for this eighty-six year old certainly had the ability to distract her.

The café called itself the English Café; it wasn't just a name adopted by locals who thought it an obvious name for a place that put tea above coffee. A quaint sign of a teapot, in Union Jack costume, hung over the heads of passers-by, perfectly still or wafting to and fro if a breeze took hold. It sold tea of sorts imaginable and not quite so, with plants and fruits proud to stand alone or dancing with one another to produce wonderfully different flavours and cakes, generally of the sponge and filling variety, which looked far too delicious to remain where they were. The books were written, without exception, in English, and she found she was greatly comforted by this familiarity. It struck a homesick note, as if someone had tapped her shoulder and uttered, "Mind the gap."

Madame Maes had had one thing in common with Martha. She wished to know another language better. They were both aiming for what they agreed was a workable fluency. For madame, it had largely something to do with the war, an everlasting gratitude to English speakers, who had saved her country and returned her family to a way of life that was bearable and lacking in fear. For Martha, she had always loved this country, its art and fashion and culture, and hoped, if she ever felt better, she would love it again. They agreed, therefore, to speak half of each meeting using the other's language and there was usually a natural point at which the changeover took place.

The bell of the shop door tinkled and madame entered, waving as soon as she spotted her friend. It wasn't unkind to say she looked like a witch because this was truly the kind of witch you would want to get to know. There was a difficulty in not thinking it when even taking a cursory glance. A lithe, slender figure that, though it was in its eighties, could, more than likely, nip up a mountain smartly or cycle as quickly as an Olympian. At the very least, give them a run for their money. She had long white hair that fell not only downwards onto a slightly tatty cardigan but also had a way of travelling outwards, a smile that showed barely any teeth while those on view rose or fell individually like separate stalagmites or stalactites in a dark cave, these a musty yellow, peppered with little black spots. Her eyes were dark and stared at everyone inquisitively, but far from fearful; they were like the promise of a warm fire from black coals, encouraging the subject of her attention to feel alive and keen to deliver, probably because there was rarely anyone else who expressed such an interest in what they were about to say. Martha smiled to herself as she came nearer and thought a broomstick should, without doubt, be madame's transport of choice. She got up, walked towards where her French friend was standing by the counter and offered to buy her a cup of tea. But her heart was heavy. Like every conversation, this would be hard work and the problem was entirely hers for Mme Maes was easy company.

Mme Maes adored coming here, and looked forward to each visit as she might a holiday, because everything about it offered a contrast to her traffic-noisy flat, with its quiet tones and delicate teacups and the fact that reading was one of its main *raisons d'être*. Her own life hadn't had as many books in it as she would have wished, which had been brought on by a combination of reasons, some of her own making, like laziness or a desire to fit in too much with those who had no desire to pick up a book. But she loved a challenge and was both enthralled and amused at her inability to understand many of the titles, which wasn't because she couldn't understand the words but was unaware of the cultural nuances.

"Please may I have a cup of Earl Grey tea?" she answered in perfect English and with great ceremony. She enjoyed the eccentricity of a tea that not only paired up with the English aristocracy but had a delicate perfume, which could be properly enjoyed only, she'd always thought, as an afternoon delight. "Yes," she then said, "Thank you," when Martha asked if she would like a slice of cake. "A piece of Victoria Sponge would be beautiful," and her thoughts turned to their queen of that name and dirty, Dickensian streets, many of which she now suspected had been made-over and looked nothing of the sort. She looked at Martha who might as well have had on a T-shirt with "I have a broken heart" written all over it. Her eyes were teary and her lips quivered. Thank God she was too old for all of that. There were some things that adorned younger adulthood that she'd put in the rubbish bin long ago and never regretted a minute of it.

They sat down. She offered Martha some of the sponge but wasn't surprised when her friend declined. Broken hearts had never given her an appetite. She would attempt to take Martha's mind to other thoughts, hard though that might be. In French she said, before not quite finishing her first delicious mouthful, "Who do you think's going to be a film star?" They invariably began in madame's language as she maintained she always had much to tell and wanted to make sure she got it out before she forgot it. Today was no exception.

"You, madame?" Martha replied, her mouth moving slightly upwards, though it remained uncertain.

"Get away with you, my dear friend," the octogenarian retorted, but she was enjoying the thought. "No, Hercule," she continued with great enthusiasm.

"Who?" Martha couldn't think of a Hercule that both she and madame knew. There was the owner of the patisserie they liked, but she was certain he was Raoul. And even if Hercule had been his name, it wouldn't have suited him. There was the guy who came here who madame was convinced was a spy working for the British on the basis that he'd been visiting the café more often since a local newspaper had mentioned how vulnerable French cities had become to the threat of terrorism and he asked very odd questions like had she walked to the café by the underground tunnel too small for humans? She'd suggested to madame that probably the monsieur had mental health problems, something she'd quickly dismissed, telling her quite curtly that madness wasn't the answer to everything. She was sure it wasn't. And she was even more certain this wasn't the guy destined for stardom.

She shrugged. This was too much like hard work. Didn't madame know the pain she was in? How relevant was this conversation to anything she was experiencing? She hated this effort. She didn't care. She really didn't care. She thought madame could distract her, but she was wrong. This was just barmy. She drank some tea and tried to calm herself. The state she was in had nothing to do with madame and everything to do with that arsehole, so she tried to make an effort, even though every word fell from her lips as heavy as a case of books. She said she didn't think it was either Raoul or the guy they'd seen here. Who else did they both know?

"We know Madame Laurent," she replied and she gently prodded Martha's shoulder, as she sometimes did. It was a signal to her that she knew something Martha didn't. Then she did as she often did and held her hands tightly against her ears and asked her please not to tell if she'd already found the fact out on the Facebook thingy. Couldn't an eighty-six year old ever be the first to convey news?

"Madame Laurent?" she asked, feeling weary of madame's penchant for quizzes as a form of conversation.

Madame was tickled. Hah! She did know something before a computer. "But not her. Think who is always with madame."

She thought for a few seconds and then it came to her. "Oh." She smiled at her French friend for she had solved the mystery.

Madame nodded and said, "Woof, woof." It was pretty much the same in both languages.

"But how?" she continued, now genuinely curious as to how the Labrador had succeeded where thousands had failed.

"I don't know," madame replied. "You'd have to ask Madame Laurent that."

"I don't really know her to speak to."

Madame smiled to herself. The English and their politeness. "Well, then, I don't know. All I do know is that Hercule is going to be in this film they're making. Monsieur De Clercq, you know Monsieur De Clercq, he's the one I told you about whose son got knocked down a year or so ago by some idiotic driver. He's all right now by the way, but anyhow,

Monsieur De Clercq and I were sitting having a chat down by the fountain, you know how we natter, blah, blah, blah, and Madame Laurent walks by, you know the way she has, long and lean, head up in the air so you feel like you're a little bee, buzzing round her feet? Well, she was walking past us, I waved, 'Hello, madame,' but she didn't hear me. Hah! Well, I'm sure you know this about madame, she doesn't tend to 'hear' everyone, and old Hercule was plodding along faithfully by her and monsieur goes, 'Lucky dog,' and I said, 'What, with madame as his mistress? I'd say, poor dog, poor dog.' 'Oh well, yes, sure,' he says. 'No, not that. Old Hercule's in this film they're making that there's so much goddamn fuss about. I tell you, my son, he says there's not a chance for any guy at the moment with all these foreign film stars and their entourages running about.'"

Martha wanted to say stop to madame as she was, at best, only catching half of this, but she didn't have the energy to understand or call a halt.

She hoped she'd caught some things madame had said or this whole meeting would be a waste of time. So, without anyone to stop her, madame continued, though she was picking up on a slightly perplexed expression coming from the other side of the table, so she slowed down as she did when she drove and spotted a police car. Not once had she ever been caught.

"My dear friend, it suddenly clicked. Clicked. It means, I suddenly knew, I realised. I realised that here's my poor heartbroken English friend and here, right here, is a film crew."

Far from showing a drop of enthusiasm, Martha just remained stony faced and took another sip of her drink. Madame could see this was going to be a long haul, involving many more meetings. Undeterred, she carried on.

"But to return to your question, my dear friend, I'm not

exactly clear from what Monsieur De Clercq said what were the thoughts in the director's head when he decided to put Hercule in his film. I think it's only a walk-on part," and she grinned. "So, what of this broken heart of yours?" she asked in English, for she could see that this was going to be the only subject that would be of any interest to Martha and broken-hearted conversation needed, she was of the opinion, to be spoken in the language of the one whose heart is scattered about. If repair was needed, she wasn't sure that a second language could do the job.

She looked earnestly at the broken face, eyes as full as any she'd ever seen. An insect could swim in them. Her poor English friend was in a mess and there wasn't much she felt she could do, but she did teach her the French for "time heals" and "you'll get through this". She had the words but also the experience. The problem was, she wasn't sure if her friend was listening. And she didn't want to get too "wise old birdy" about it because there was nothing more annoying to young ones and, frankly, nothing more depressing to her because she didn't want to feel she knew everything. If that was the case, what was the point of her sad little life?

"I don't believe you don't care," she said when Martha said she didn't care about anything. She had that English sentence perfectly and she was quite pleased with herself, not without any thought of Martha's sadness but because she was glad her friend didn't have to make the effort of correcting her when she was at such a low ebb. It was true to say, though, that she had to content herself with not learning any new words today. Martha could barely manage a word.

★

It was another day and another sponge. This time coffee and walnut, which was a real pleasure in madame's eyes, not to mention her stomach, because, though she did appreciate a cup of tea, she would've been dishonest if she said she didn't miss a little taste of the old café. Books were being read, cutlery tinkled and English words floated all around her, some whispered, others more assured, offering apologies for being late, thoughts on the rain and the odd recommendation. "Have you read this? I think you'd love it." *Well, that's fraught with danger.* Madame smiled to herself, remembering a friend who'd scolded her for a recommendation she'd once given, asking madame if she could possibly give her those ten hours and twenty minutes – she'd actually counted – back again as she'd hated every bit of the book. Madame had just sat quietly and patiently through this diatribe because she obviously couldn't give those hours back to her friend as a gift and, if she'd had a closer friendship, could have edged towards mentioning that her friend didn't have to finish it and that, in general, she might do well to veer towards the opinion that reading, even if it is not entirely enjoyable in a particular instance, is never wasted. What the experience had taught her was not to recommend anything to that person again who had chosen a rather disparaging honesty over any sense of graciousness.

She was waiting for Martha but had deliberately arrived early so she could soak up an hour or so listening to others and give herself permission to eat and drink alone. It felt wonderfully modern. Her mother would never have approved, not even in such a respectable establishment as this. Martha had done this for her. She had forced her out of her… what was it she said? Comfort zone, that was it, and she wondered what that was in English. She would ask her. As she was pondering comfort zones and being separated from them, Martha walked in. The door tinkled, in a quaint English way, and one or two people looked up for a moment or two, then carried on with what they were doing when they saw the latest entrance was nothing to do with them.

"I'm sorry, I started…" Madame Maes coughed over a bit of walnut that was tucked discreetly in the sponge. She quickly cleared her throat while Martha unwrapped a scarf from her neck. "I started without you, I hope you don't think I was being rude. I was just interested to see what it felt like being here on my—"

"That's fine," Martha said quietly.

"I was out of my comfort zone. How do you say that?"

Martha told her.

"Comfort zone," she repeated.

They then reverted back to French, maintaining the unspoken tradition of beginning in madame's language.

"Can I get you anything?" Martha asked.

"Another cup of tea would be good. Here." Madame reached for her bag. "It's my turn." There were protests on either side, but it was finally agreed that madame should do the honours and as she watched Martha walk to the counter, she couldn't help notice the poor girl's weight loss. She needed to get some food inside her, that was for sure.

When the drinks and the very slim – no, thin – girl returned, madame started the conversation. She knew from the last time not to ask Martha how she was and she certainly wasn't going to comment on the jumper that was now far too big for her.

"So, the filming's begun. Down, as you might expect, by the fountain. But five o'clock in the morning! Monsieur De Clercq, he said you can't get a quiet cup of coffee first thing in the morning. Well, you know, normal first thing, seven, seven-thirty. No, and the other day, he said he went down to his favourite café around his usual time and they'd actually run out of his favourite almond croissants because there's so many busy bodies down there trying to get a look-in before they start their day's business. Have you seen them?"

Martha said she hadn't, but a friend of hers had. It was

the friend whose face she'd turned into a series of the letter Q with a small 10 by each for a board-game-themed party she was going to. As she painted them, she kept thinking, *Hey, shitbag, here's ten questions for you,* but she got to question one, "How long have you known her?" and got stuck there for the entire painting session, forgetting to answer her friend's question, "Why don't you come to this party?" because she was so engrossed in answering the question for the bastard, which at the lowest point was, "As long as we've been together." She told madame they might go down tomorrow or the next day, but she was pretty sure she wasn't going to bother.

"You should, you should. I think you'd enjoy it, especially with all your interest in make-up. I'm a bit old for that sort of thing, but if I were young..." and she smiled at the thought of what that might be.

Martha, despite occasional lapses in concentration, felt she'd understood most of what Madame Maes was saying, more than the last time they had met, which surprised her as she felt she was so unreceptive to just about anything at the moment. She watched madame smile to herself and knew her French friend would have been up as early as the film crew, no problem.

"You like films, then, madame?"

"I do, I do. But, for goodness's sake, call me Sybille. Yes, I fell in love with them after the war and have enjoyed them ever since. The first film I saw was, well, it was all about... well, I just loved it and was hooked from that point on. I used to go with a friend and we'd swoon over the male leads, how we'd swoon," and she clasped a spidery hand on her chest and looked skywards. "I also love your films and the American ones. That was when I started to take an interest in English." She took a sip of English breakfast tea. "Ooh, that's lovely. Goes down a treat," and she put the cup back on the saucer. "How's the make-up going?"

"OK," Martha replied, grimacing slightly to indicate this wasn't entirely the case. "I'm practising on friends, but I haven't been to college for a couple of weeks. Can't face it. But I know I have to go back."

Sybille could hardly wait to intervene. "Too blooming right, you do. You're very talented. I've seen some of the work you've done. You're not going to let that... that... so-and-so get the better of you, are you? I hope not. What a waste, you trundling back to England, with nothing to show for it. Just a few conversations with a silly old woman in a tea shop. No, my girl. That is not going to happen," and she wagged a wrinkly finger in Martha's direction, as if casting a spell. "By hook or by crook" was almost in the air. "What are you supposed to be working on at the moment?" Sybille continued and Martha, shaken slightly by this sudden directness of her companion, said one of her friends had given her their latest assignment, which was dolls. She had to find a model and make them up as some kind of doll. "Well?" Sybille pursued.

God, this was hard work. She just didn't have any enthusiasm for the assignment. She was sure it wasn't going to happen. But one idea had come her way.

"Well?" Sybille offered a smile this time.

"I have this idea of a Russian doll. Is that the right word?"

"Yes, yes," and Sybille said, "Russian," in English to confirm what they were both talking about.

"I think it might work quite well."

"Oh, yes," replied Sybille. She smiled. "Yes, very well." She took another sip of tea. "I used to have a set. Beautiful they were. Eight of them. I can see them now. Smiley faces. Black hair peeping out from yellow scarves. Red dresses and flowery aprons. The smallest was so tiny. You wouldn't believe it. I loved taking them apart, then putting them back, one inside the other, again. I used to put them on my windowsill and my mother, she used to say, 'Sybille, why do you put them there?

They get so dusty in the sun. And it's not you who has to do the dusting, is it?' Eventually, she gave up and said, 'You can do your windowsill, my girl. All those dolls. Don't know why your grandmother gave you them.' But I was glad she had."

Martha's mind transported itself to another grandmother, the one who belonged to her ex-boyfriend. She hated that. She hated how one word could re-awaken heartbreak, just at a moment when it seemed to have temporarily taken a backseat.

"Don't let him sit at that computer so long," she'd say to anyone who was listening. "Sometimes I wonder if he'll wake up one day and forget how to string a sentence together. The world was meant for all of us to get along, find out things from one another, get along, have conversations. I can't think why we all bothered to spend so much time talking to him when he was a little boy." Yes, she hated people gate-crashing her head, particularly when she was so fond of them.

"You know," said Sybille, "I swear I'm going to have to bring a whole box of tissues every time I meet you." She smiled and scrabbled in her bag for a tiny, unopened packet she knew she had somewhere. "Here," she said, "you're welcome to all of these."

Martha gave a nod of gratitude and blew her nose. That she was sorry went without saying, which was good because she was unable to utter a syllable. She was sobbing now to the point where breathing was almost a problem.

Sybille took her hands and held them in her spindly, arthritic digits and told her to take some deep breaths.

"If you're anything like me," she said in perfect English, "you wish this had never happened and you were still with this James, but now he's hurt you so badly you don't want him back because you know deep down that's not going to work. So, really, just at the moment, you can't wish for anything. When my heart was in pieces I used to wish I was someone else. I'd look at other people and think, *You don't know the half of it*, because I thought my pain was unique. No one else could have possibly experienced as much hurt as this because I'd have heard about it or someone would have told me."

She drank some more tea. Unburdening herself was thirsty work. There was silence for a few minutes as there can be between friends who know one another well enough. There were just the murmurs of others and the delicate sound of cups being carefully placed on saucers or the gentle stirring of tea. It took this quiet for her mind to deliver some painful memories she hadn't experienced quite so sharply for a long while. It was as if heartbreak was contagious and she'd caught Martha's, just as she might her cold. She turned them into a smile, though. Time could do that and she gave a little experience of the disease back because an old heartbreak, one that had seen its best days, could perhaps help a new one, could show its lack of fatality and here she was to prove it.

She told of a boyfriend for whom one woman wasn't enough and of the silliness of this old biddy who kept on forgiving in the hope that a generous spirit would be rewarded. It was three dalliances later when she finally realised if any reward was coming her way, it wasn't from someone who looked at her and saw only what he could get away with.

"All I can say is, you're better off as you are. I know, I know, don't look at me like that. But God forbid you should ever have to cope with heartbreak and a couple of children making demands on you." She could see she wasn't making any inroads, but she said this anyway. "The right man will never want to leave and nor will he take the you-know-what. He won't believe his luck. Anyway," she continued, this time in French; she needed to get Martha's mind going again. "This make-up. Here's a story for you."

She sat up in her chair, tall and straight, as if defying the forthcoming words and caught up in her little rebellion. As far as she could remember, she didn't think she'd ever spoken of this before.

"There was one time," she started nervously in her own language, "I was still living at home, even though I was twenty-five; my brother and sister had left by then, they were both married with children. I was living at home and I'd just got in from work. The girls and I had been mucking about a bit, er, being silly, in our lunch hour and one of them said to me, 'You know, Sybille, I think you'd look really nice in a bit of make-up. You have very nice eyes.' I laughed. I'd never worn it, mainly because my parents took a very dim view of it. They didn't approve, my dad in particular. And also, I suppose, because I didn't think I had a face worth making up."

"That's silly," Martha interjected, blowing her nose. "You have a lovely face," she said and wiped her eyes dry.

Sybille smiled. "Well, thank you, but no amount of paint could improve things, I thought. But they were friendly girls…"

"Where did you work?"

"Oh, the town hall. Just office work. Typewriters then, of course, clackety-clack. The noise, you wouldn't believe it. The building was beautiful, though. Old, timbered-looking, like something out of a fairytale."

"Typewriters look such hard work."

"They were, they were. Your fingers ached. And your nails, well, you were always breaking them. Anyway, we'd always got on really well, so when they asked if they could do my face, I said, 'Yes, OK, if you want,' so they had a right old time putting this eye shadow on, that lipstick, trying out different colours and, I had to admit, I enjoyed the experience a lot more than I thought I would. I suppose I felt a bit pampered and that never does any harm, does it? And when they'd finished and I looked in the mirror, well, I couldn't believe what I saw. Do you know, I didn't look half-bad? We were all very giggly, very happy and this continued right into the afternoon, especially as others in the office passed me by looking as though they'd seen a ghost or something."

"So you enjoyed wearing make-up."

"Yes," Sybille answered thoughtfully. "If I'm being honest, much more than I'd expected. It certainly gives you a bit of confidence, doesn't it? Puts a layer between you and the world."

"It always makes me feel better, though at the moment probably not such a great idea." She pointed to her tear-stained face that was gradually recovering and slightly smiled. Sybille touched her left hand and was pleased to see the glimmer of hope.

"So," she continued, "when I was walking home, I felt quite pleased with myself. It had been a good day and I was one of the girls in a way I hadn't been before. But, sad to say, it didn't last. As soon as my dad saw me, well, all hell let loose. He asked me what on earth I had plastered all over my face and ordered me to go and wipe it all off. He said it was disgusting. 'Red lipstick,' he shouted. 'Do you know what sort of women wear red lipstick? Not the sort of woman I want anywhere near my family, let alone in it.'"

"But he must've known his daughter wasn't like that?"

"Oh, I don't think parents thought like that, certainly not my dad. There were just rules, ways of behaving…"

"But the other women you worked with…"

"Oh, he would've just dismissed them. Not worth bothering with, not from the right sort of family. I'm surprised, looking back, he didn't demand that I leave the place when he realised what 'sort', as he described it, I was mixing with…"

"Demand that you leave?"

"Believe me, if he'd said I had to leave, that would've been it. I'd have had to go. Otherwise, I would've been out on my ear, nowhere to live…"

"His own daughter?"

"Oh yes. Those days, it was always, 'while you're under my roof'. I can't tell you how many times I heard that one. And nine times out of ten I hadn't done anything wrong. Not even by his standards. It was just his way of reminding everyone, and that included my mother, who was boss."

Martha was shocked that a young life could be so prescribed, probably because she hadn't heard anyone of Sybille's generation talk like this before. There had always been a silent acceptance coupled with a wry smile in both her grandmothers' stories, but Sybille's words encouraged a feeling of relief that her own birth had coincided with a different time.

"I can't imagine that," she said.

"What?"

"I can't imagine what it's like to have a parent tell me what I can or can't put on my face."

Sybille laughed. "Different times," she said, echoing Martha's exact thoughts. "Different times." She sighed with a mixture of envy and pride that she'd had to reach for a courage young people nowadays didn't have to but were nevertheless in awe of.

She returned to her story.

"He demanded to know if anyone had seen me walking home and even though I'd waved at the baker and said 'Hello' to someone in our street, I said they hadn't because God alone knows what he'd have done if I had said 'Yes'. By this time, I was crying so much I almost didn't need to wash the make-up off," and she smiled in recognition. "How quickly things change. It was horrible, and it was as if the lovely day I'd had hadn't happened. I'll always remember how he terrified the life out of me that evening. You never lose that."

She paused for a moment and felt the dark, dull colours of the living room where all this had happened.

"Suffice to say, I never wore make-up again. Even after my mum and dad died, I still never did. I was frightened, I suppose, as to what would have happened if I had. It would have been like touching a hot plate.

"But the dolls, dusty or not, now they were helpful. Often, I'd use them to help me sort something out so they could be the people in my life and I'd get them to have imaginary conversations with one another. Even at twenty-five I was still doing it, believe it or not. So that night, when I'd done all my crying, I unscrewed all the dolls and the ones I'd usually used for my brother and sister I put to one side – after all, they didn't live with us anymore – and Mum I put a little away from my dad and me because that was where she was, quietly looking on. My dad and me, well, he was the biggest doll, and I, as usual, was the smallest and he was standing over me, but instead of all the unpleasant nonsense he'd come out with, he just said, 'You look nice, Sybille. Are you and the girls going out tonight?'"

Martha tried to imagine Sybille's face when it was its younger, ironed-out self. Her eyes would have still been warm and engaging and the twinkle as bright, but there would be a smooth canvas of skin showing off their rich colour, allowing them to be the first point of anyone's attention. She could see what her colleagues must have meant. She imagined a smile that included a perfect set of teeth framed by a bright crimson lipstick and madame's hair, thicker and curly, falling more tidily than it did now, in hope of a suitor, perhaps.

"What I was going to say to you also was" – Sybille had changed the subject – "that apparently Hercule's enjoying himself no end. Madame Laurent stands on the side, would you believe, doing as she's told but, of course, smoking, nonchalantly, casually, the odd cigarette so she doesn't look as if she's obeying orders in any way. Monsieur De Clercq said it's quite funny. It's as if the poor dog's finding his feet. Instead of lumbering along at madame's side, he's quickened

his pace. He's making the film crew work hard. He said to his mate, 'I think Hercule's taking that bloke for a walk.' Aah. It must be so exciting, that world." She paused before she said, "I've always loved the theatre. I loved going to puppet shows as a child, though, of course, there wasn't much happening during the war, but then, after that, I was brought up in the north, Houlgate, by the sea, and we would go to Deauville occasionally, not far away, where there was sometimes a show. I loved it. Deauville has a film festival there now, for those who can't get to Cannes. You must've gone to quite a lot of theatre. I always imagine everyone does in England."

"Not quite everyone," Martha said, "but I do."

"There, I knew it, what with your interests and everything."

"It's very expensive, though. Or it can be. There are some seats that aren't too bad."

"Where have you seen it?"

"London. Sometimes you can get cheap seats at the last minute. And I've seen Shakespeare," she said with a question mark in her voice.

"Oh, of course I know Shakespeare. Who doesn't? What have you seen?" And she wore that very interested look she had the whole time Martha told her about a production of *A Midsummer Night's Dream* she'd seen a while ago, which was more like a nightmare than a dream in that it conjured up a strangeness that was almost frightening. And nobody wore very much.

She smiled and Sybille burst out laughing. In French, Martha said, "Do you know what, Sybille? I think I should paint your face."

★

Martha looked at the six dolls, with their identical expressions, standing attentively in a line on the table. They were like the physical representation of an unsuccessful therapeutic process, one that had been fiercely resisted and after many attempts to bring something to light had, in the final hour, shown little, if anything, that was new. How much more interesting it would be, she thought, if, in the opening up of each one, a layer of anger, despair or excitement could be found. She remembered Sybille rearranging her dolls to make sense of things that weren't organising themselves well in her head, but the passive faces just made Martha angry and she couldn't imagine them offering her the same support, though she agreed with Sybille that the polite, small smiles were true of much human interaction.

★

The hallway was dark, even though daylight was inviting itself in and Sybille, with her eyes to the ground, because a fall was always a good possibility these days, could only just make out a patterned floor, whose tiles, with their tiny yellow stars, belonged to another century and a time requiring something quite hardy. From what she could see, they were beautifully preserved and possibly polished, so she would need to take great care. She stood for a second or two in the darkness and her eyes took her to a small area of light at the back of the house that had found its way in from a small courtyard perhaps, with the help of an open door. It cast its warmth on a bicycle, nestled comfortably against a wall that propped it up as one would a drunken or troubled friend. Proud and dark wooden stairs led up to what she guessed must have been other flats and as she walked behind Martha to her friend's place on the ground floor, she felt a shiver from the past and was thankful that her own modern apartment had never had to bear the stomping feet of occupying soldiers or the sharp bristle in the air when the door knocked and, with it, the sound of words nobody understood.

Martha's flat was surprisingly neat, she thought, not because her friend's youth or personality determined it should be otherwise, more that it had been shown greater care than she would have expected from a broken heart. But then she remembered another friend from long ago who quite viciously plumped up cushions and swept floors whenever she was miserable or had had enough of the world.

The entire flat, except the toilet and shower, which Martha explained were behind a small door in the far corner, was one room. Martha's bed, apparently horribly uncomfortable until she'd added a top-up mattress, was to Sybille's left while a tiny kitchen lay to her right. A bar divided the two and was decorated with multi-coloured lights, a feature that combined cosiness and an element of the theatrical effectively. A work table sat opposite the bed, the surface of which had on it Martha's computer and more make-up than Sybille thought she'd ever seen in her life. Tube upon tube was lined up obediently in various rows, perhaps according to colour or shade, ready to do their work, and she thought how a face is just another canvas for anyone artistic like Martha, something that had never occurred to her as clearly before.

There were posters and artwork everywhere she looked. One was very familiar: the post-war Parisian kiss that paid scant regard to passers-by and didn't care about the bespectacled and beret-donned man who seemed to disapprove. Others she didn't quite understand and whether generational difference, taste or her educational shortcomings were the cause, she didn't really know. But she loved a large, purple canvas that bore a collage of pink and grey painted flowers, their Latin names written beautifully across them. She told Martha so, who smiled and thanked her. It was her own work. Sybille had suspected as much and was pleased that her pleasure at the spectacle had preceded that thought.

Martha put the tap on and let a gush of cold water thud

into the saucepan she was holding, then lit one of the two rings on her small stove and put the saucepan on it.

"Tea?" she enquired of her visitor.

"Of course," came the reply. It was, after all, a tradition. "I'm warning you," Sybille said with a grin all over her face. She was excited that a young woman wanted to spend time making up this craggy old excuse for a face, but old, unsettling memories were tucked in there somewhere and she didn't want them unfolded. "I don't want to be glammed up, I don't want any of that…" She was speaking French and Martha was looking curiously at her. "I don't want to look as if I'm going out for a night out. I don't want any of that…"

"I know, I know." Martha's voice was reassuring and Sybille watched her pour the boiled water into a pot. She believed her and quietly sighed with relief.

"I don't mind being one of your animals, something like that. But I'll wipe it off before I leave, if you don't mind. I don't want people thinking, *That silly old fool, what does she think she's doing?*"

Martha handed her a cup of tea. She was an observant girl, despite her heart breaking. It was just the right strength.

Martha couldn't honestly say she relished anything these days; taking delight in something was a bit beyond her experience at the moment, but she did consider the prospect of making up an older face at the very least distracting in its novelty. She'd read the theory and listened to the lectures on the older skin but hadn't had the opportunity to put her knowledge into practice. She made a cup for herself, then plonked down on the end of her bed.

"Actually, I was thinking about a Russian doll," she said and reached over to the other side of the bed where a packet of biscuits lay in wait.

Sybille was shrieking. "Oh Lord, I'm going to look a right…"

"Charlie?" Martha offered. "No, you're not," and there was

a real certainty about her tone. Sybille laughed and accepted the chocolatey biscuits that were offered. She enthusiastically took two because she hadn't had much lunch. Secretly delighted at an idea that was kilometres away from any notion her father had of glamour, she suddenly felt a hunger taking hold and thought it wouldn't be long before she asked Martha for another couple of biscuits. It would be like being in the theatre. She could play a part.

Martha got up and walked to the other side of the bed, bent down and produced a Russian doll from somewhere on the floor where she must have been keeping it. Sybille gave a broad smile. It was as if seventy odd years had melted away and when Martha brought it round for her to see, her mind could picture only the windowsill again with her own six dolls perched on it, some faded a little by the sun and ever so slightly dusty. And there was her mother looking on, no smile and raised eyebrows.

Martha checked the brushes, powders and colours she needed.

"How have you been, madame?" she asked in English.

Madame answered in French. How she was always best answered in her own language. "OK, I think. Let's just say, as well as anyone can be at eighty-six." She must seem like a museum piece to Martha. "My doctor said my blood pressure was a bit up, but she doesn't seem too bothered, so I'm thinking, if she seems all right about it, I'm not going to worry. How about you?"

Martha shrugged her shoulders. There was nothing to say that she hadn't already probably bored Sybille to death with and there was no significant change to report.

Sybille offered her English. "I wish I could go to England and tell that blooming so-and-so what he's put you through. You are going to be fine, you know. It just doesn't seem it at the moment, does it?"

Martha's head went from side to side.

"I'm going to see to it that you will feel better at some point. These things take time," and she smiled her virtually toothless grin, which did slightly improve Martha's state of mind, and she managed to smile back. "Take my Jean, for instance. After that horrible boyfriend I told you about, I thought I'd never find anyone. I just resigned myself to a single life because I never thought I'd trust anyone again. But he was lovely, kind, thoughtful and I could always have trusted him with my life. I never wore make-up, he knew that story of my dad, so he didn't push me to do anything I didn't want to. He knew these things run deep." She paused. "You'll find a Jean. I know you will."

It was very convincing and Martha had no intention of saying she didn't believe her.

Martha invited her model to sit down on a chair near the window, which she'd placed at an angle that had enough light to show her face in its natural colour but without the harshness of too much sun.

"I do love the theatre," Sybille said as she settled herself in the allotted position. It was a conversation she'd decided to continue from their last meeting, as if a minute hadn't passed since the last sentence and nor had several nights' sleep and a few more meals.

"It's pure escapism; you can just lose yourself in another world, forget your troubles." She was enjoying this attention. "Don't laugh, I often wished I'd gone into that world myself. Well, when I was little. Of course, my dad wouldn't have approved. Been almost akin to me deciding to be a lady of the night. So I settled for office work." She paused and allowed herself to be re-positioned by Martha. "God, if I were young now," she said and smiled at the thought of her young self in a generation not guided by parental wishes. Who the hell would she have been?

Martha put plenty of foundation on Sybille's face and under-eye cream to lighten the darkness there. Sybille closed her eyes as Martha gently rubbed in all the cream. Nobody had been as physically close to her as this since Jean had died twenty-three years ago. She'd forgotten how soothing a simple touch of the face could be and how transformed her thoughts. From seemingly nowhere her mind conjured up the sea that she adored and the little beach they'd usually strolled along. She could hear the crashing waves, excited children and the occasional bark of Claude, their dog, as he scampered back and forth from them, delirious at being off his lead. It wasn't easy, seeing all those children, but the sea was magnificent and could always be relied upon to shift her mood into a more positive direction. She almost felt the big grin on her face as she watched the tide.

"If you were my granddaughter," she said, "I'd blooming well ask you to do this every day."

Martha gently stroked her face with a soft brush. It was very comforting and made her realise she hadn't been cared for like this for a long time. She missed that. She particularly missed the unexpected pleasure of someone thinking of you when you didn't know they had been. Jean had been good at that. He often had had little surprises up his sleeve and enchanted her with treats he knew she'd love.

"I never had children," she heard herself saying. "Jean and me. It never happened. It's hard. You get on with life, of course you do, you don't have a choice, but first there are your friends with their children. They grow up and move out, so you feel as though you've got your mates back again and you think, at least I didn't have that heartbreak of little ones leaving, but then there are the grandchildren. And you can't help feeling you've been dealt a bit of a blow."

Martha applied the blusher to Sybille's cheeks, perfect red circles that had no intention of disguising their purpose. Rosy and healthy, they belonged to the pure contentment of a doll. She didn't respond to madame's revelation. It didn't seem to require one and any attempt to tell her that she was sure life had been good anyway sounded limp and unworthy. She thought about how expected children were, though voices were less clear on the subject, she supposed, since Sybille's youth. She couldn't think about them. Right now, they were about as far off the table as they could be. She carried on with Sybille's cheeks. Her skin, with its valleys and mountains, offered quite a challenge but in the last half-hour, she noted, her thoughts had been completely absorbed in her model's life.

It was an hour or so later when they both looked in the mirror. Martha was eager to see madame's reaction and she beamed when she saw her friend's delight. It was almost a shock when she saw her mouth turned upwards. A while ago, the guy in the patisserie had said he liked her smile. He even had the nerve to ask her why he hadn't seen it recently.

Sybille was extremely happy with the result; in fact, pleased as punch. First, she screamed, and then she laughed, and then she put her right hand across her mouth and touched her nose with her forefinger.

"Oh my God," she said loudly and in perfect English. The Russian doll, with its flowered scarf wrapped round its chin, though decrepit, was recognisable, with its blushed cheeks, pink lips and long lashes. The scarf was a smart move as well as a correct one. It covered her wrinkly old neck. She loved the whole thing and said so.

"Another tea?" Martha asked and she nodded. Water was put in the saucepan and onto the oven.

"Tomorrow," Sybille said firmly, for the attention she'd received had given her confidence, "you and me, we're going down to the fountain. We're going to see the filming. If nothing else, it'll be a laugh."

"We'll have to get up early," came the reply. Martha's French was perfect, Sybille thought. If she closed her eyes, she could barely detect an English accent.

ACKNOWLEDGEMENTS

I would like to thank friends who have read previous drafts of some of these stories and given very helpful advice, and one friend in particular who has read every word and who has always supported me. I would also like to thank my husband for the many, many hours he has spent reading the manuscript and for all his love and support, and my daughter, whose enthusiasm spurs me on.